vol.2___

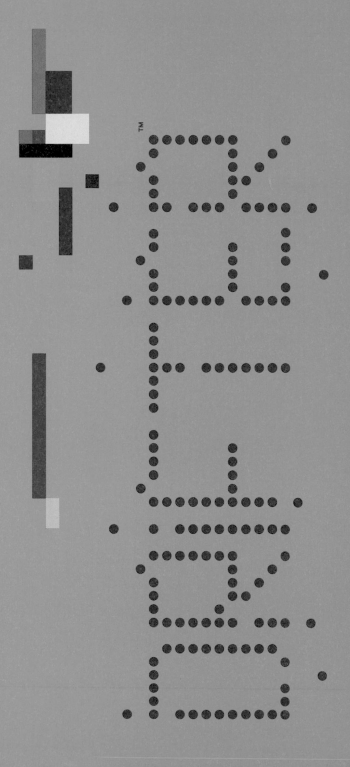

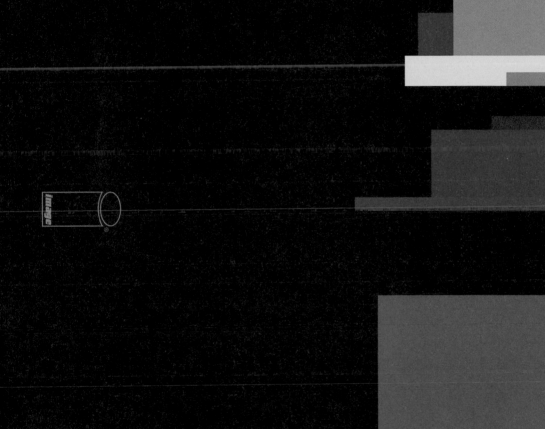

IMAGECOMICS.COM
ISBN: 978-1-63215-501-6

DRIFTER VOL 2. First Printing. December 2015. Published by Image Comics, Inc. Office of publication: 2001 Center Street, Sixth Floor, Berkeley, CA
94704. Copyright © 2015 Againdemon, LLC & Nicolas Klein. All rights reserved. DRIFTER™ (including all prominent characters featured herein), its logo
and all character likenesses are trademarks of Againdemon, LLC & Nicolas Klein, unless otherwise noted. Image Comics® and its logos are registered
trademarks of Image Comics, Inc. No part of this publication may be reproduced or transmitted, in any form or by any means (except short excerpts for
review purposes) without the express written permission of Againdemon, LLC, Nicolas Klein, or Image Comics, Inc. All names, characters, events, and
locales in this publication are entirely fictional. Any resemblance to actual persons (living or dead), events, or places, without satiric intent, is coincidental.
First printed in single magazine format as DRIFTER #6-9 by Image Comics, Inc. Printed in the USA. For information regarding The CPSIA on this printed
material call: 203-595-3636 and provide reference #RICH–656562.
Representation: Law Offices of Harris M. Miller II, P.C.

Drifter Volume 02
Originally published as DRIFTER #6-9

Script: Ivan Brandon
Full color art and cover: Nic Klein
Lettering: Clem Robins
Logo and design: Tom Muller
Editor: Sebastian Girner
Special thanks to Kristyn Ferretti
Wind Beneath Our Wings: Kieron Dwyer

Original cover artists: Nic Klein, Eduardo Risso,
Tom Muller, Daniel Krall, and Paul Azaceta

DRIFTER created by Ivan Brandon and Nic Klein
AN OFFSET COMICS PRODUCTION

CHAPTER 6
TRACK THE STARS

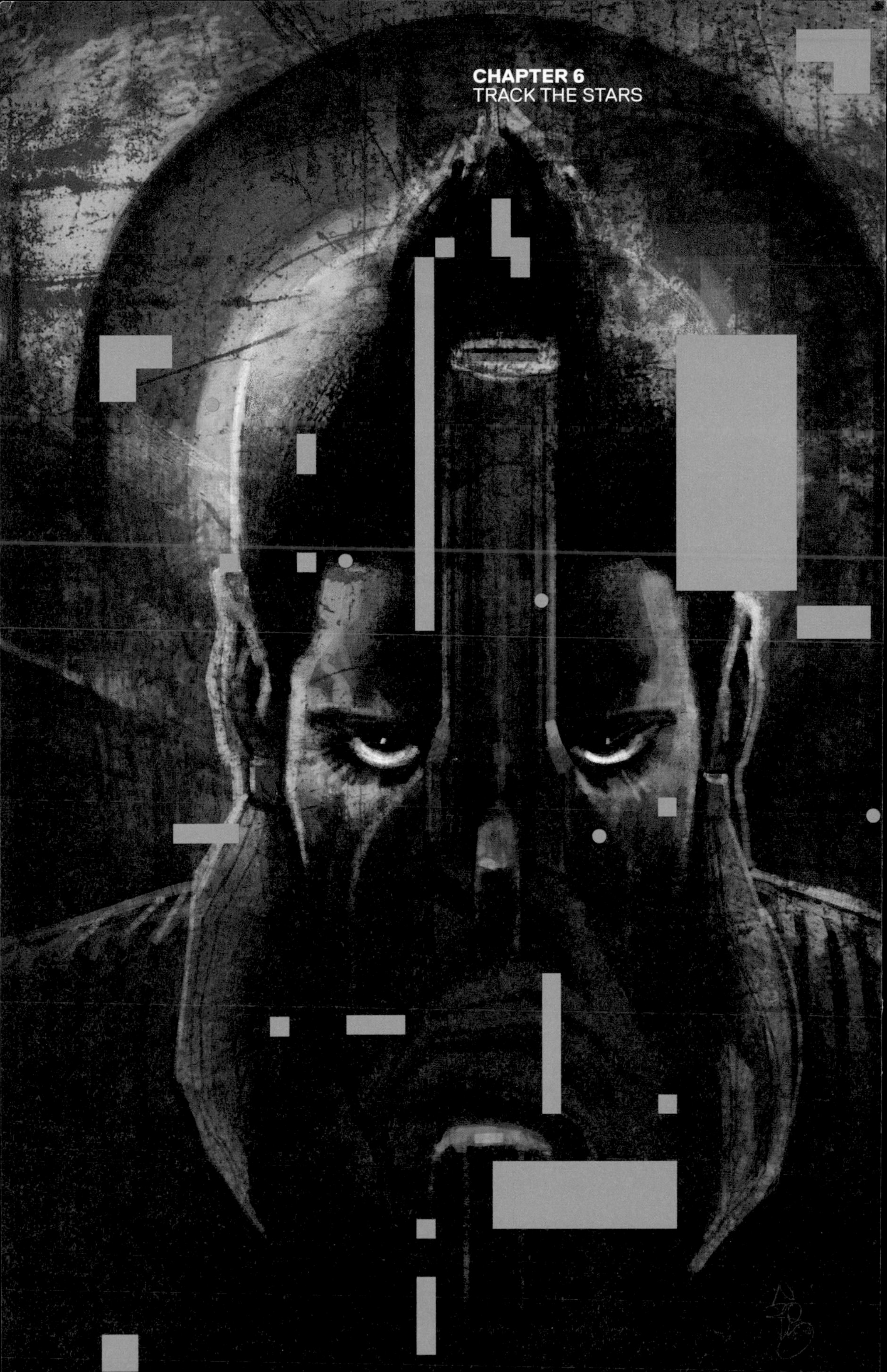

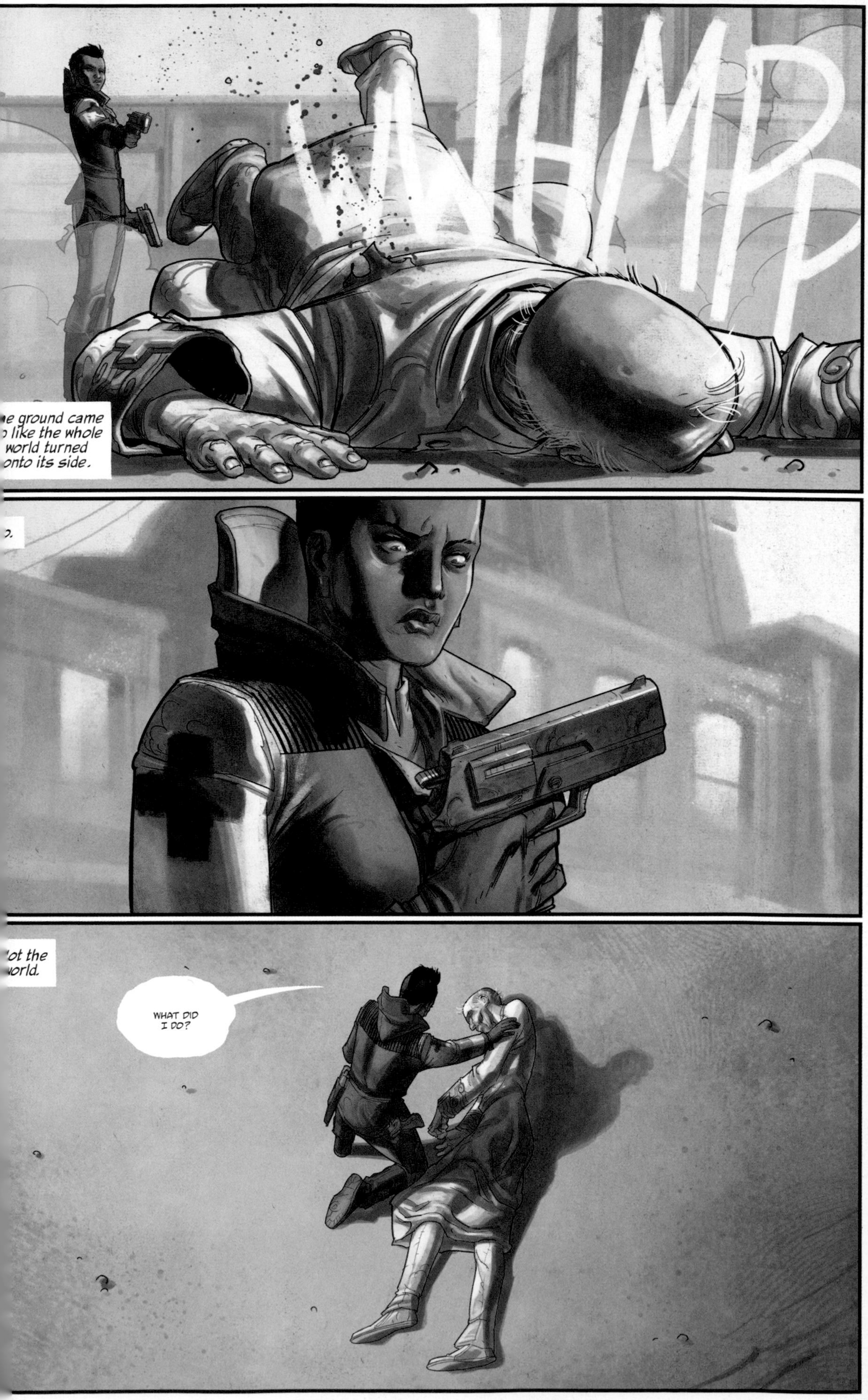
WHMPP
e ground came
o like the whole
world turned
onto its side.
o.
ot the
world.
WHAT DID I DO?

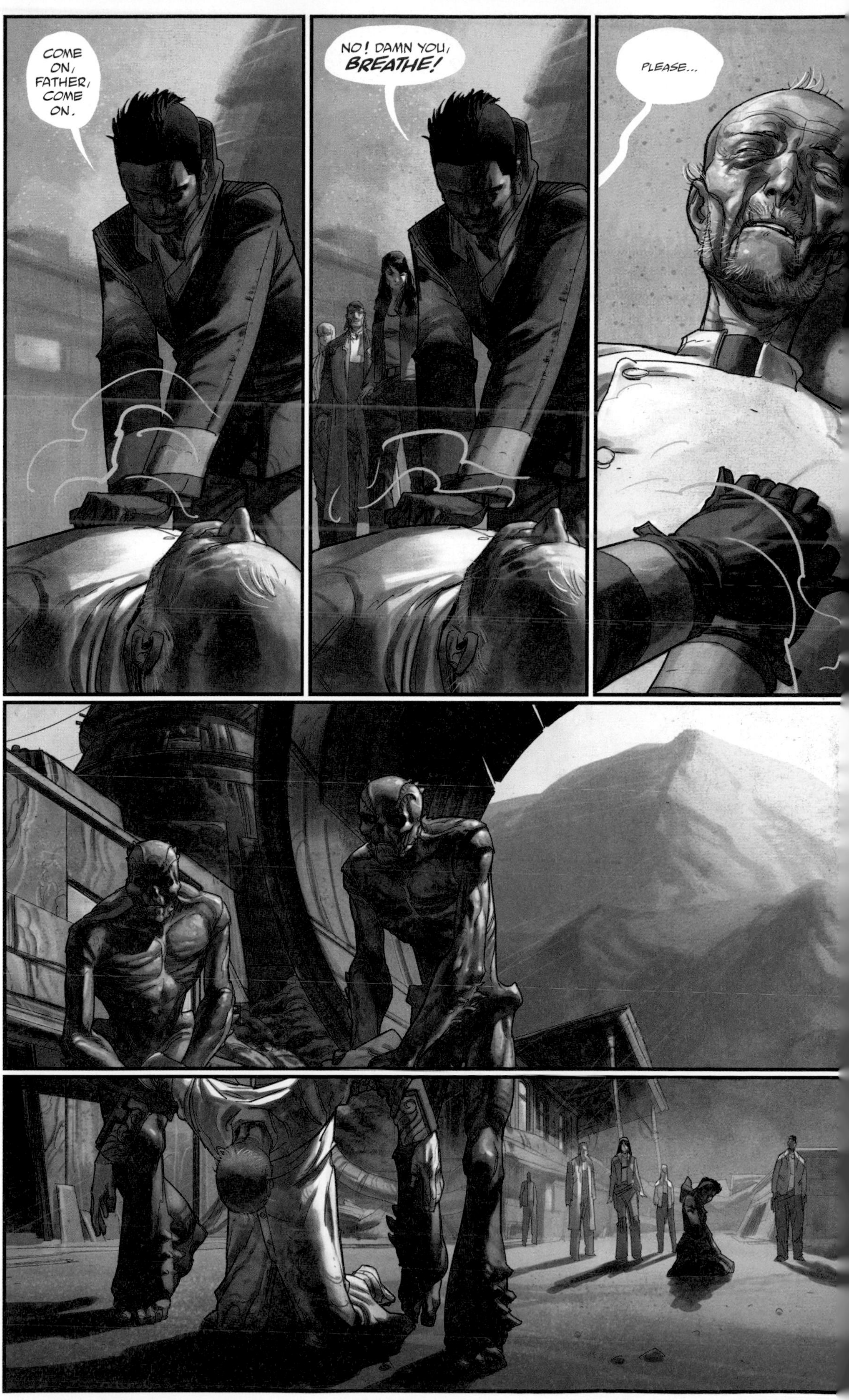
COME ON, FATHER, COME ON.
NO! DAMN YOU, BREATHE!
PLEASE...

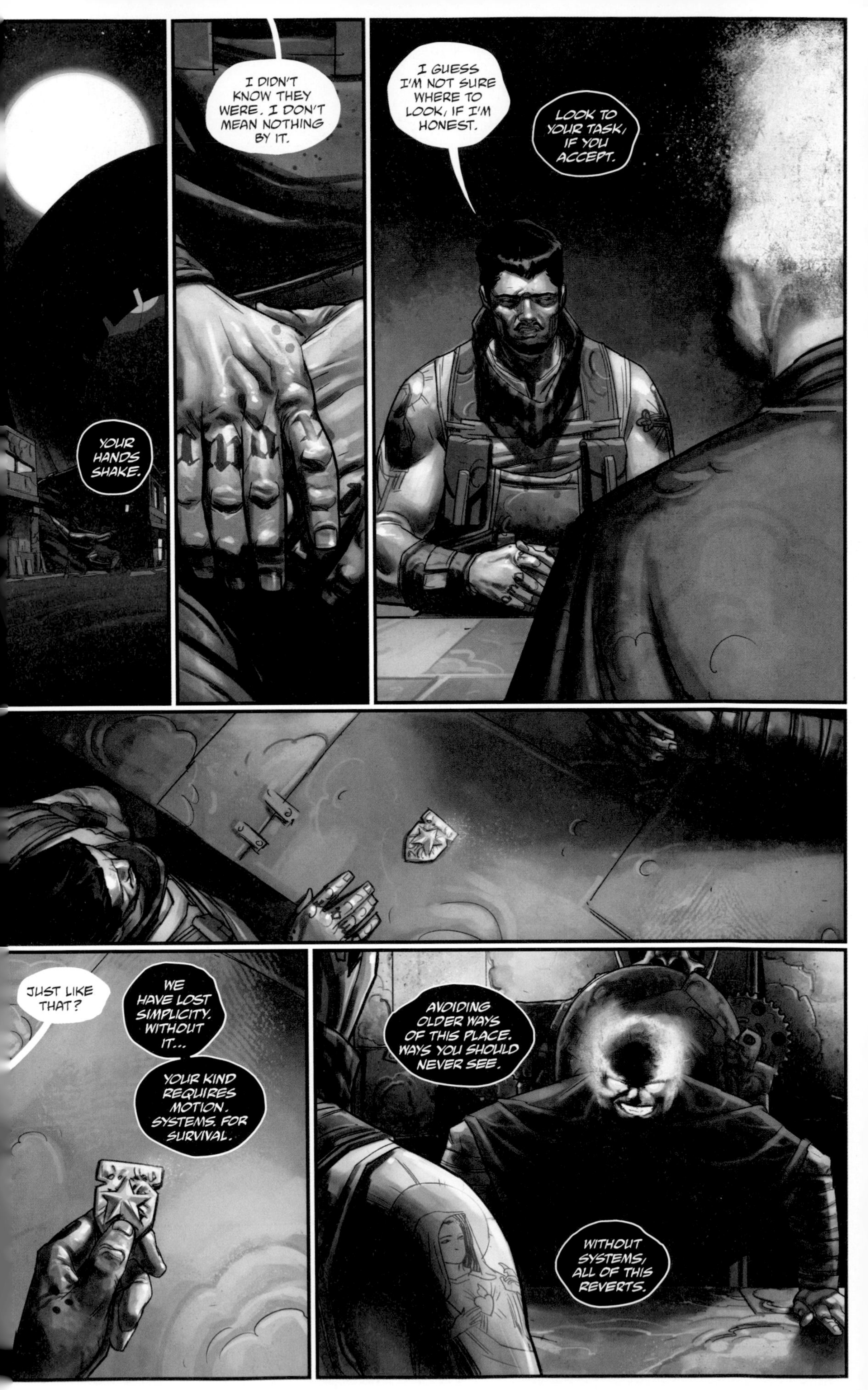
I DIDN'T KNOW THEY WERE. I DON'T MEAN NOTHING BY IT.
I GUESS I'M NOT SURE WHERE TO LOOK, IF I'M HONEST.
LOOK TO YOUR TASK, IF YOU ACCEPT.
YOUR HANDS SHAKE.
JUST LIKE THAT?
WE HAVE LOST SIMPLICITY. WITHOUT IT...
YOUR KIND REQUIRES MOTION. SYSTEMS. FOR SURVIVAL.
AVOIDING OLDER WAYS OF THIS PLACE. WAYS YOU SHOULD NEVER SEE.
WITHOUT SYSTEMS, ALL OF THIS REVERTS.

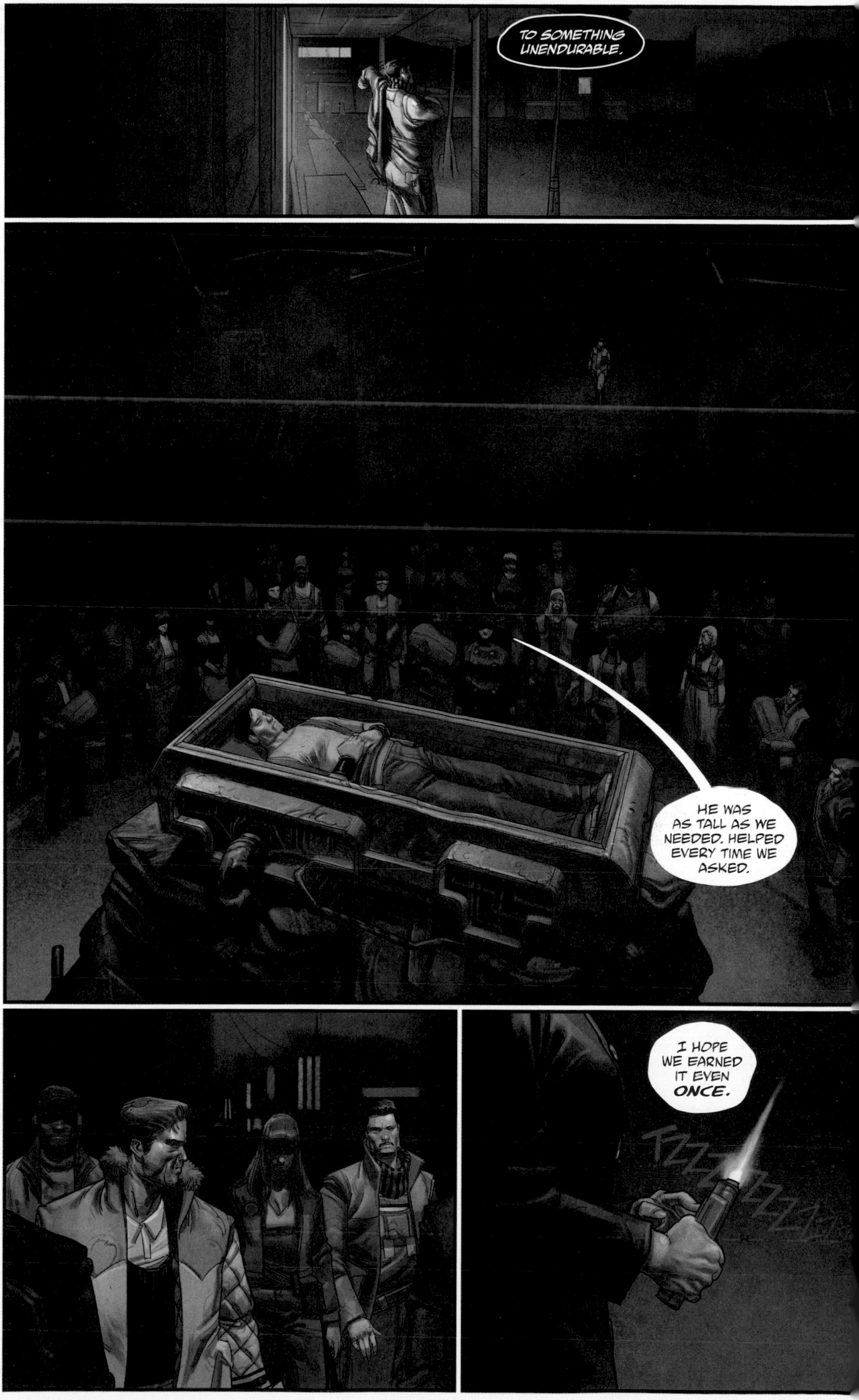
TO SOMETHING UNENDURABLE.
HE WAS AS TALL AS WE NEEDED. HELPED EVERY TIME WE ASKED.
I HOPE WE EARNED IT EVEN ONCE.

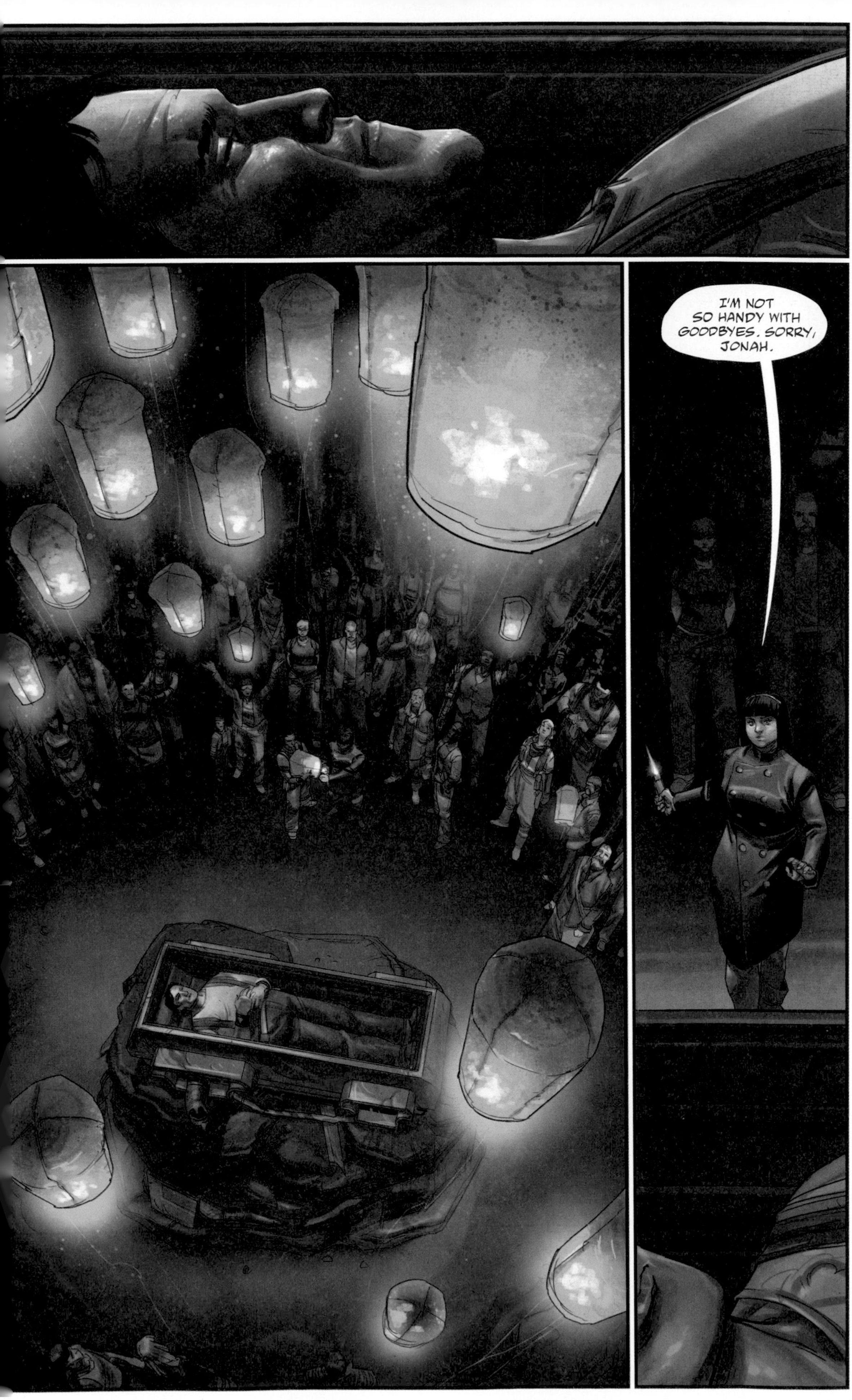
I'M NOT SO HANDY WITH GOODBYES. SORRY, JONAH.

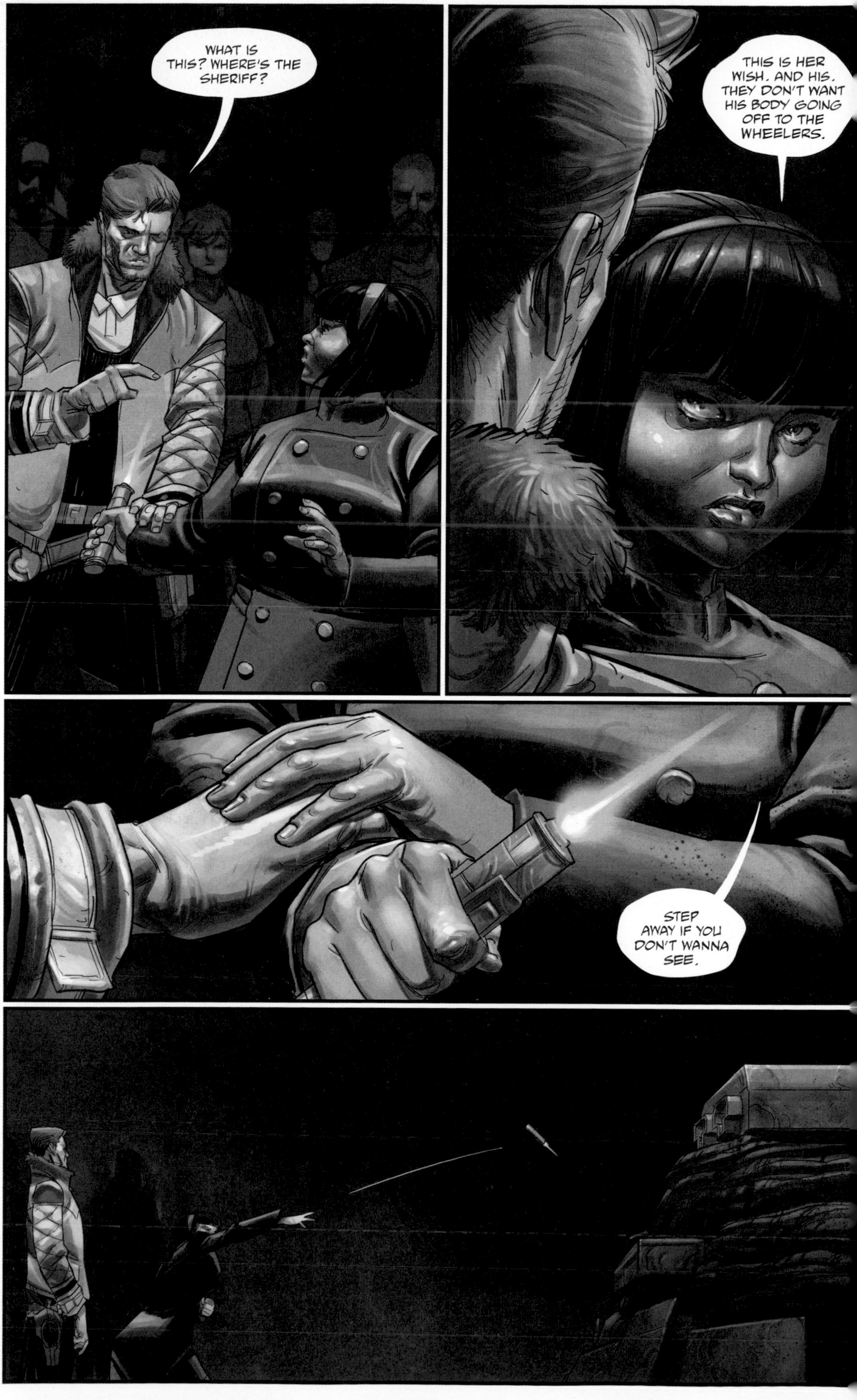
WHAT IS THIS? WHERE'S THE SHERIFF?
THIS IS HER WISH. AND HIS. THEY DON'T WANT HIS BODY GOING OFF TO THE WHEELERS.
STEP AWAY IF YOU DON'T WANNA SEE.

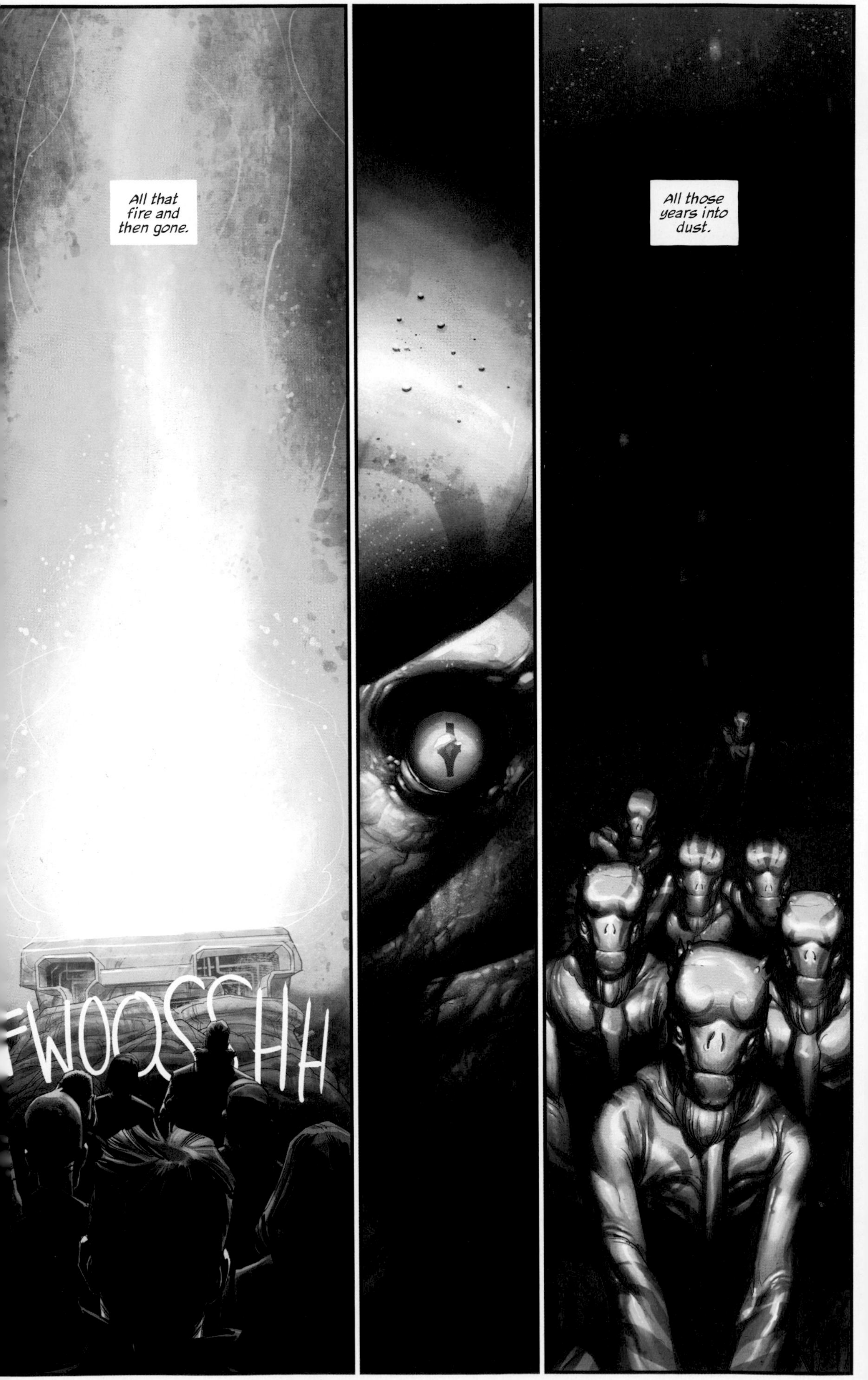
All that fire and then gone.
FWOOSSHH
All those years into dust.

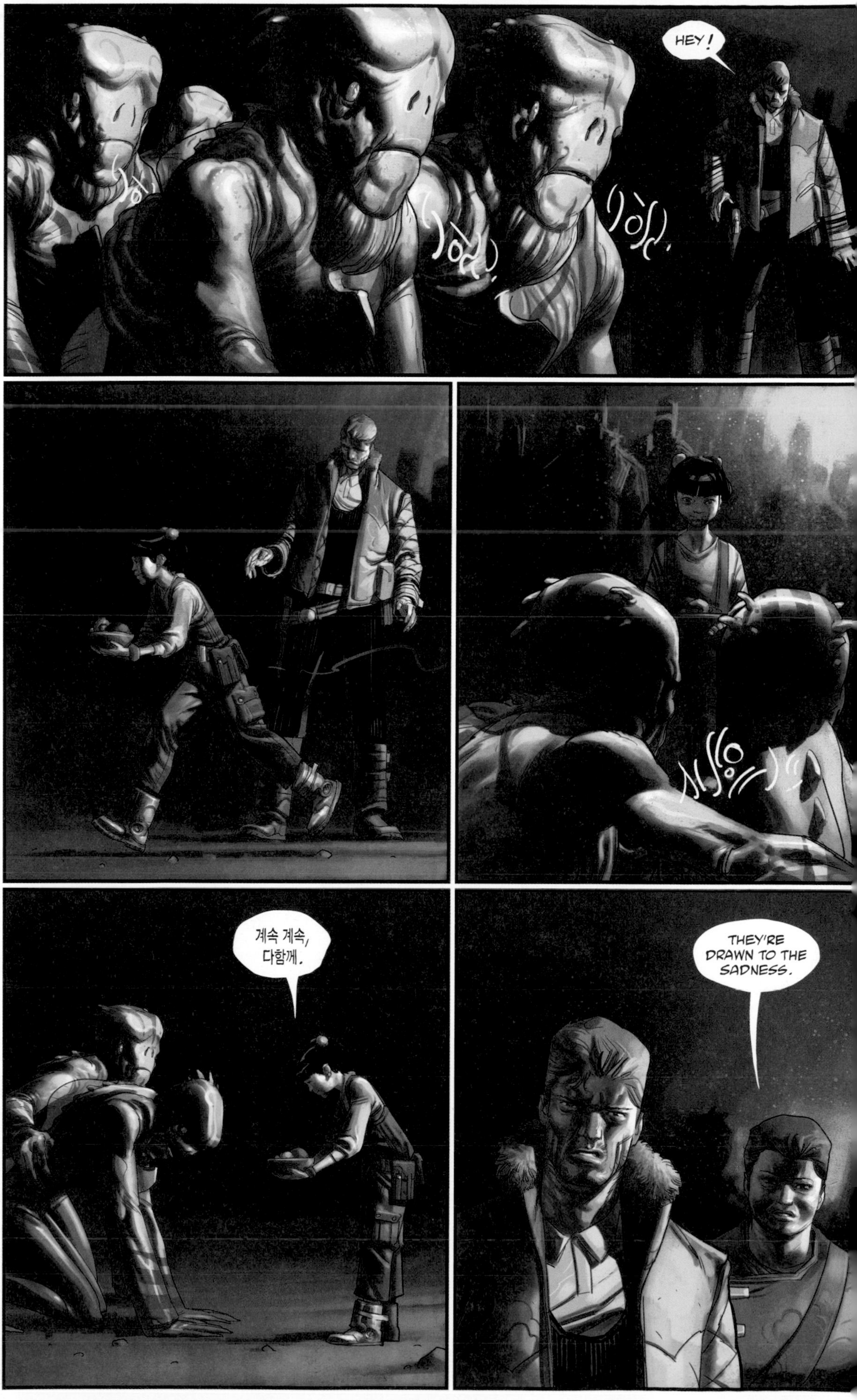
HEY!
계속 계속,
다함께.
THEY'RE DRAWN TO THE SADNESS.

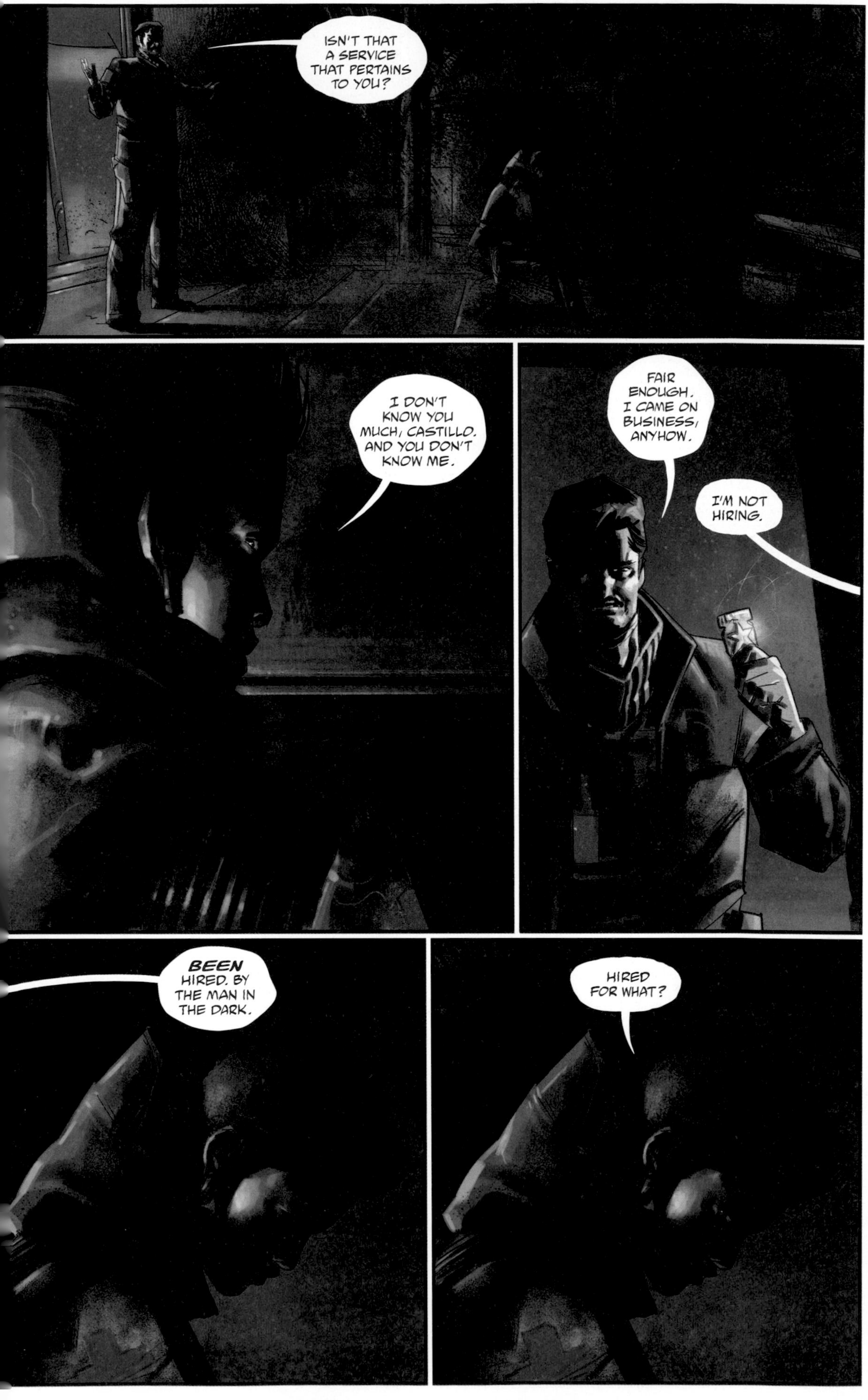
ISN'T THAT A SERVICE THAT PERTAINS TO YOU?
I DON'T KNOW YOU MUCH, CASTILLO. AND YOU DON'T KNOW ME.
FAIR ENOUGH. I CAME ON BUSINESS, ANYHOW.
I'M NOT HIRING.
BEEN HIRED. BY THE MAN IN THE DARK.
HIRED FOR WHAT?

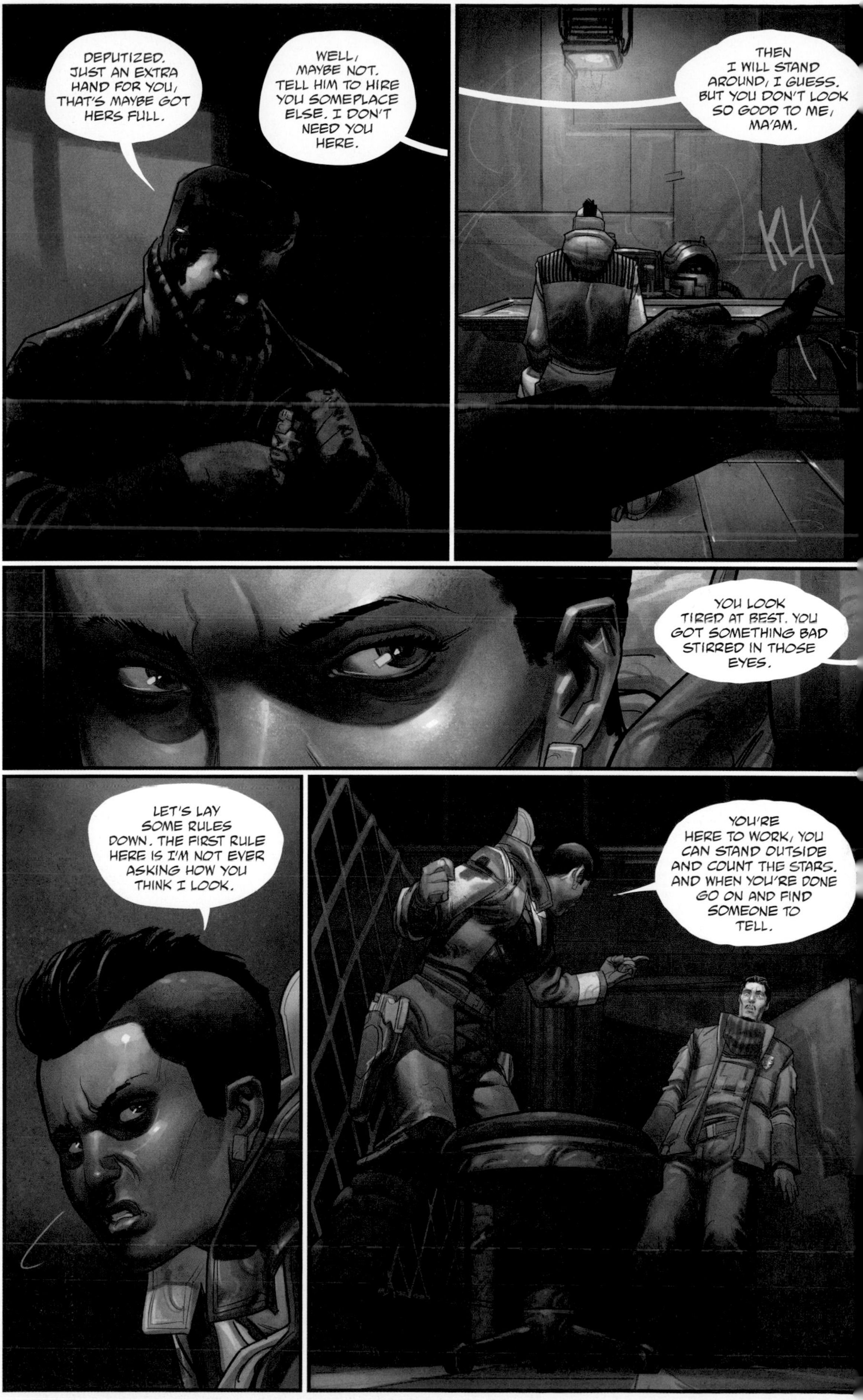
DEPUTIZED. JUST AN EXTRA HAND FOR YOU, THAT'S MAYBE GOT HERS FULL.
WELL, MAYBE NOT. TELL HIM TO HIRE YOU SOMEPLACE ELSE. I DON'T NEED YOU HERE.
THEN I WILL STAND AROUND, I GUESS. BUT YOU DON'T LOOK SO GOOD TO ME, MA'AM.
KLK
YOU LOOK TIRED AT BEST. YOU GOT SOMETHING BAD STIRRED IN THOSE EYES.
LET'S LAY SOME RULES DOWN. THE FIRST RULE HERE IS I'M NOT EVER ASKING HOW YOU THINK I LOOK.
YOU'RE HERE TO WORK, YOU CAN STAND OUTSIDE AND COUNT THE STARS. AND WHEN YOU'RE DONE GO ON AND FIND SOMEONE TO TELL.

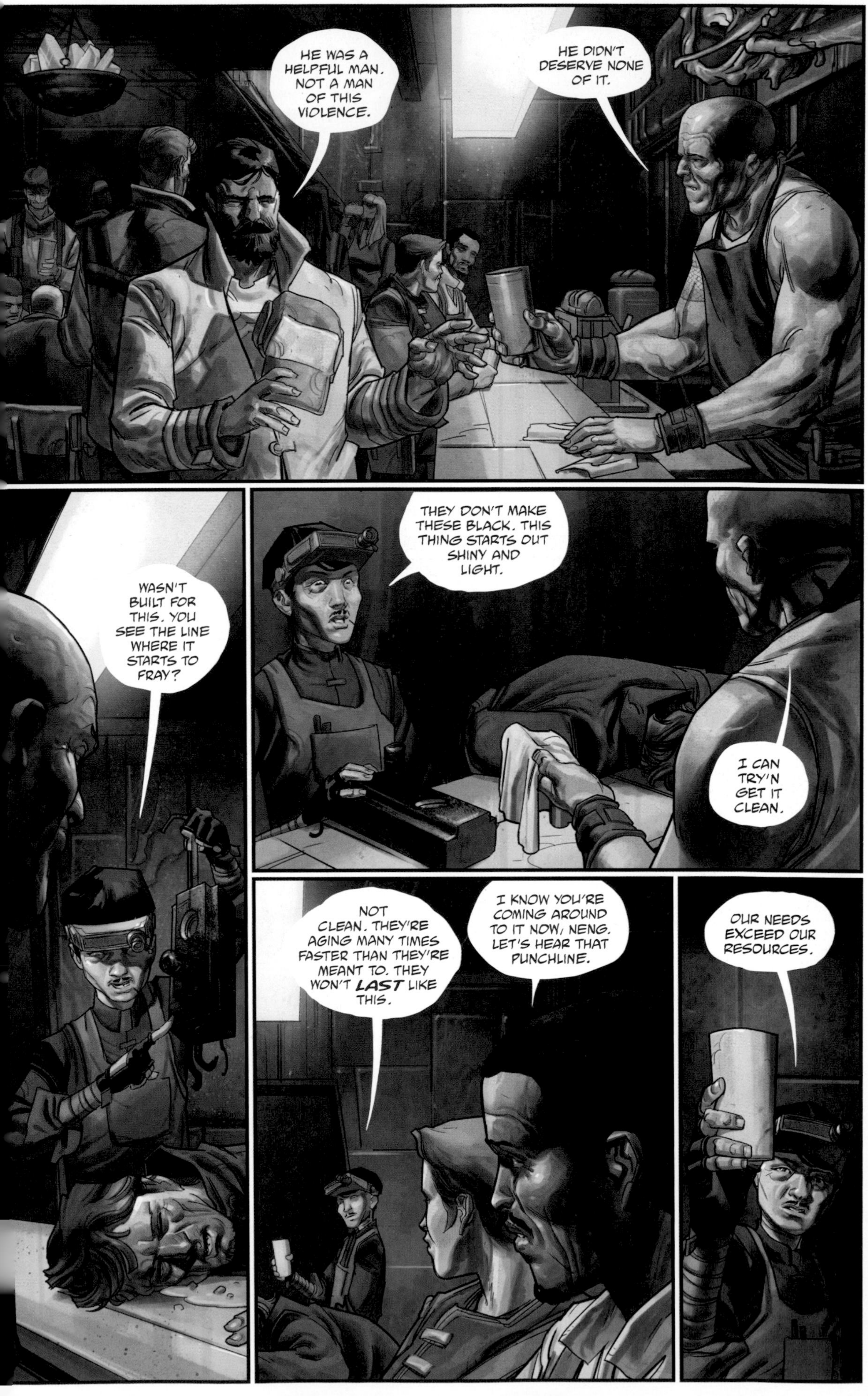
HE WAS A HELPFUL MAN. NOT A MAN OF THIS VIOLENCE.
HE DIDN'T DESERVE NONE OF IT.
WASN'T BUILT FOR THIS. YOU SEE THE LINE WHERE IT STARTS TO FRAY?
THEY DON'T MAKE THESE BLACK. THIS THING STARTS OUT SHINY AND LIGHT.
I CAN TRY'N GET IT CLEAN.
NOT CLEAN. THEY'RE AGING MANY TIMES FASTER THAN THEY'RE MEANT TO. THEY WON'T LAST LIKE THIS.
I KNOW YOU'RE COMING AROUND TO IT NOW, NENG. LET'S HEAR THAT PUNCHLINE.
OUR NEEDS EXCEED OUR RESOURCES.

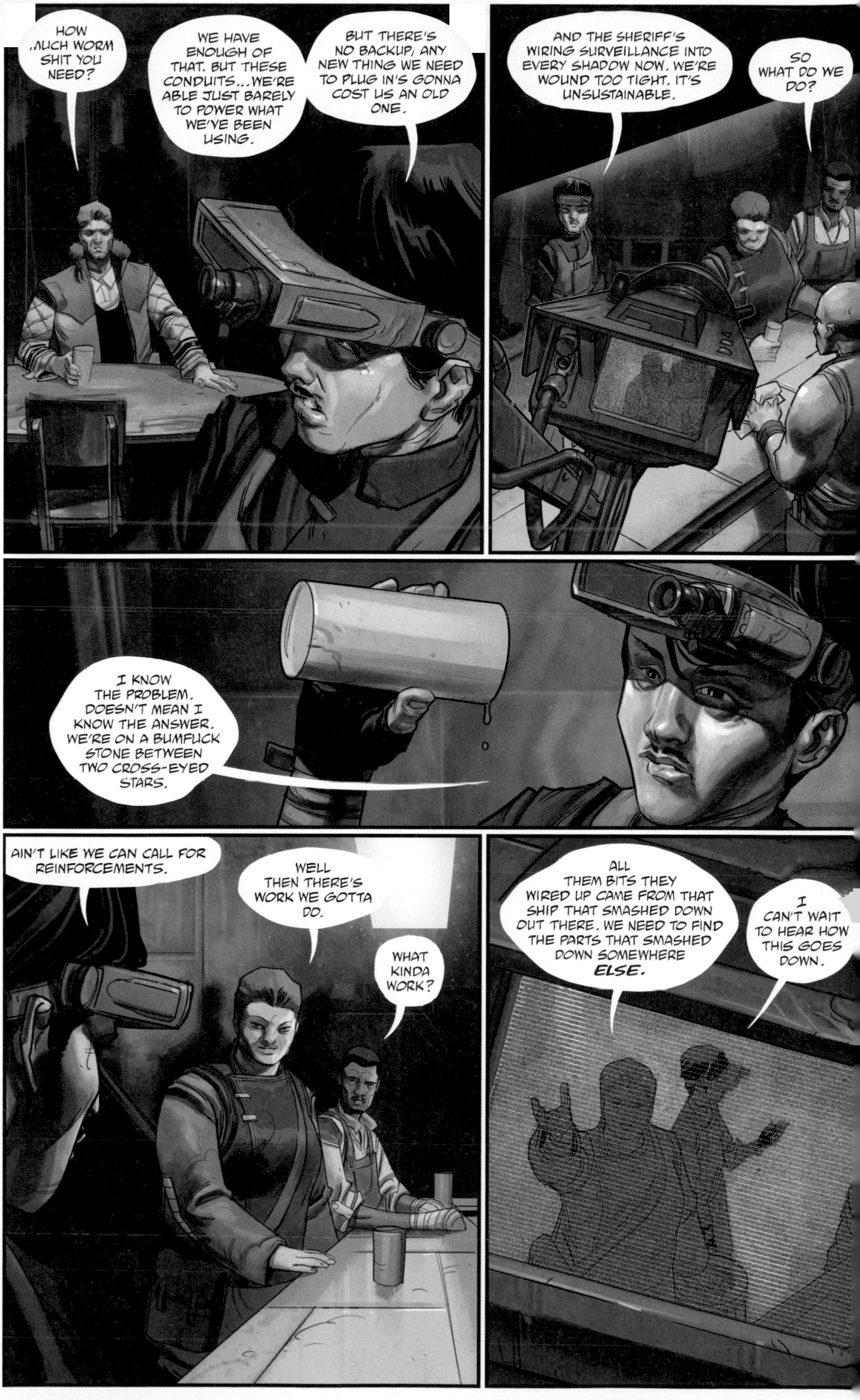
HOW MUCH WORM SHIT YOU NEED?
WE HAVE ENOUGH OF THAT. BUT THESE CONDUITS... WE'RE ABLE JUST BARELY TO POWER WHAT WE'VE BEEN USING.
BUT THERE'S NO BACKUP, ANY NEW THING WE NEED TO PLUG IN'S GONNA COST US AN OLD ONE.
AND THE SHERIFF'S WIRING SURVEILLANCE INTO EVERY SHADOW NOW. WE'RE WOUND TOO TIGHT. IT'S UNSUSTAINABLE.
SO WHAT DO WE DO?
I KNOW THE PROBLEM. DOESN'T MEAN I KNOW THE ANSWER. WE'RE ON A BUMFUCK STONE BETWEEN TWO CROSS-EYED STARS.
AIN'T LIKE WE CAN CALL FOR REINFORCEMENTS.
WELL THEN THERE'S WORK WE GOTTA DO.
WHAT KINDA WORK?
ALL THEM BITS THEY WIRED UP CAME FROM THAT SHIP THAT SMASHED DOWN OUT THERE. WE NEED TO FIND THE PARTS THAT SMASHED DOWN SOMEWHERE ELSE.
I CAN'T WAIT TO HEAR HOW THIS GOES DOWN.

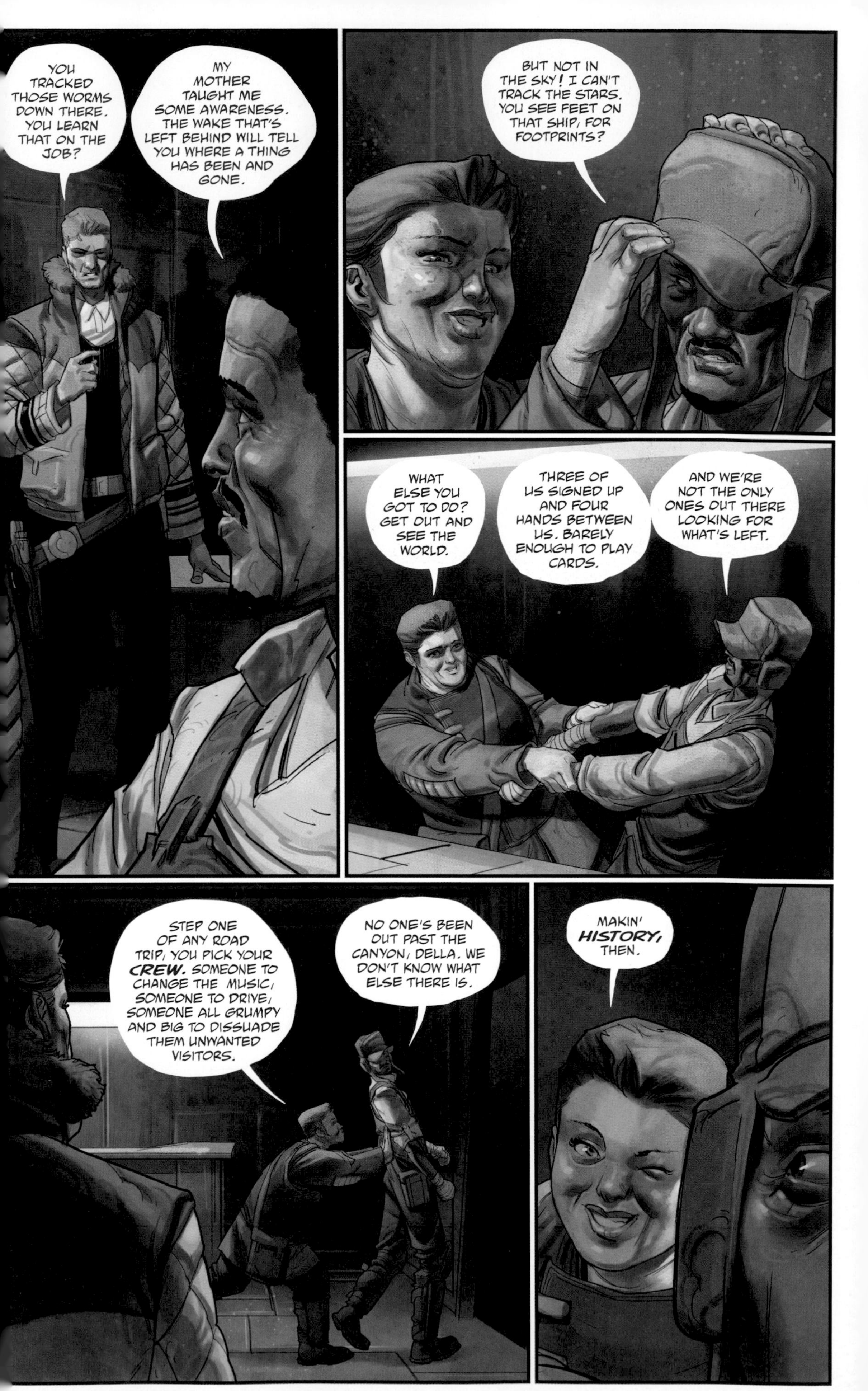
YOU TRACKED THOSE WORMS DOWN THERE. YOU LEARN THAT ON THE JOB?
MY MOTHER TAUGHT ME SOME AWARENESS. THE WAKE THAT'S LEFT BEHIND WILL TELL YOU WHERE A THING HAS BEEN AND GONE.
BUT NOT IN THE SKY! I CAN'T TRACK THE STARS. YOU SEE FEET ON THAT SHIP, FOR FOOTPRINTS?
WHAT ELSE YOU GOT TO DO? GET OUT AND SEE THE WORLD.
THREE OF US SIGNED UP AND FOUR HANDS BETWEEN US. BARELY ENOUGH TO PLAY CARDS.
AND WE'RE NOT THE ONLY ONES OUT THERE LOOKING FOR WHAT'S LEFT.
STEP ONE OF ANY ROAD TRIP, YOU PICK YOUR **CREW.** SOMEONE TO CHANGE THE MUSIC, SOMEONE TO DRIVE, SOMEONE ALL GRUMPY AND BIG TO DISSUADE THEM UNWANTED VISITORS.
NO ONE'S BEEN OUT PAST THE CANYON, DELLA. WE DON'T KNOW WHAT ELSE THERE IS.
MAKIN' ***HISTORY,*** THEN.

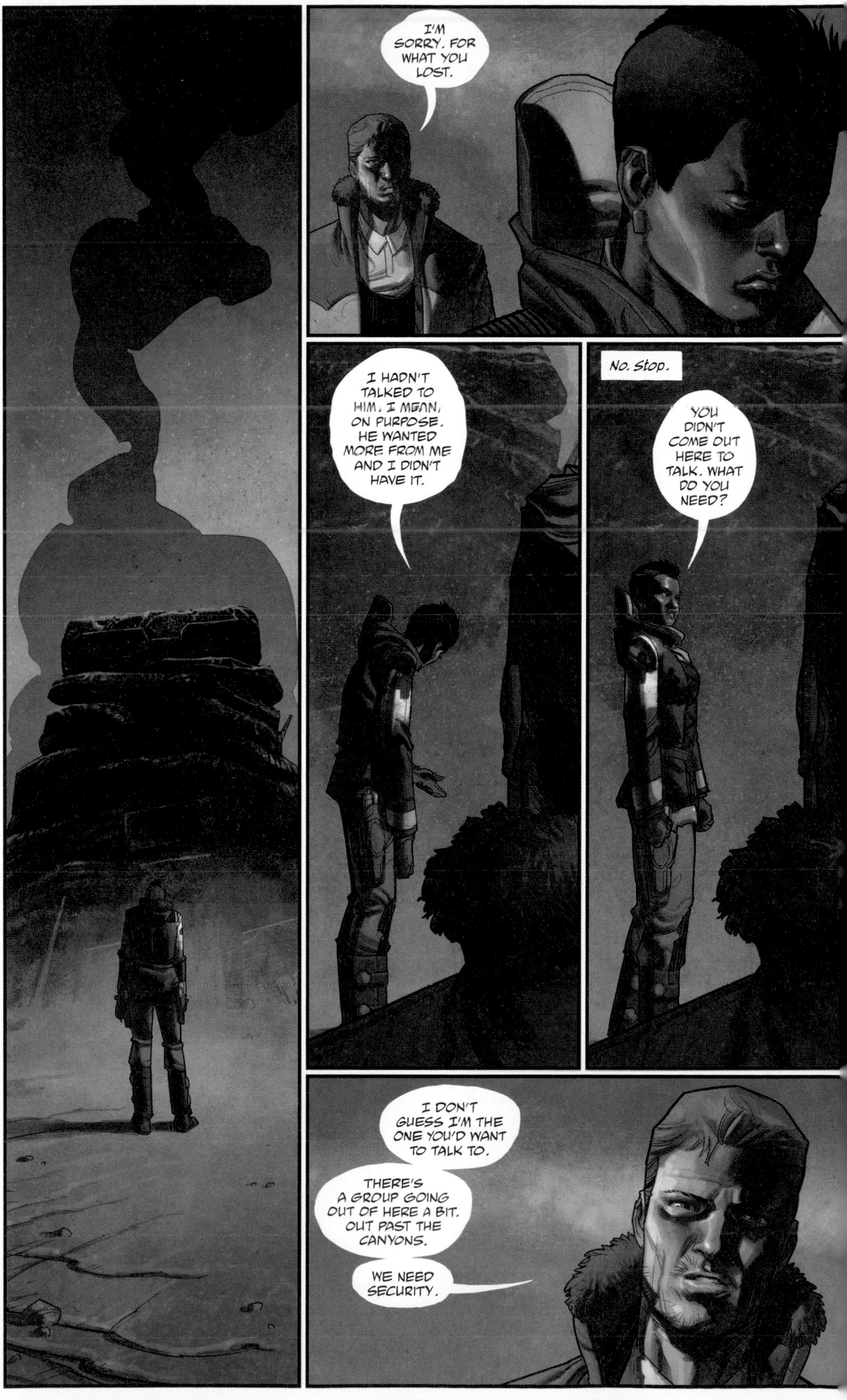
I'M SORRY. FOR WHAT YOU LOST.
I HADN'T TALKED TO HIM. I MEAN, ON PURPOSE. HE WANTED MORE FROM ME AND I DIDN'T HAVE IT.
No. Stop.
YOU DIDN'T COME OUT HERE TO TALK. WHAT DO YOU NEED?
I DON'T GUESS I'M THE ONE YOU'D WANT TO TALK TO.
THERE'S A GROUP GOING OUT OF HERE A BIT. OUT PAST THE CANYONS.
WE NEED SECURITY.

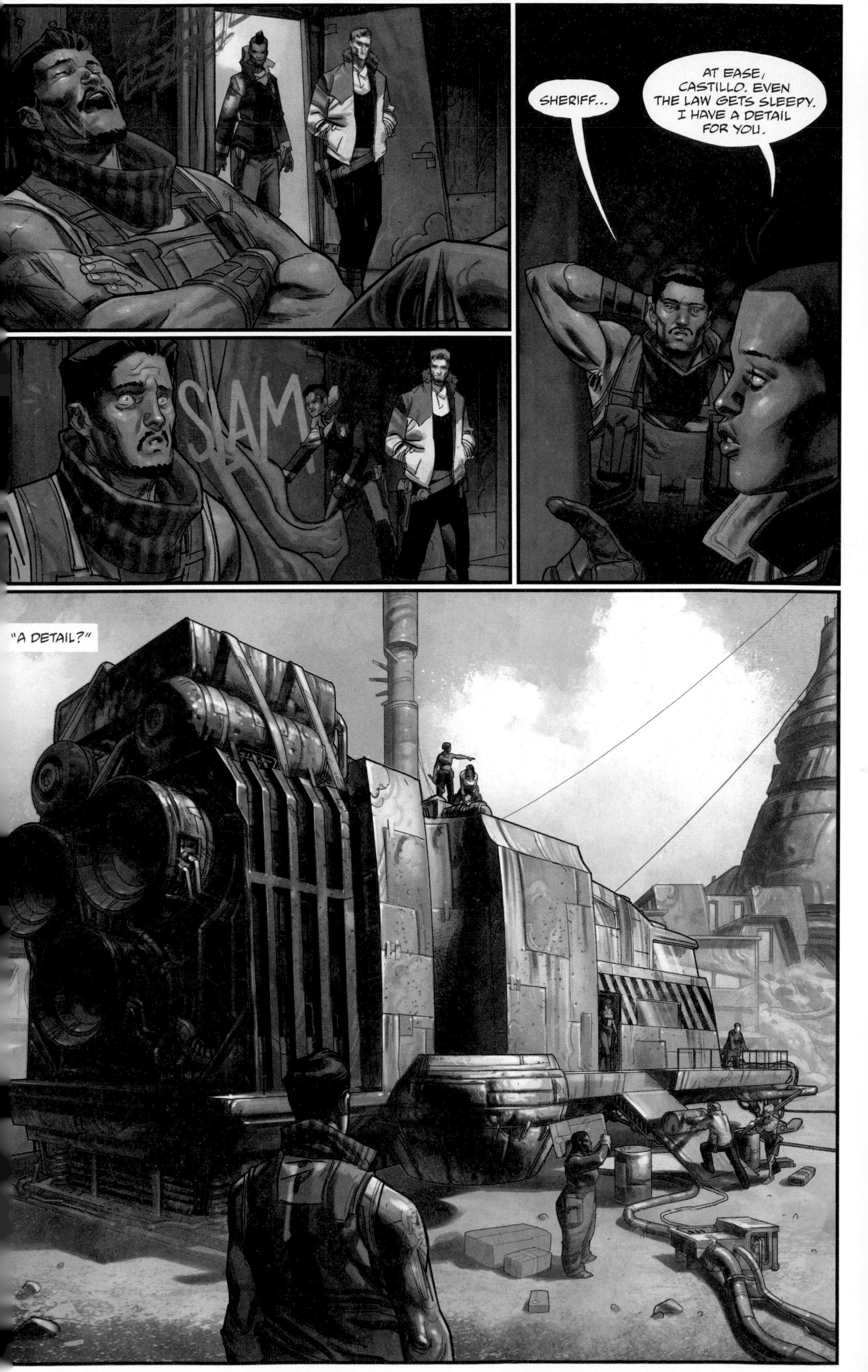
SHERIFF...
AT EASE, CASTILLO. EVEN THE LAW GETS SLEEPY. I HAVE A DETAIL FOR YOU.
SLAM
"A DETAIL?"

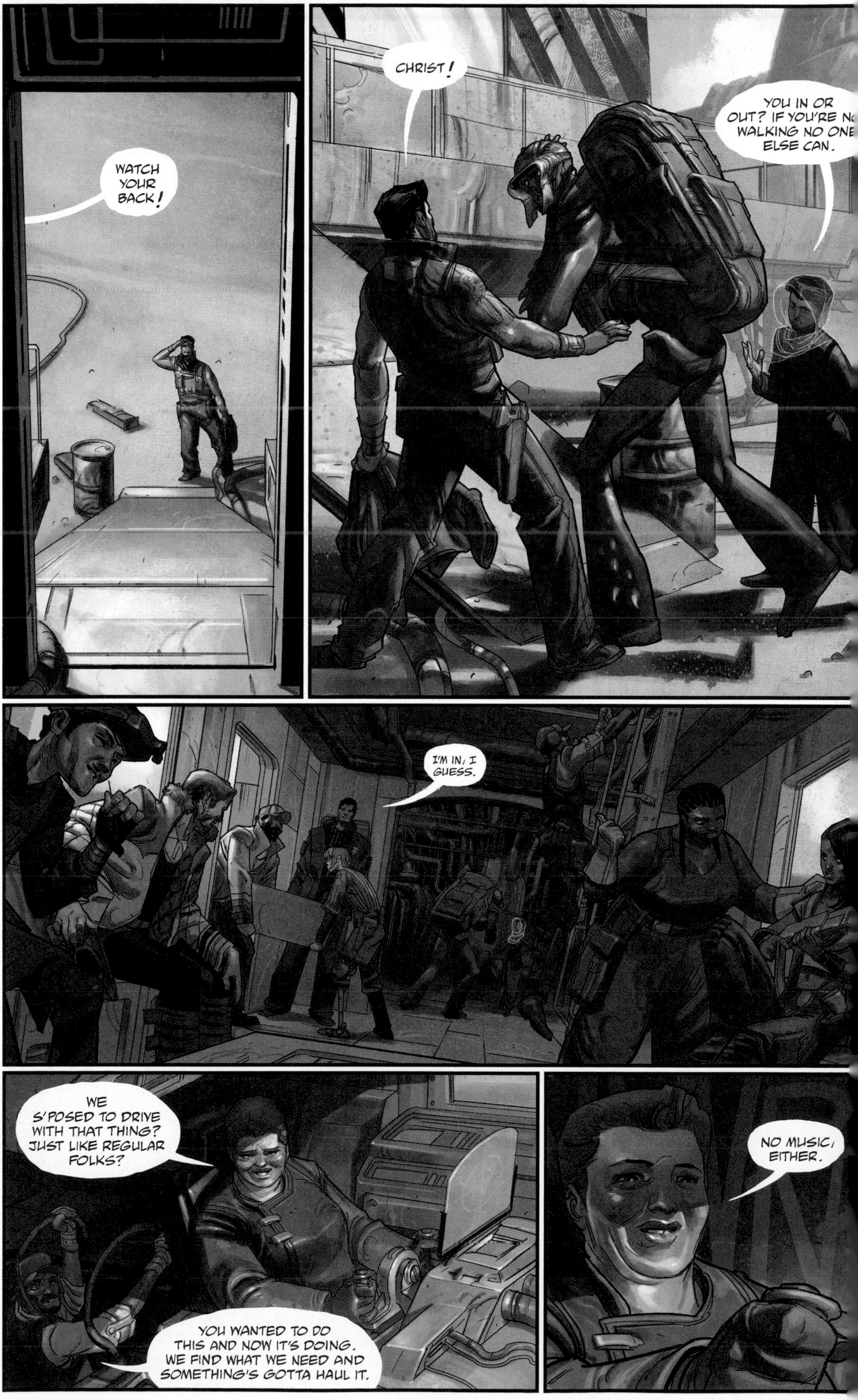
WATCH YOUR BACK!
CHRIST!
YOU IN OR OUT? IF YOU'RE NO WALKING NO ONE ELSE CAN.
I'M IN, I GUESS.
WE S'POSED TO DRIVE WITH THAT THING? JUST LIKE REGULAR FOLKS?
YOU WANTED TO DO THIS AND NOW IT'S DOING. WE FIND WHAT WE NEED AND SOMETHING'S GOTTA HAUL IT.
NO MUSIC, EITHER.

SHE GRINDS THE GEARS JUST THE ONCE. LEANS IN AND RIDES US PAST THE SUNS.

PAST WHAT'S FAMILIAR.

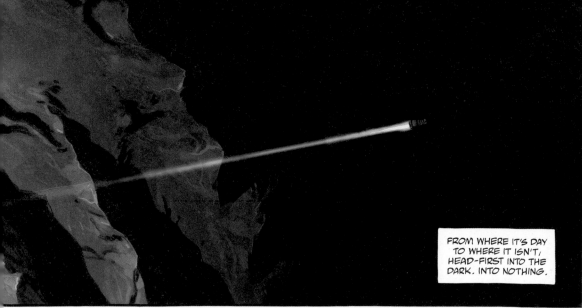

FROM WHERE IT'S DAY TO WHERE IT ISN'T, HEAD-FIRST INTO THE DARK. INTO NOTHING.

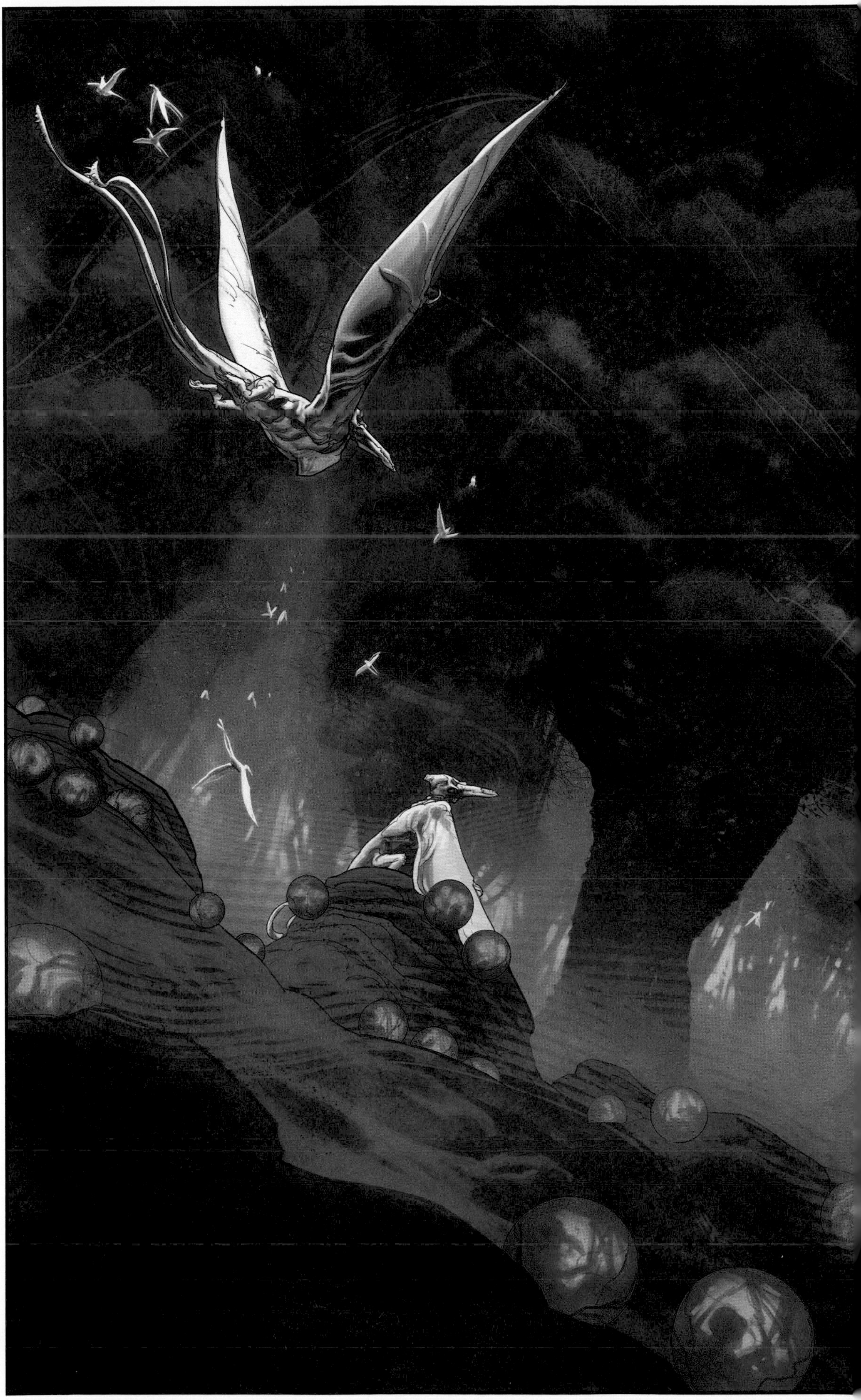

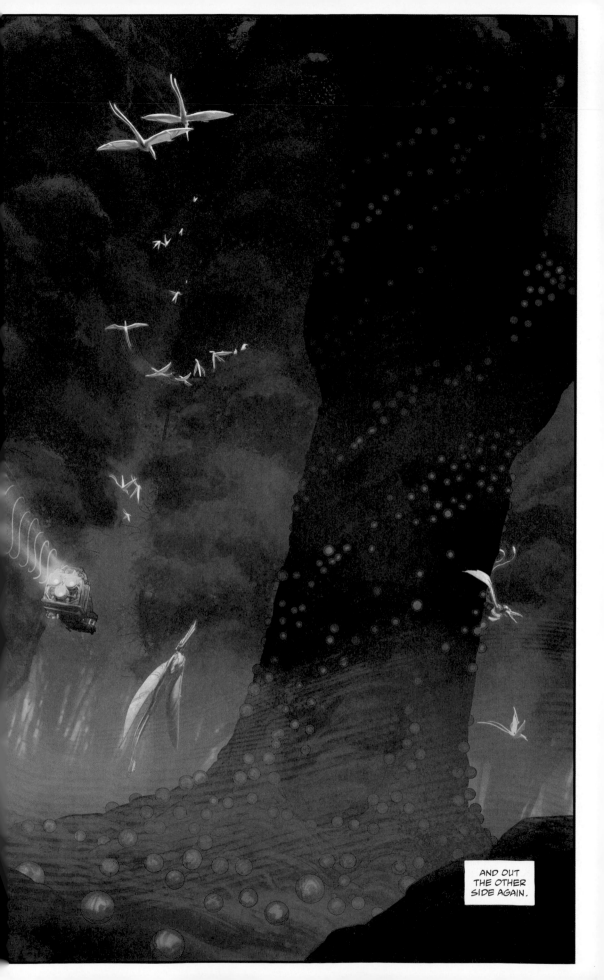

AND OUT
THE OTHER
SIDE AGAIN.

CHAPTER 7
A ROTTEN SOUND

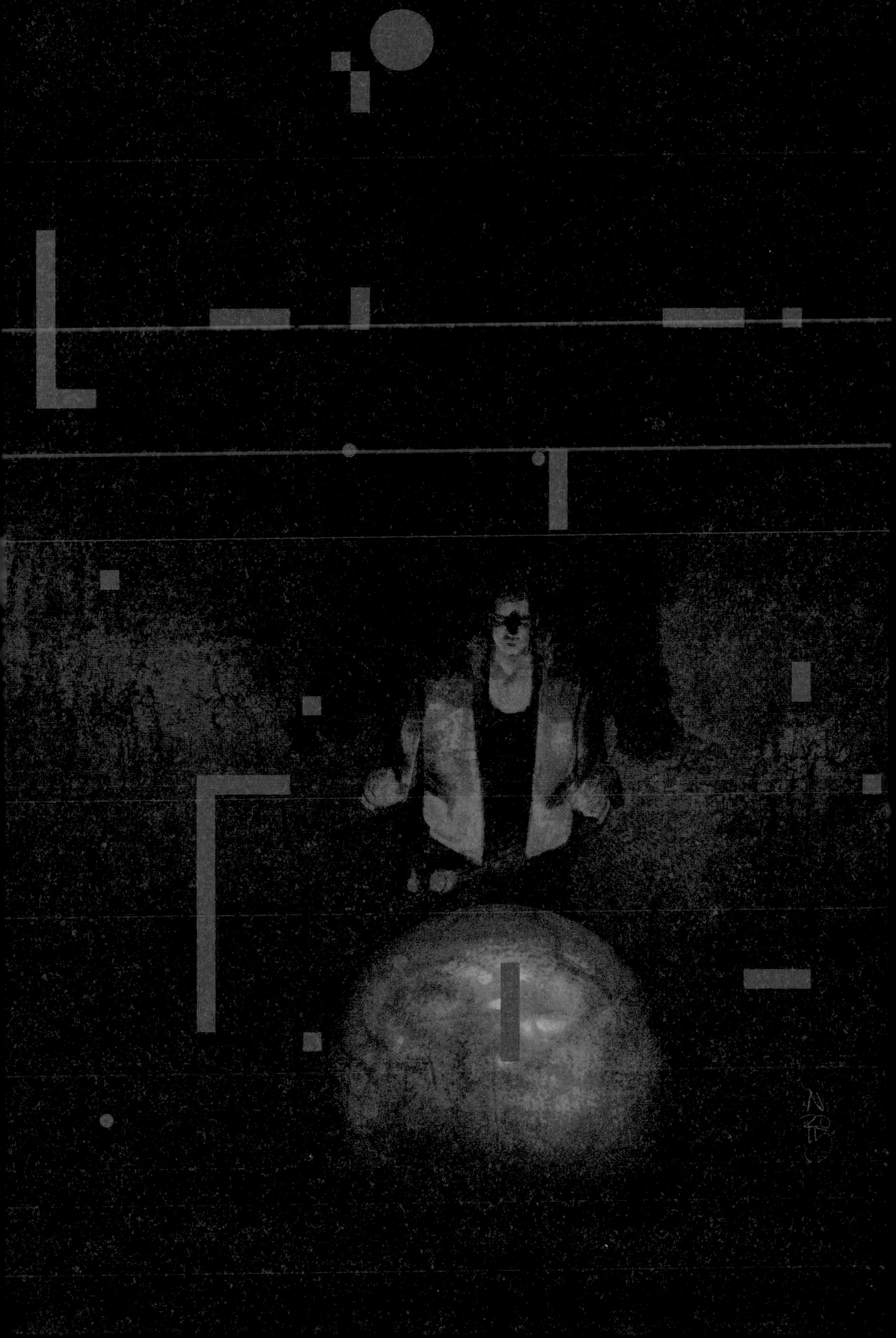

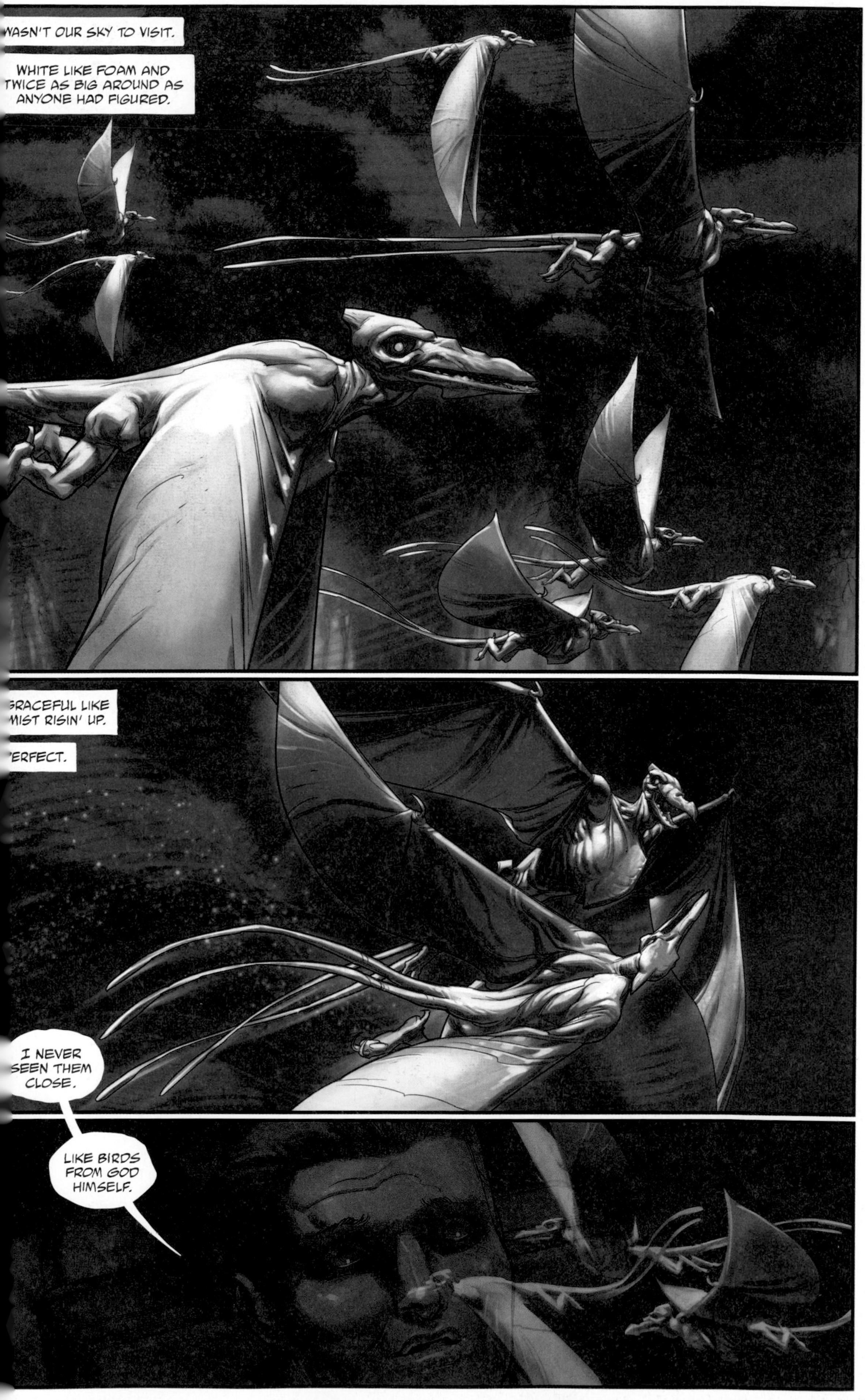
WASN'T OUR SKY TO VISIT.
WHITE LIKE FOAM AND TWICE AS BIG AROUND AS ANYONE HAD FIGURED.
GRACEFUL LIKE MIST RISIN' UP.
PERFECT.
I NEVER SEEN THEM CLOSE.
LIKE BIRDS FROM GOD HIMSELF.

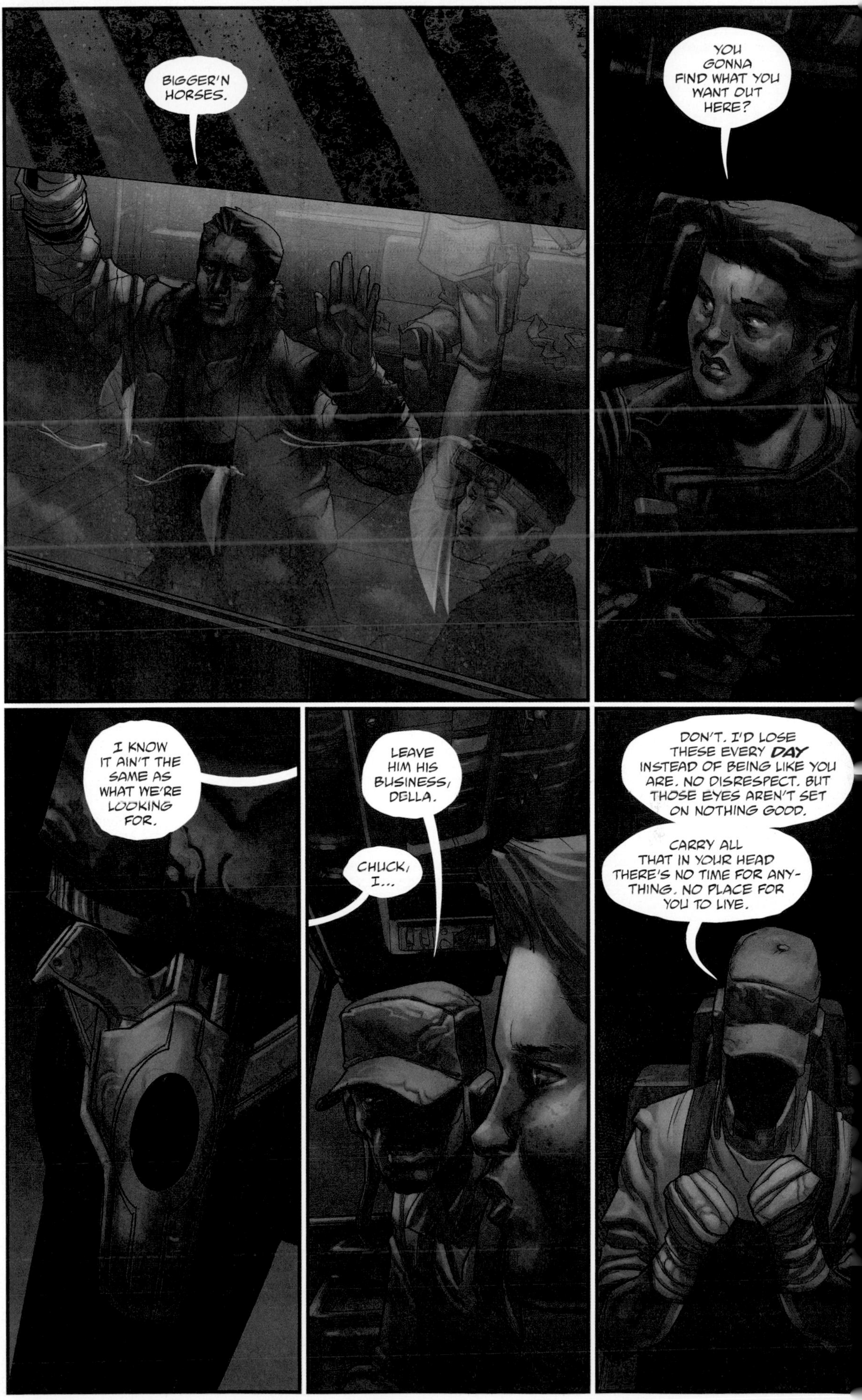
BIGGER'N HORSES.
YOU GONNA FIND WHAT YOU WANT OUT HERE?
I KNOW IT AIN'T THE SAME AS WHAT WE'RE LOOKING FOR.
LEAVE HIM HIS BUSINESS, DELLA.
CHUCK, I...
DON'T. I'D LOSE THESE EVERY DAY INSTEAD OF BEING LIKE YOU ARE. NO DISRESPECT. BUT THOSE EYES AREN'T SET ON NOTHING GOOD.
CARRY ALL THAT IN YOUR HEAD THERE'S NO TIME FOR ANY-THING. NO PLACE FOR YOU TO LIVE.

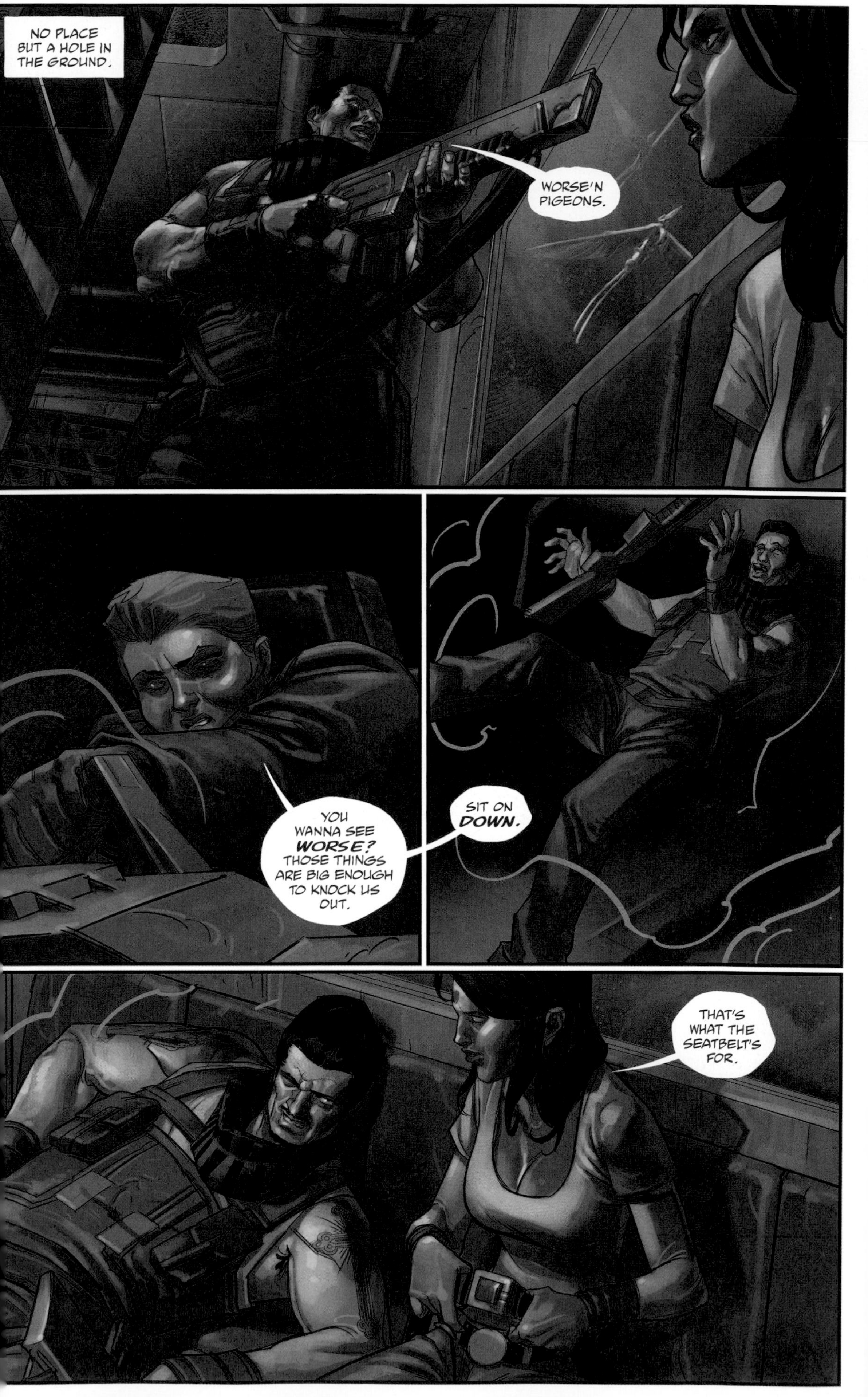
NO PLACE BUT A HOLE IN THE GROUND.
WORSE'N PIGEONS.
YOU WANNA SEE WORSE? THOSE THINGS ARE BIG ENOUGH TO KNOCK US OUT.
SIT ON DOWN.
THAT'S WHAT THE SEATBELT'S FOR.

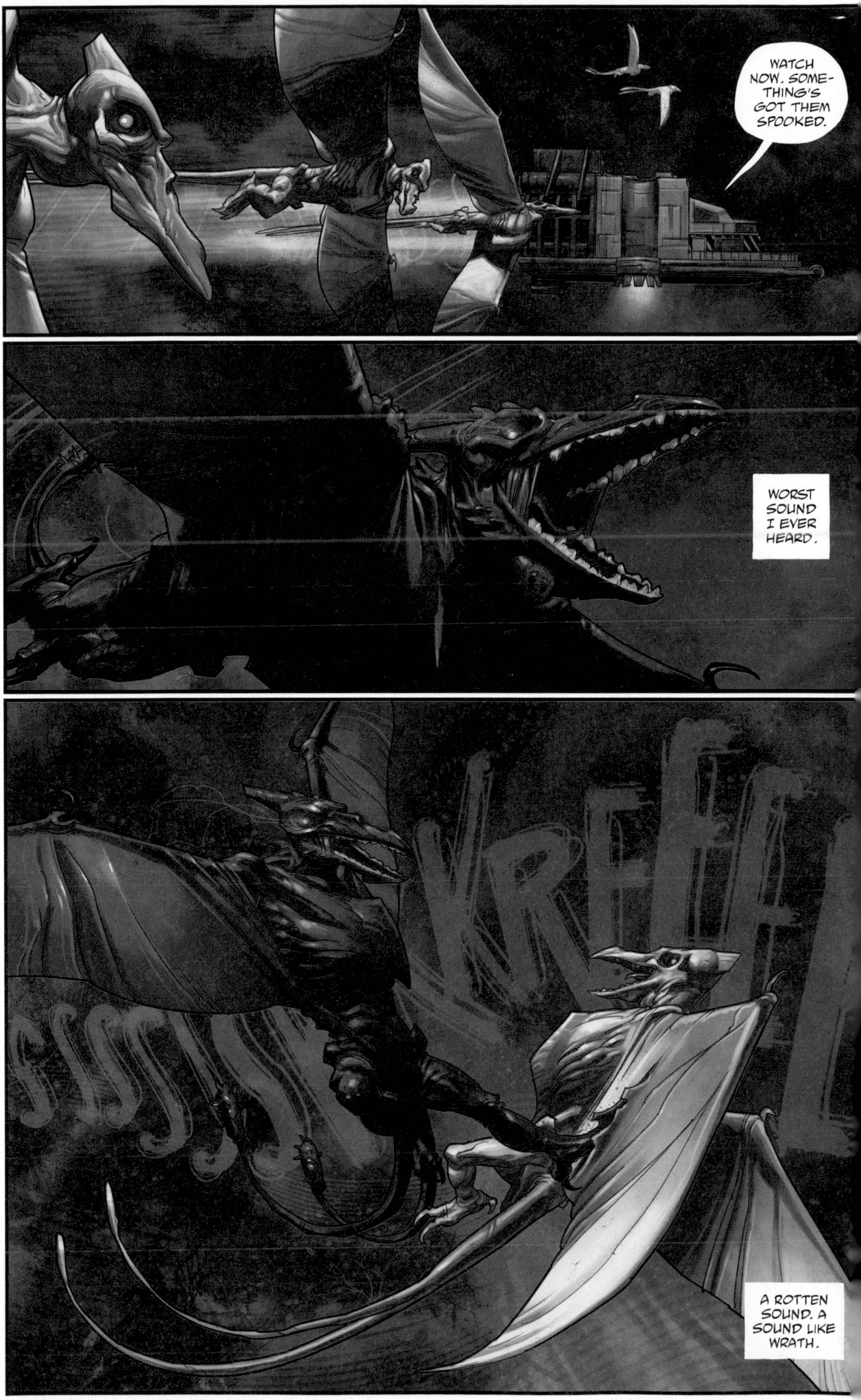
WATCH NOW. SOMETHING'S GOT THEM SPOOKED.
WORST SOUND I EVER HEARD.
A ROTTEN SOUND. A SOUND LIKE WRATH.

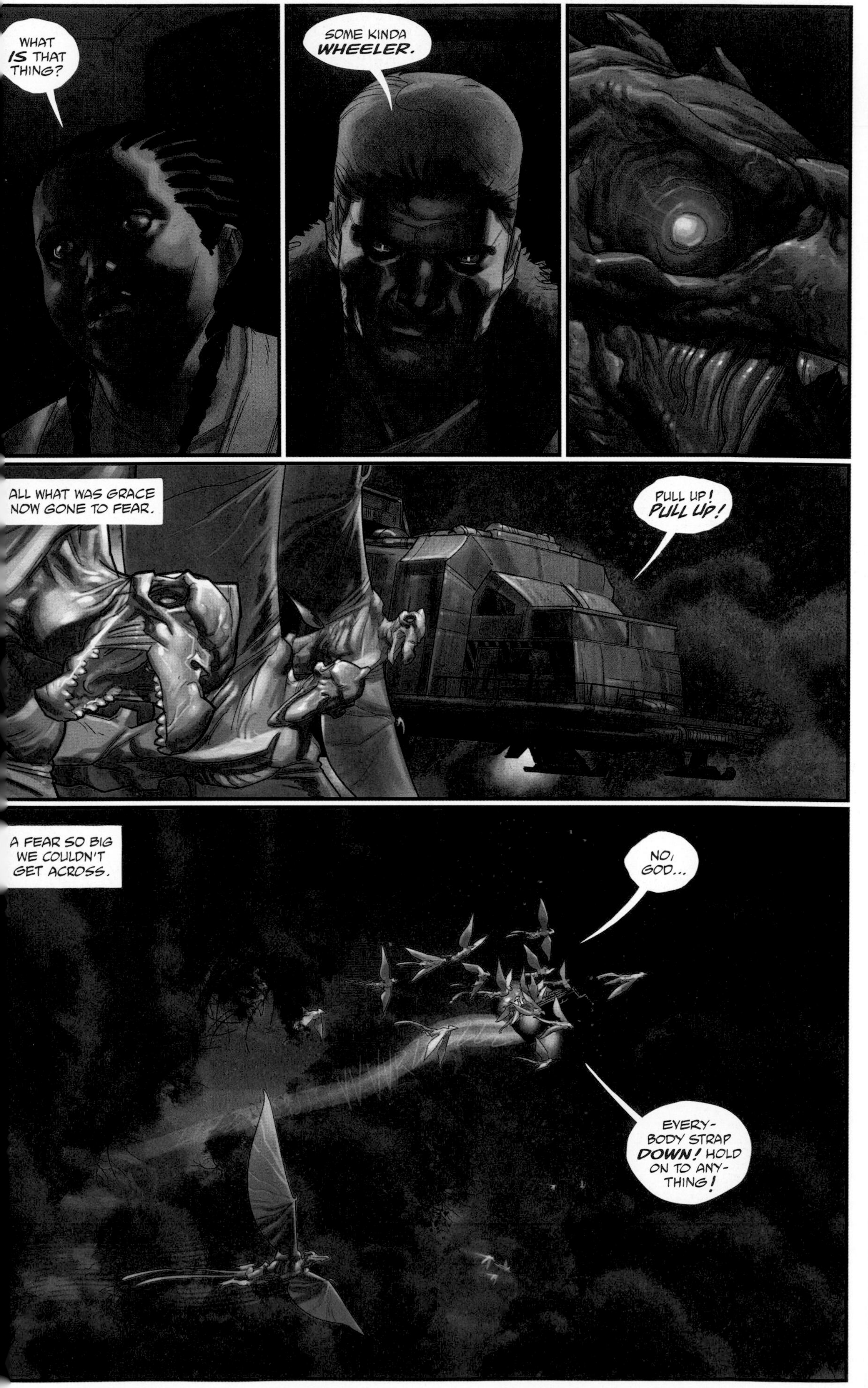
WHAT IS THAT THING?
SOME KINDA WHEELER.
ALL WHAT WAS GRACE NOW GONE TO FEAR.
PULL UP! PULL UP!
A FEAR SO BIG WE COULDN'T GET ACROSS.
NO, GOD...
EVERY-BODY STRAP DOWN! HOLD ON TO ANY-THING!

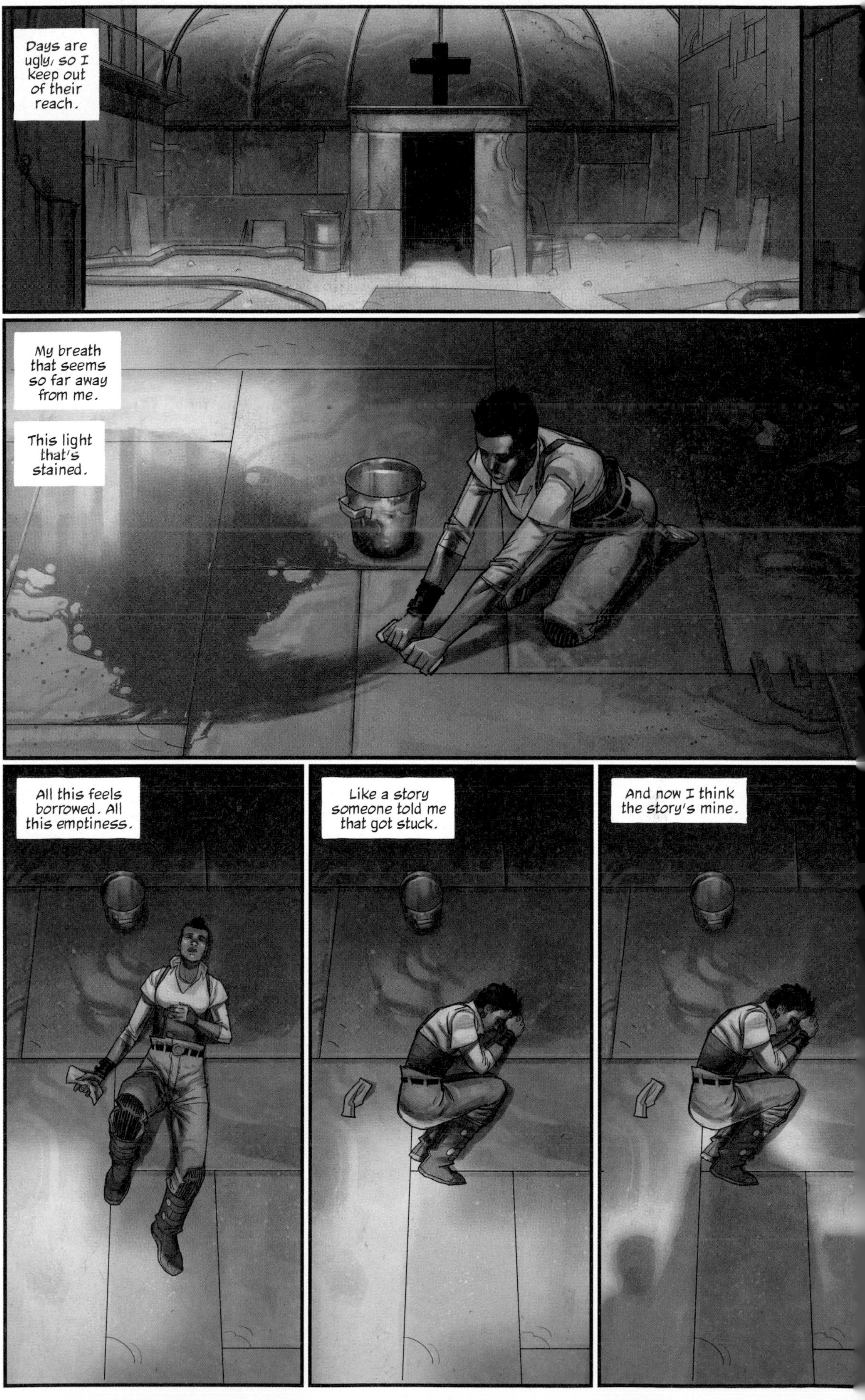

Days are ugly, so I keep out of their reach.
My breath that seems so far away from me.
This light that's stained.
All this feels borrowed. All this emptiness.
Like a story someone told me that got stuck.
And now I think the story's mine.

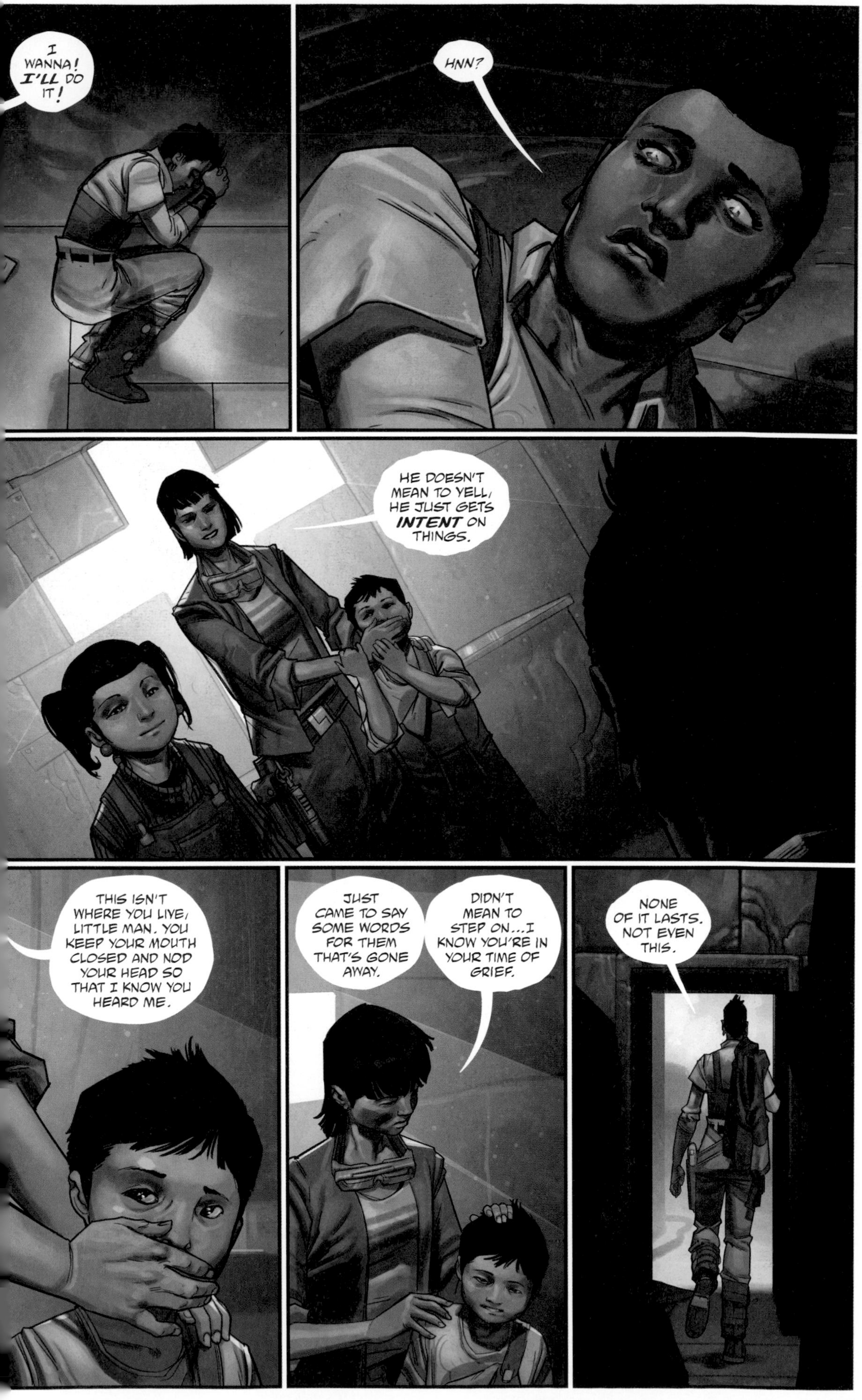
I WANNA! I'LL DO IT!
HNN?
HE DOESN'T MEAN TO YELL, HE JUST GETS INTENT ON THINGS.
THIS ISN'T WHERE YOU LIVE, LITTLE MAN. YOU KEEP YOUR MOUTH CLOSED AND NOD YOUR HEAD SO THAT I KNOW YOU HEARD ME.
JUST CAME TO SAY SOME WORDS FOR THEM THAT'S GONE AWAY.
DIDN'T MEAN TO STEP ON...I KNOW YOU'RE IN YOUR TIME OF GRIEF.
NONE OF IT LASTS. NOT EVEN THIS.

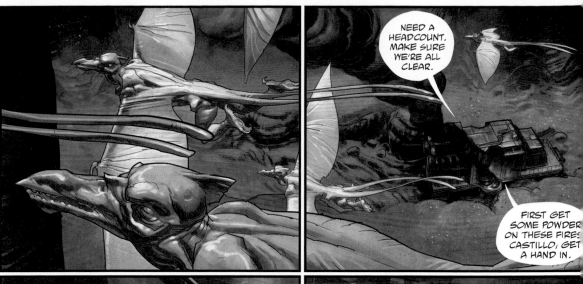

NEED A HEADCOUNT. MAKE SURE WE'RE ALL CLEAR.

FIRST GET SOME POWDER ON THESE FIRES CASTILLO, GET A HAND IN.

CASTILLO!

THAT FIRE'S *SPREADING!*

WE GOTTA GET CLEAR...

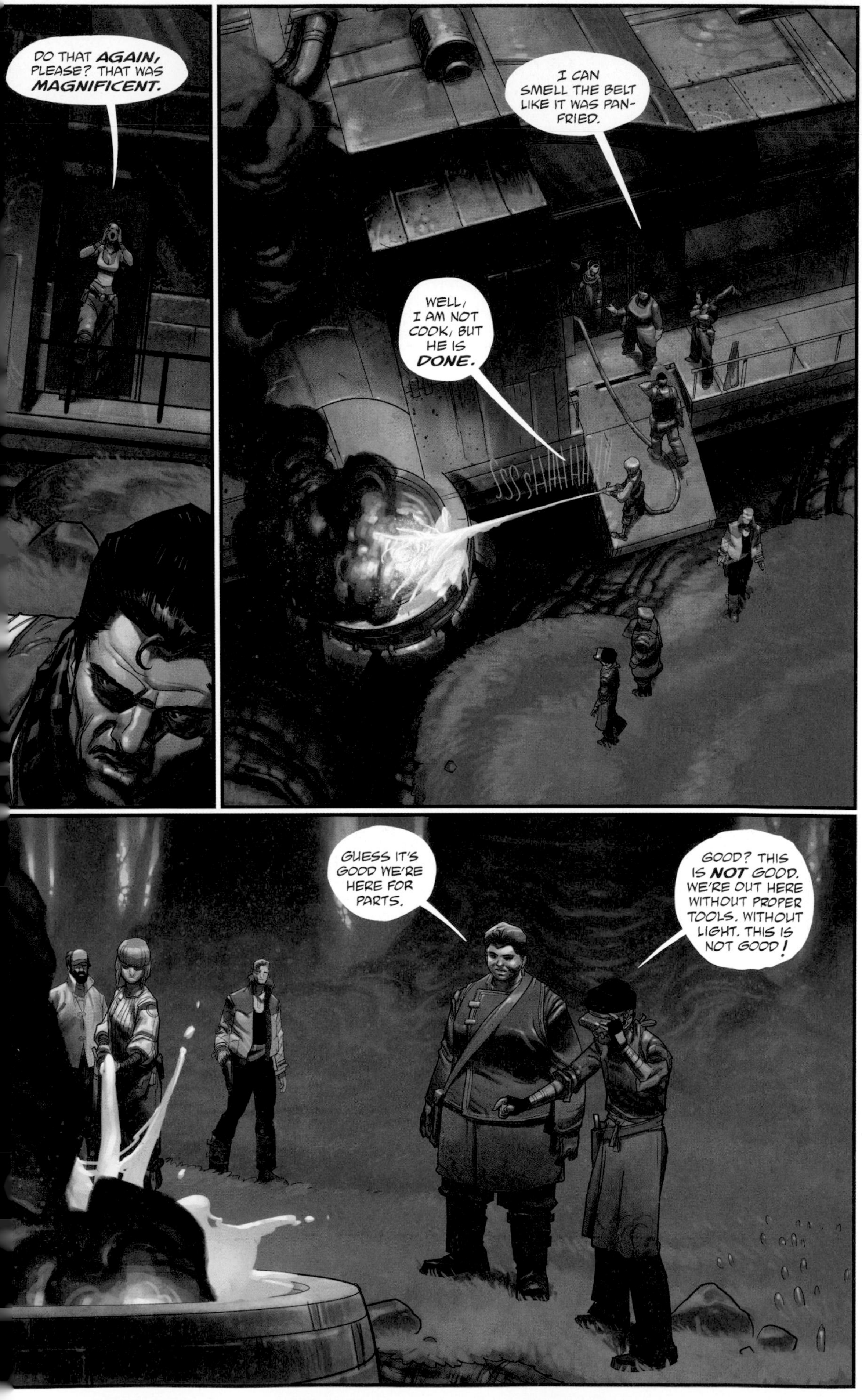
DO THAT **AGAIN,** PLEASE? THAT WAS ***MAGNIFICENT.***
I CAN SMELL THE BELT LIKE IT WAS PAN-FRIED.
WELL, I AM NOT COOK, BUT HE IS ***DONE.***
SSSSHHHHHH
GUESS IT'S GOOD WE'RE HERE FOR PARTS.
GOOD? THIS IS ***NOT*** GOOD. WE'RE OUT HERE WITHOUT PROPER TOOLS. WITHOUT LIGHT. THIS IS NOT GOOD!

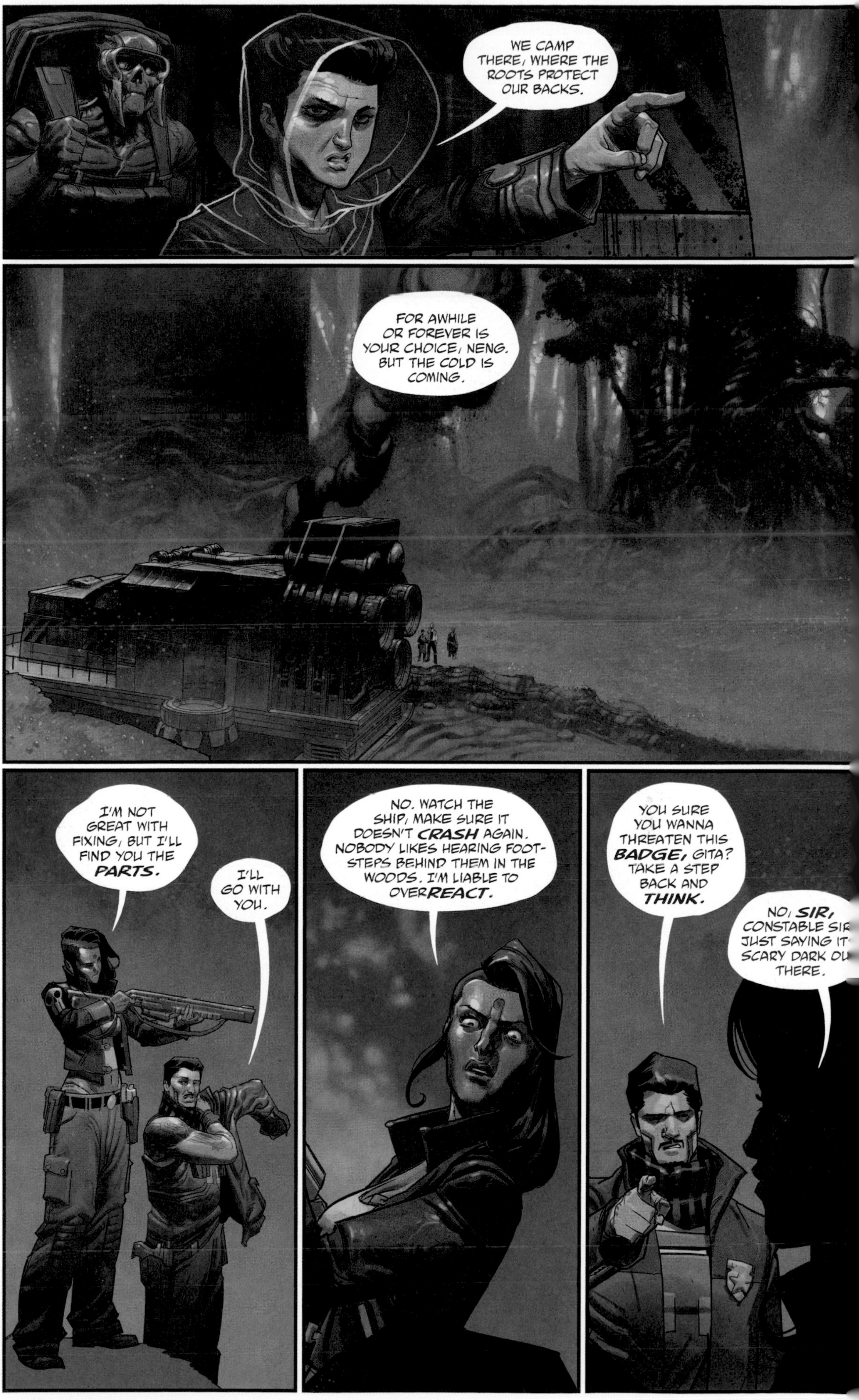
WE CAMP THERE, WHERE THE ROOTS PROTECT OUR BACKS.
FOR AWHILE OR FOREVER IS YOUR CHOICE, NENG. BUT THE COLD IS COMING.
I'M NOT GREAT WITH FIXING, BUT I'LL FIND YOU THE **PARTS.**
I'LL GO WITH YOU.
NO. WATCH THE SHIP, MAKE SURE IT DOESN'T **CRASH** AGAIN. NOBODY LIKES HEARING FOOT-STEPS BEHIND THEM IN THE WOODS. I'M LIABLE TO OVER**REACT.**
YOU SURE YOU WANNA THREATEN THIS **BADGE,** GITA? TAKE A STEP BACK AND **THINK.**
NO, **SIR,** CONSTABLE SIR JUST SAYING IT SCARY DARK OU THERE.

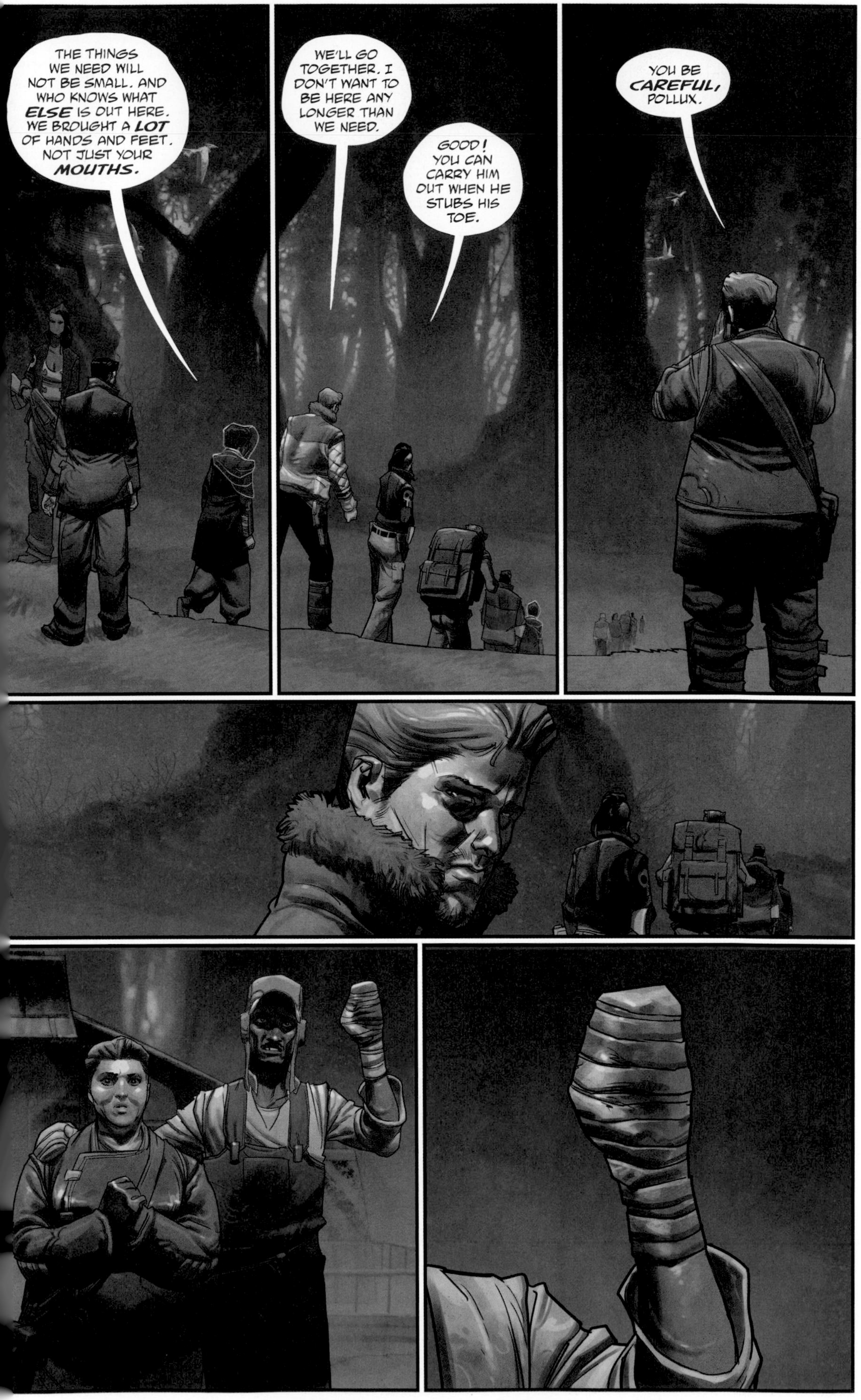
THE THINGS WE NEED WILL NOT BE SMALL. AND WHO KNOWS WHAT ELSE IS OUT HERE. WE BROUGHT A LOT OF HANDS AND FEET. NOT JUST YOUR MOUTHS.
WE'LL GO TOGETHER. I DON'T WANT TO BE HERE ANY LONGER THAN WE NEED.
GOOD! YOU CAN CARRY HIM OUT WHEN HE STUBS HIS TOE.
YOU BE CAREFUL, POLLUX.

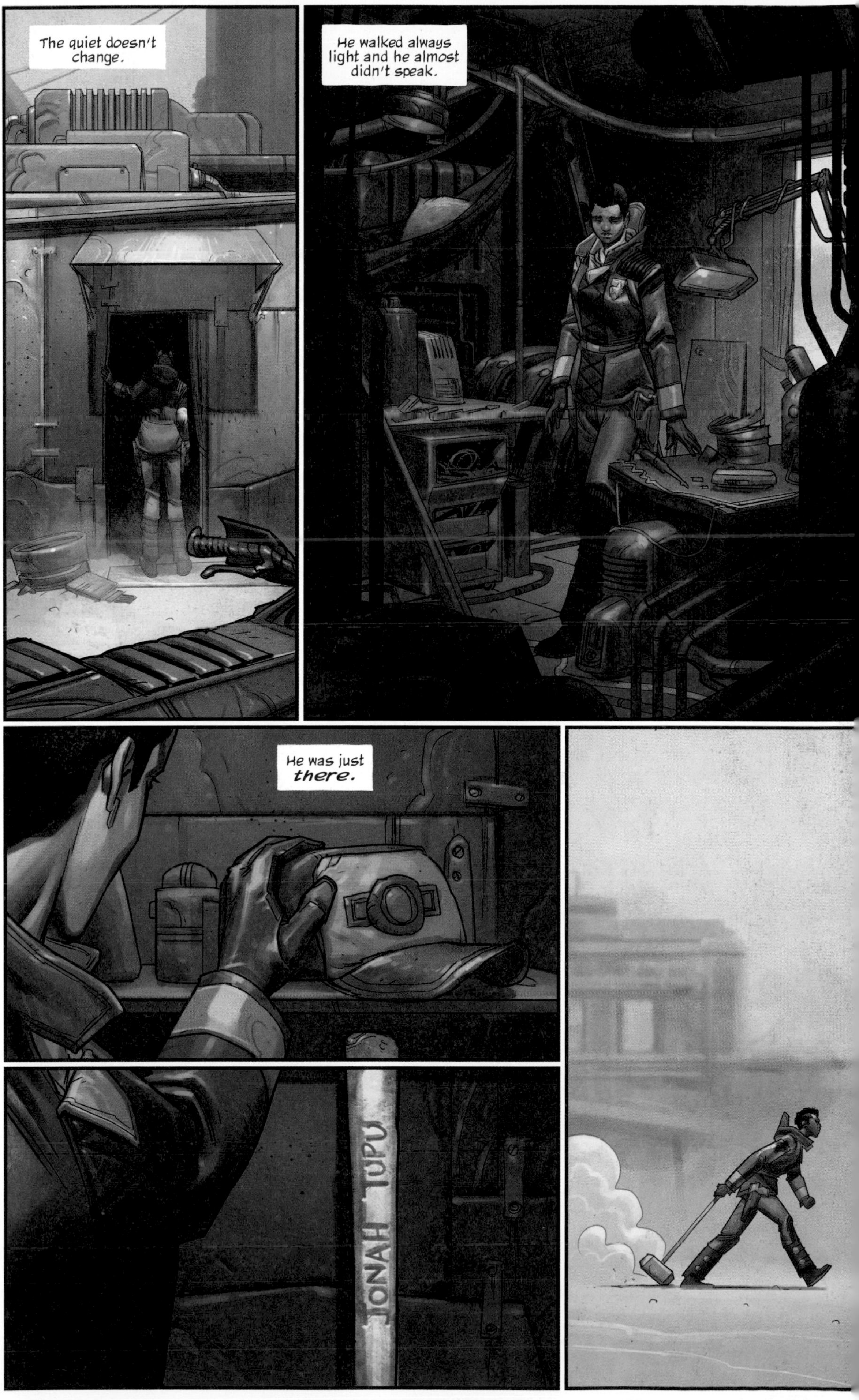
The quiet doesn't change.
He walked always light and he almost didn't speak.
He was just *there.*
JONAH TUPU

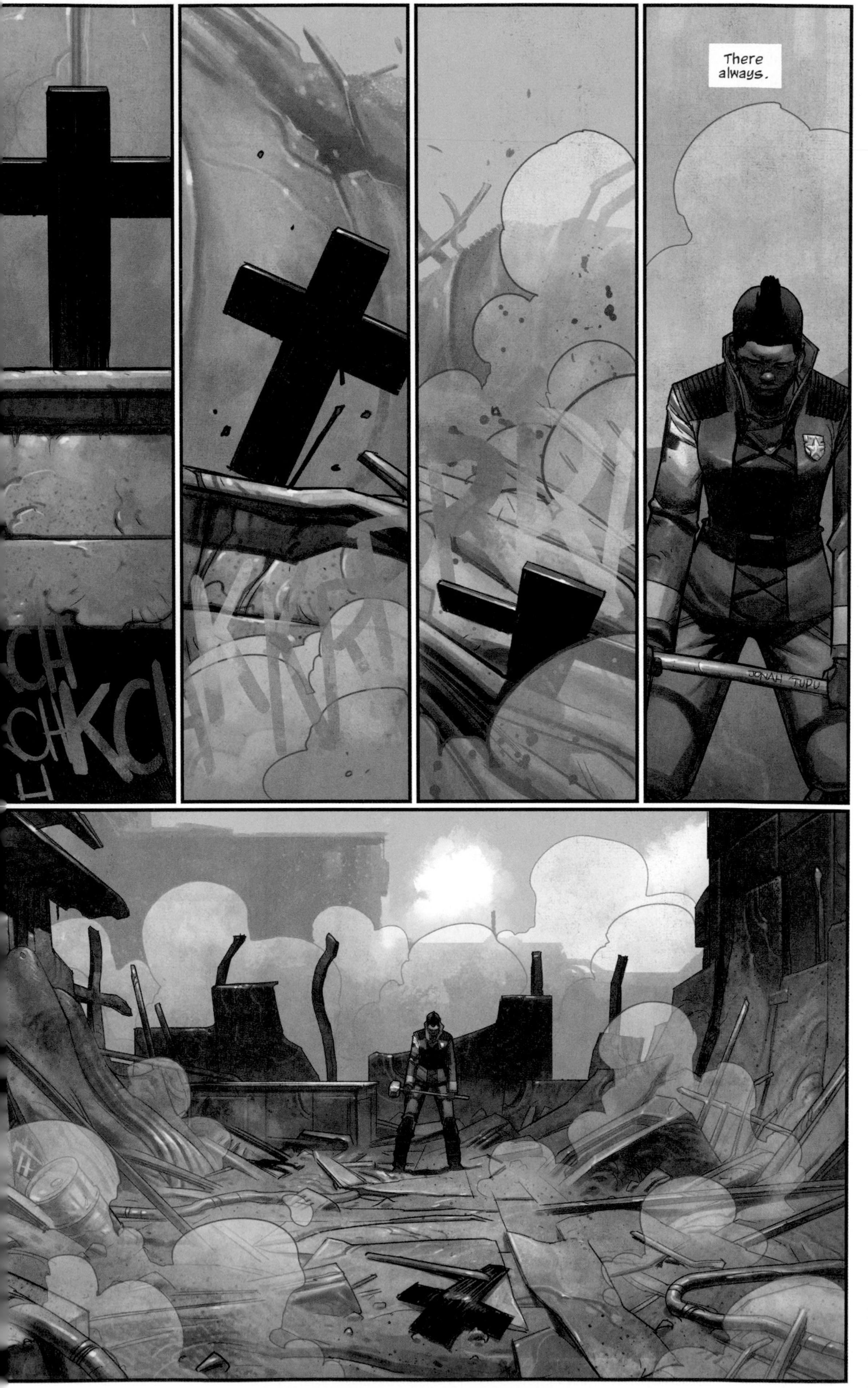
There always.
JONAH TUPU

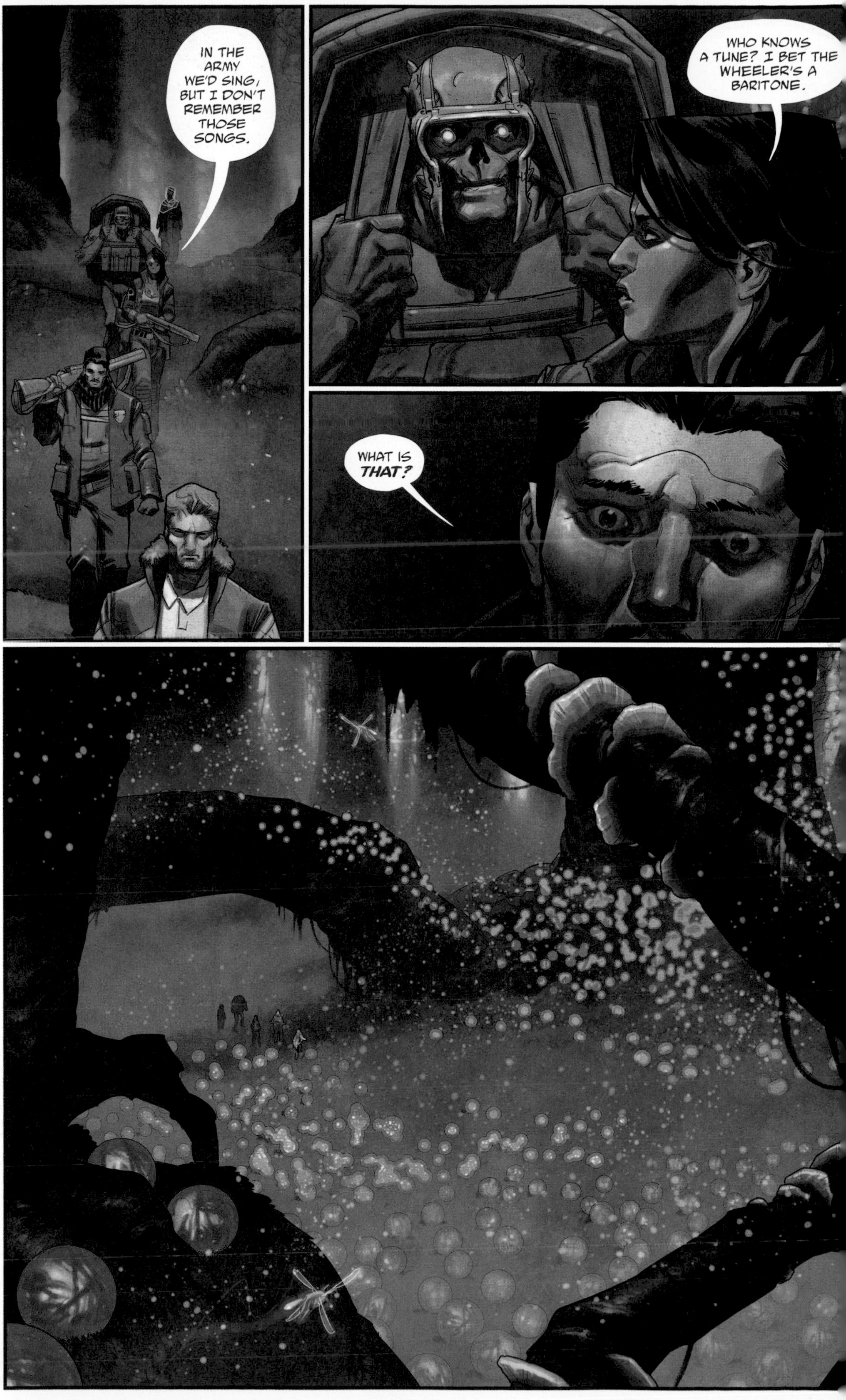
IN THE ARMY WE'D SING, BUT I DON'T REMEMBER THOSE SONGS.
WHO KNOWS A TUNE? I BET THE WHEELER'S A BARITONE.
WHAT IS *THAT?*

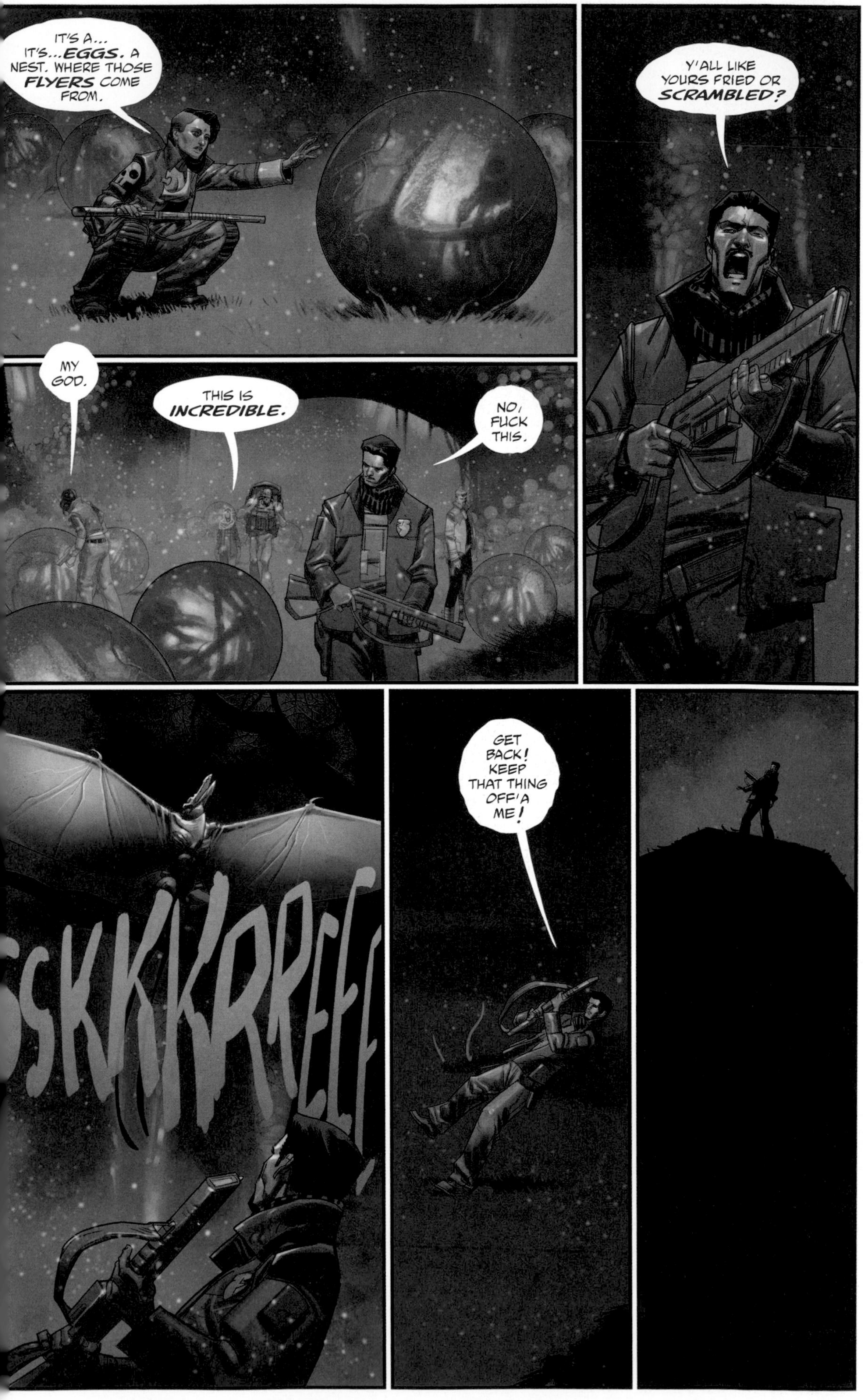
IT'S A...
IT'S...EGGS. A NEST. WHERE THOSE FLYERS COME FROM.
Y'ALL LIKE YOURS FRIED OR SCRAMBLED?
MY GOD.
THIS IS INCREDIBLE.
NO, FUCK THIS.
SKKKREEE
GET BACK! KEEP THAT THING OFF'A ME!

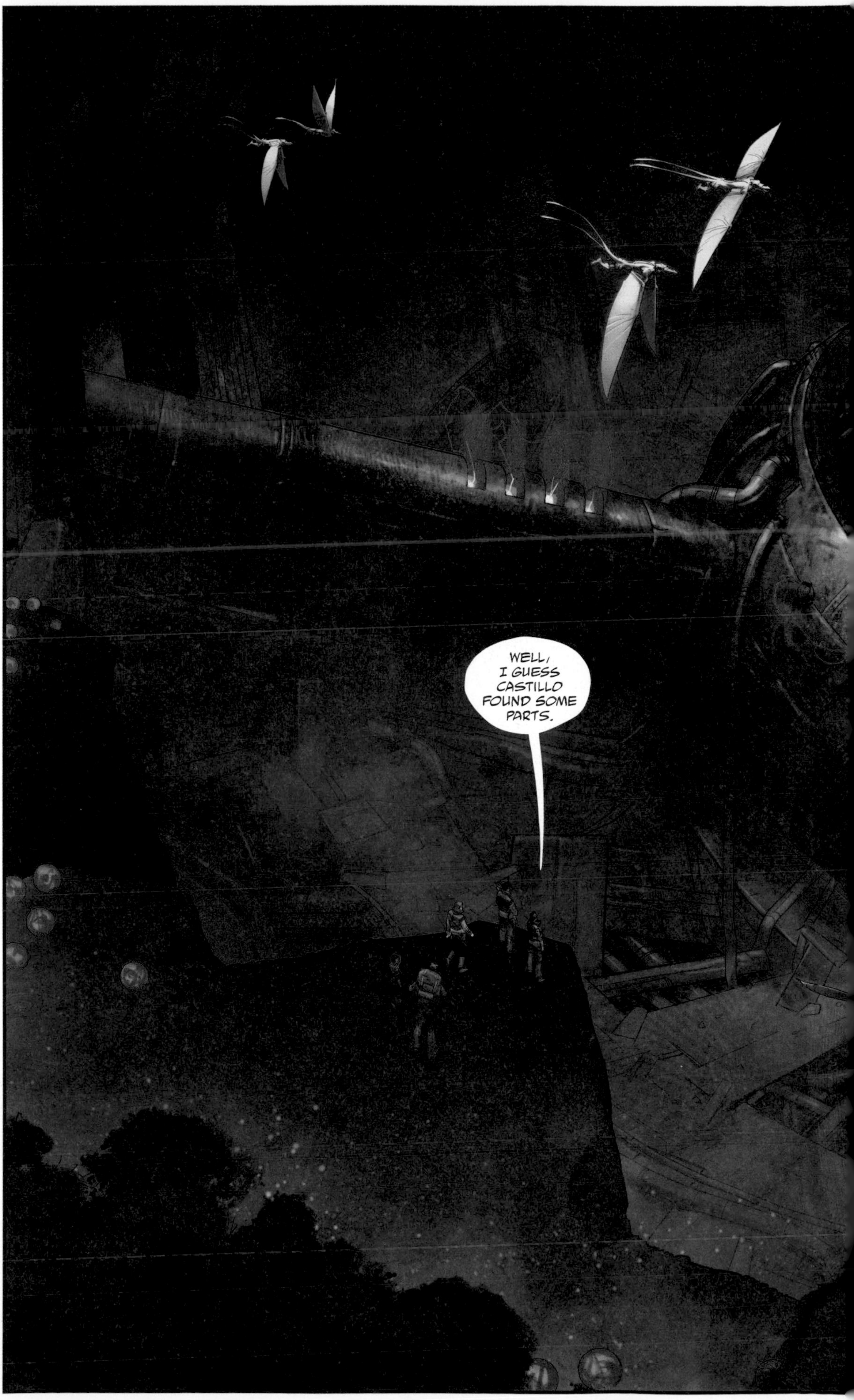
WELL, I GUESS CASTILLO FOUND SOME PARTS.

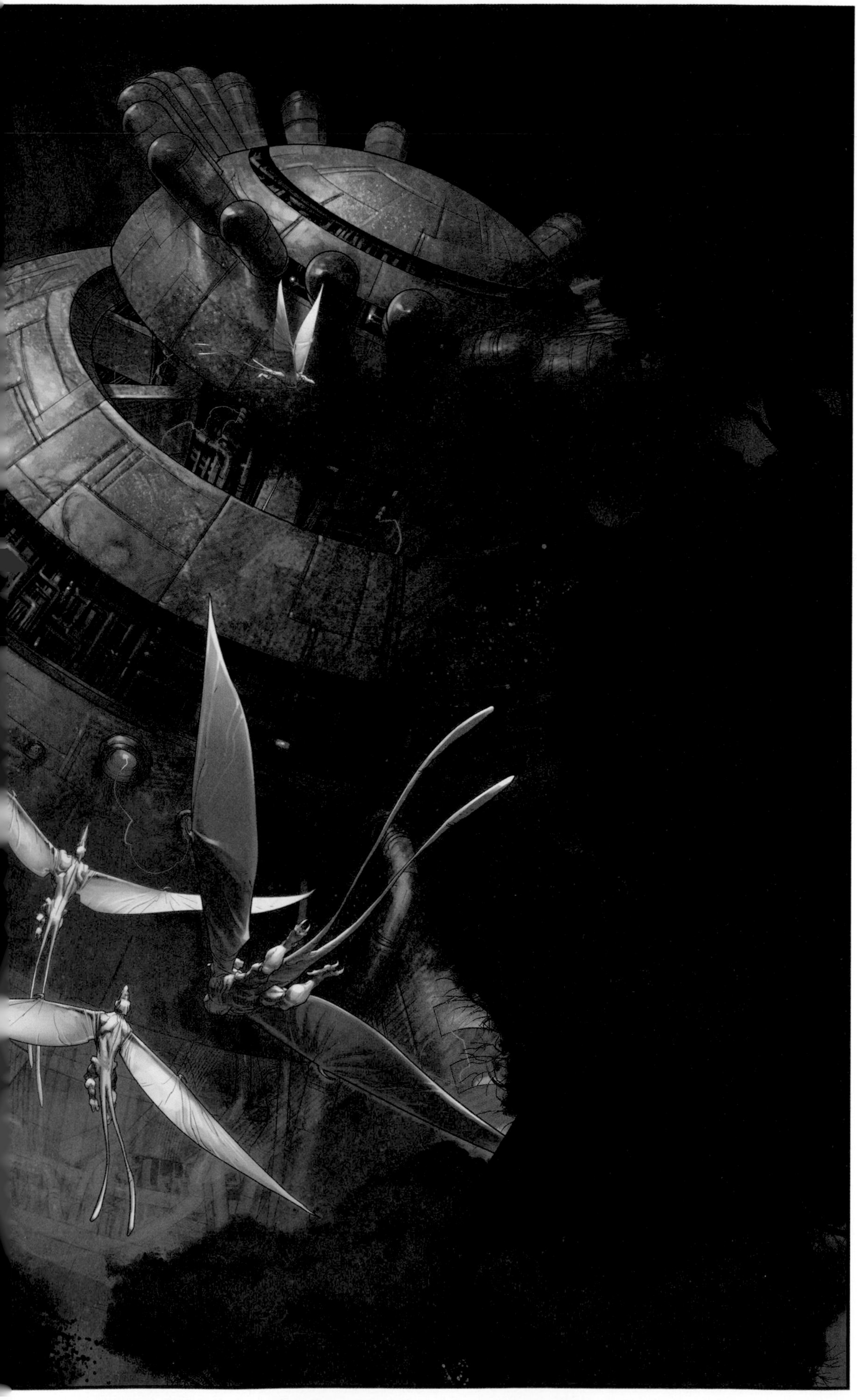

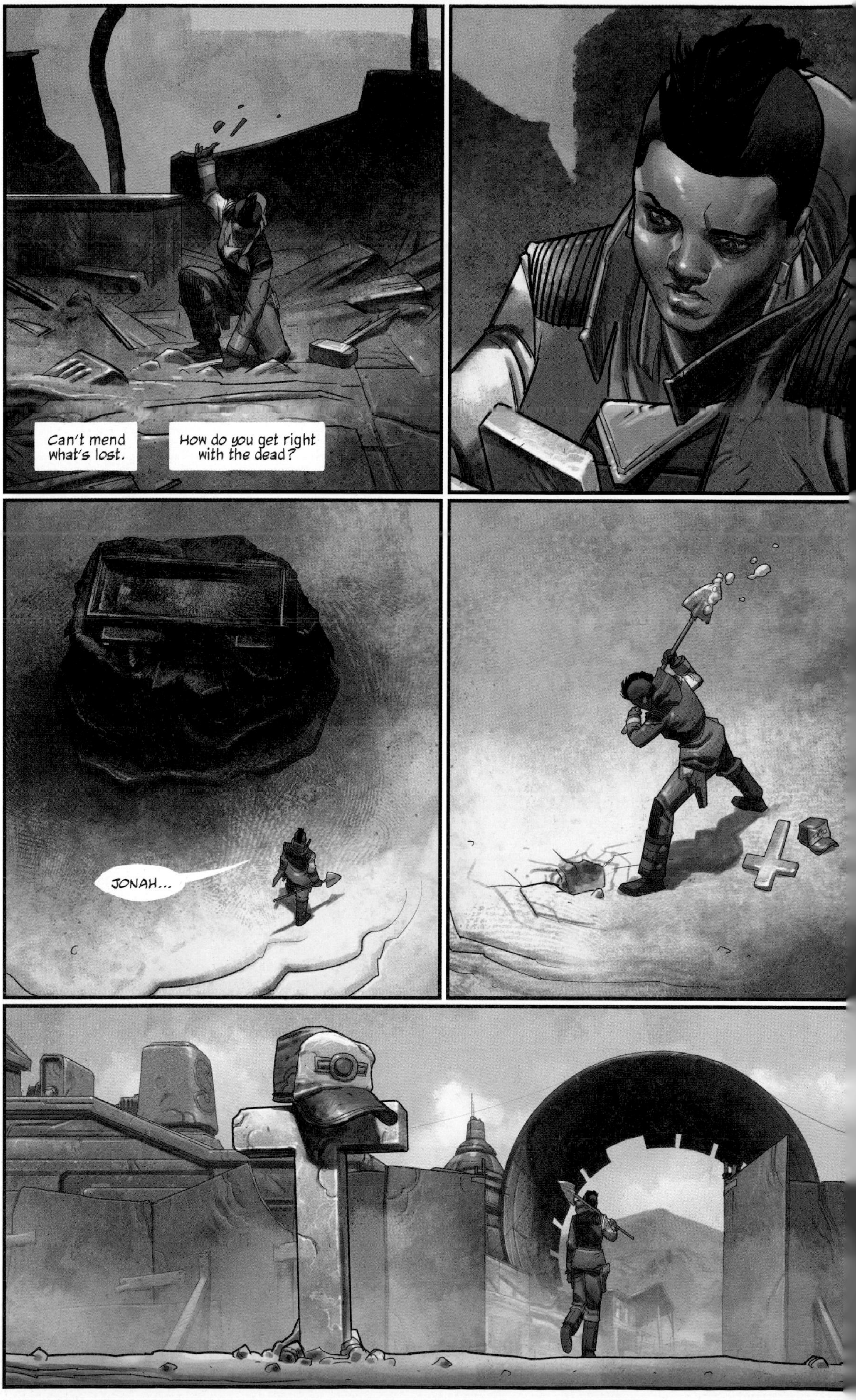
Can't mend what's lost.
How do you get right with the dead?
JONAH...

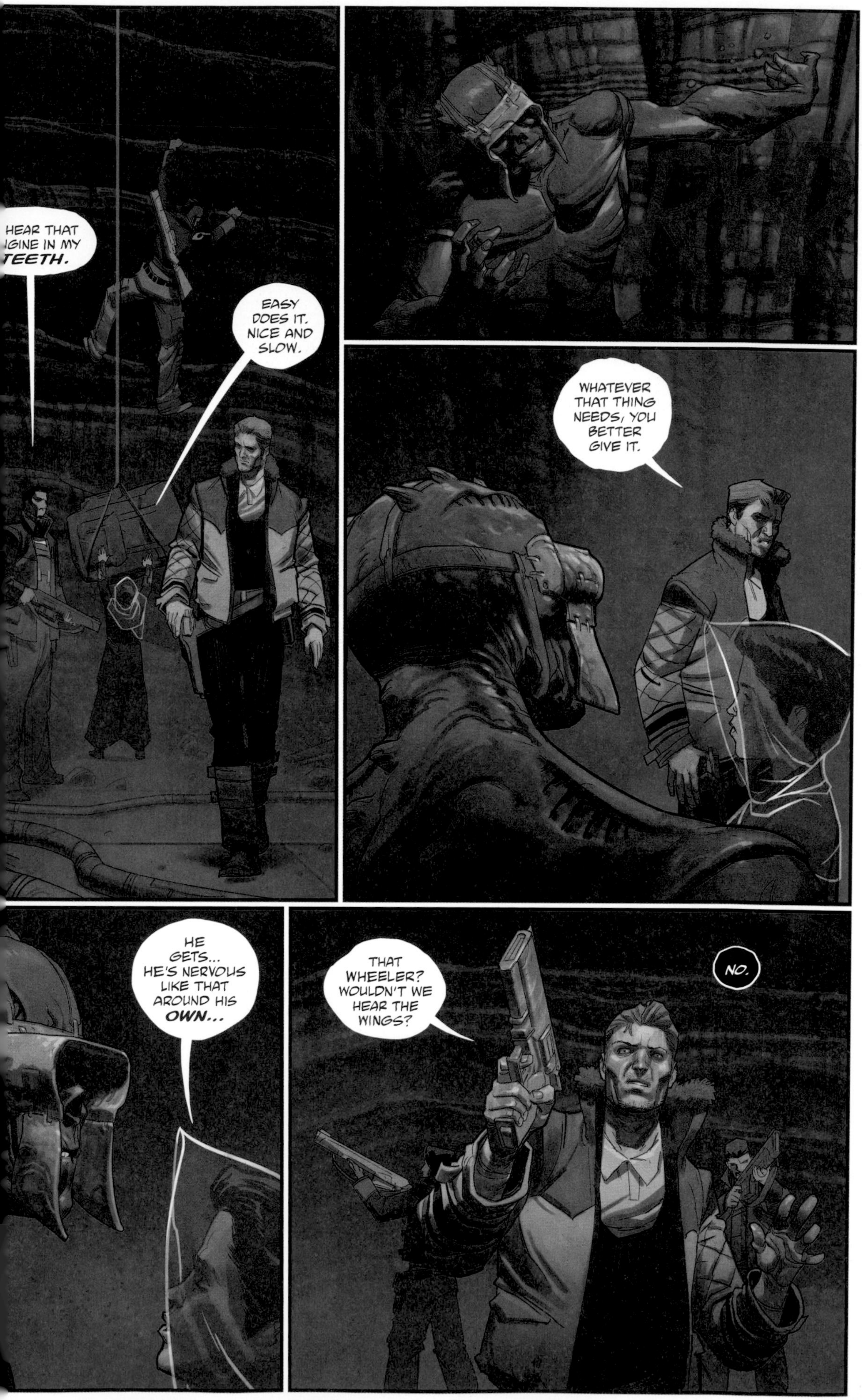
HEAR THAT
NGINE IN MY
TEETH.
EASY DOES IT. NICE AND SLOW.
WHATEVER THAT THING NEEDS, YOU BETTER GIVE IT.
HE GETS... HE'S NERVOUS LIKE THAT AROUND HIS OWN...
THAT WHEELER? WOULDN'T WE HEAR THE WINGS?
NO.

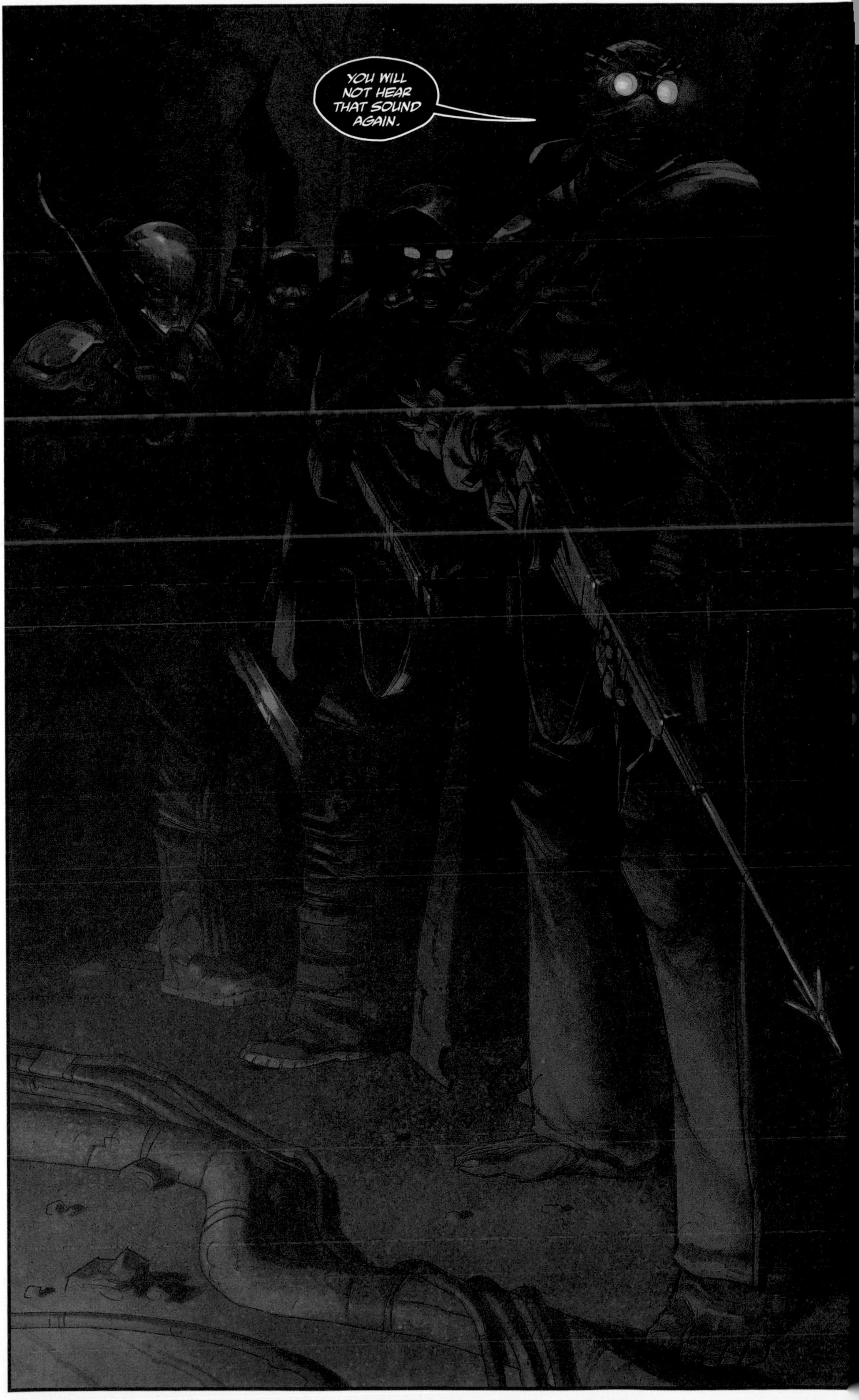
YOU WILL NOT HEAR THAT SOUND AGAIN.

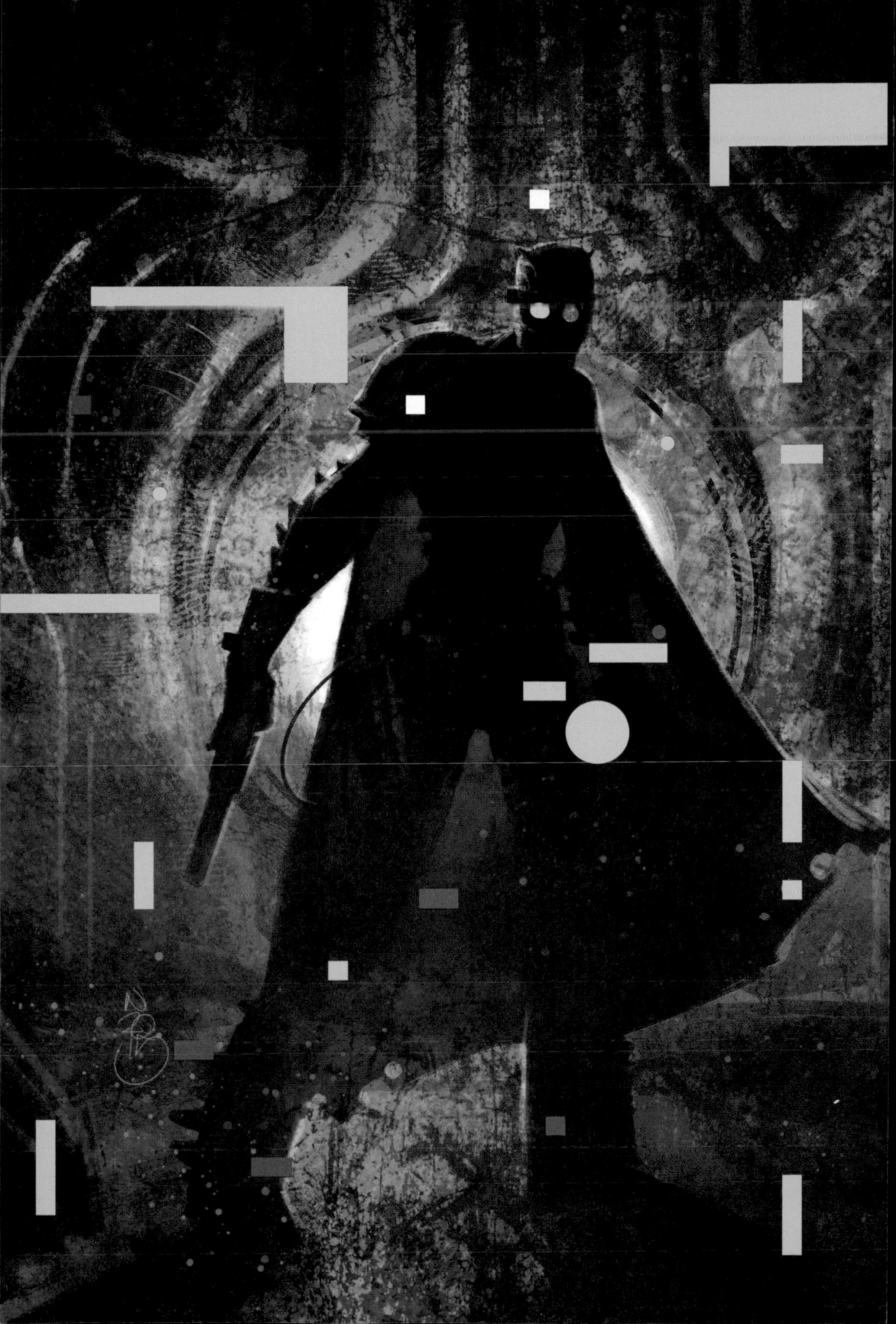

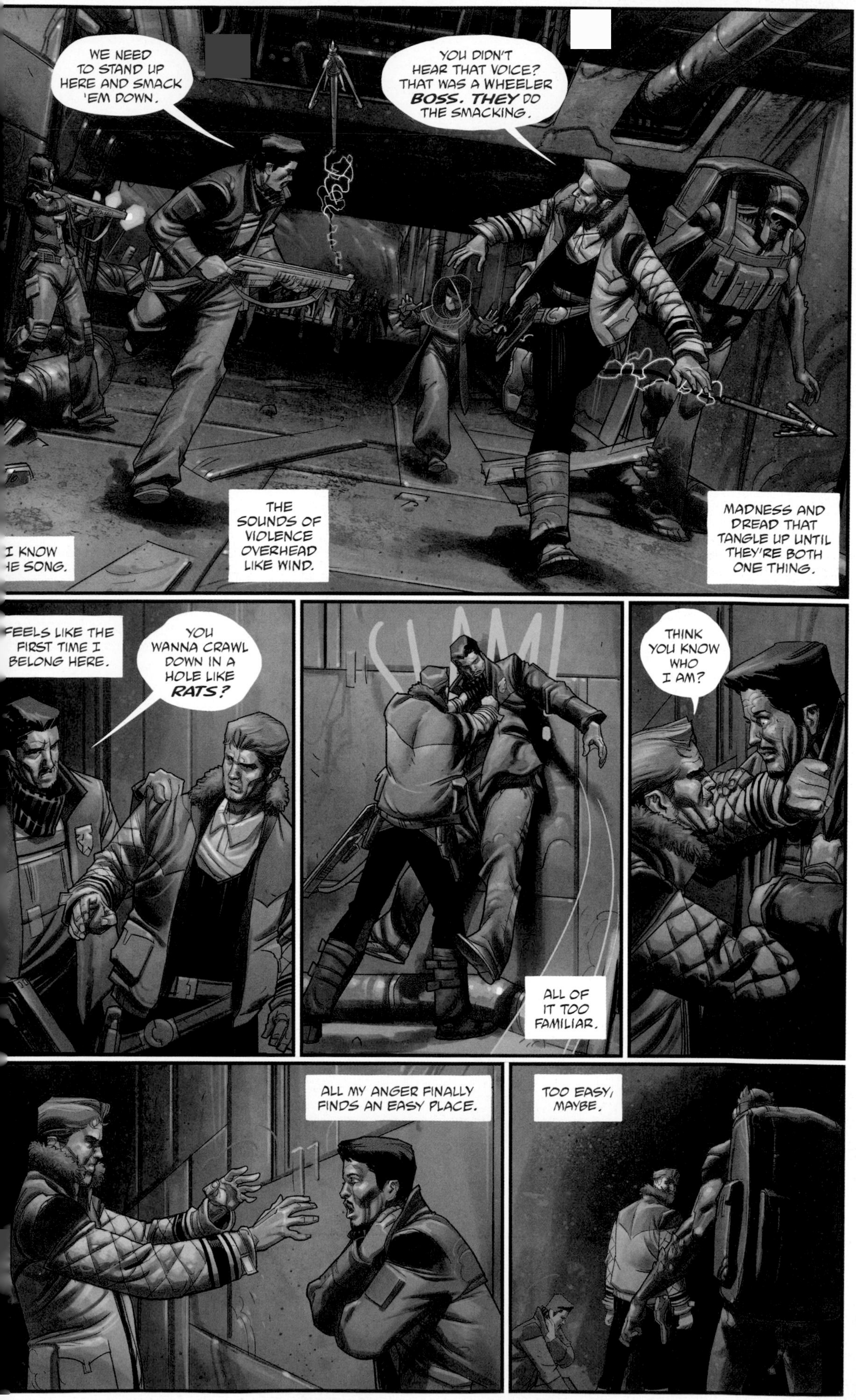
WE NEED TO STAND UP HERE AND SMACK 'EM DOWN.
YOU DIDN'T HEAR THAT VOICE? THAT WAS A WHEELER BOSS. THEY DO THE SMACKING.
I KNOW HE SONG.
THE SOUNDS OF VIOLENCE OVERHEAD LIKE WIND.
MADNESS AND DREAD THAT TANGLE UP UNTIL THEY'RE BOTH ONE THING.
FEELS LIKE THE FIRST TIME I BELONG HERE.
YOU WANNA CRAWL DOWN IN A HOLE LIKE RATS?
SLAM!
ALL OF IT TOO FAMILIAR.
THINK YOU KNOW WHO I AM?
ALL MY ANGER FINALLY FINDS AN EASY PLACE.
TOO EASY, MAYBE.

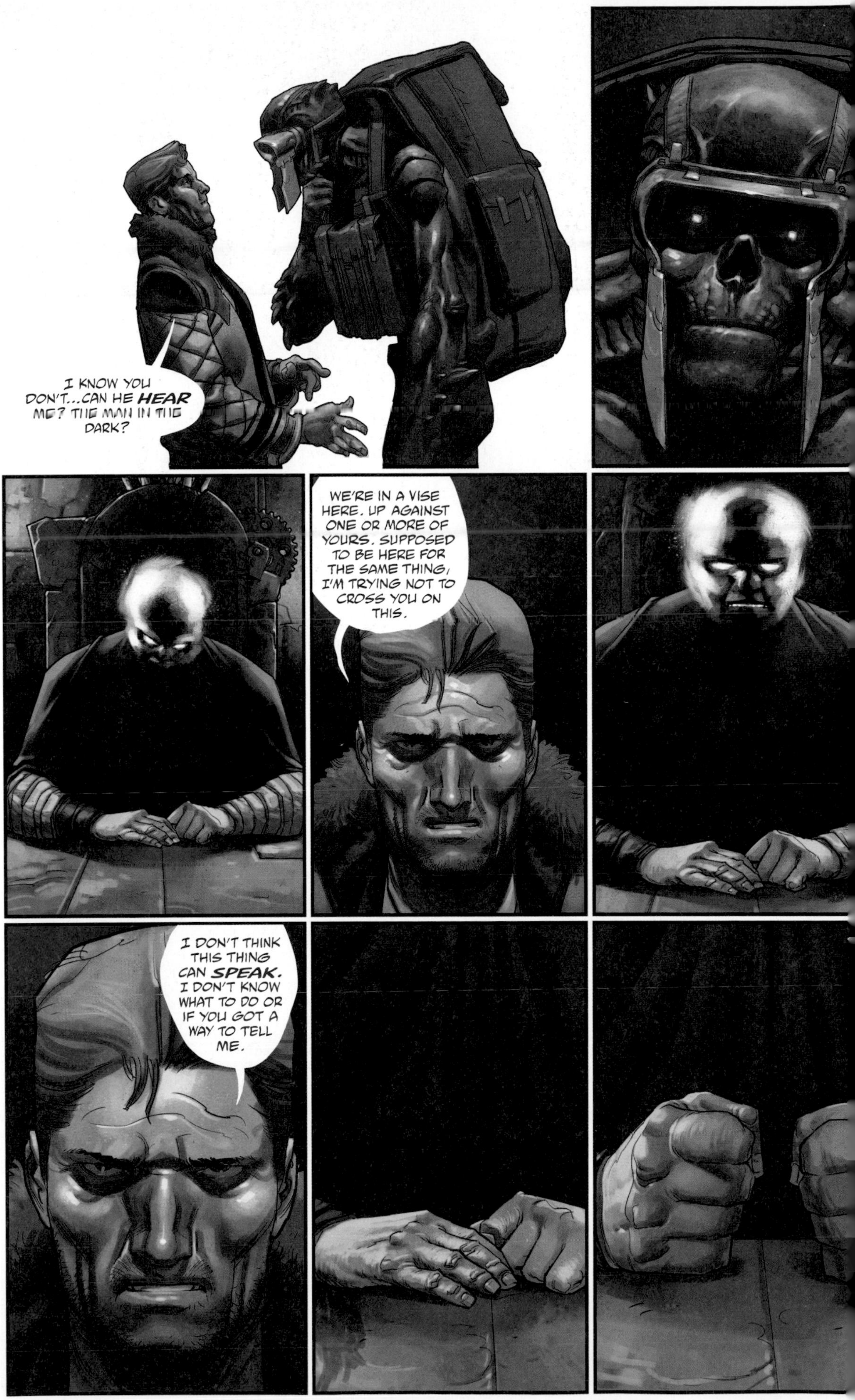
I KNOW YOU DON'T...CAN HE HEAR ME? THE MAN IN THE DARK?
WE'RE IN A VISE HERE. UP AGAINST ONE OR MORE OF YOURS. SUPPOSED TO BE HERE FOR THE SAME THING, I'M TRYING NOT TO CROSS YOU ON THIS.
I DON'T THINK THIS THING CAN SPEAK. I DON'T KNOW WHAT TO DO OR IF YOU GOT A WAY TO TELL ME.

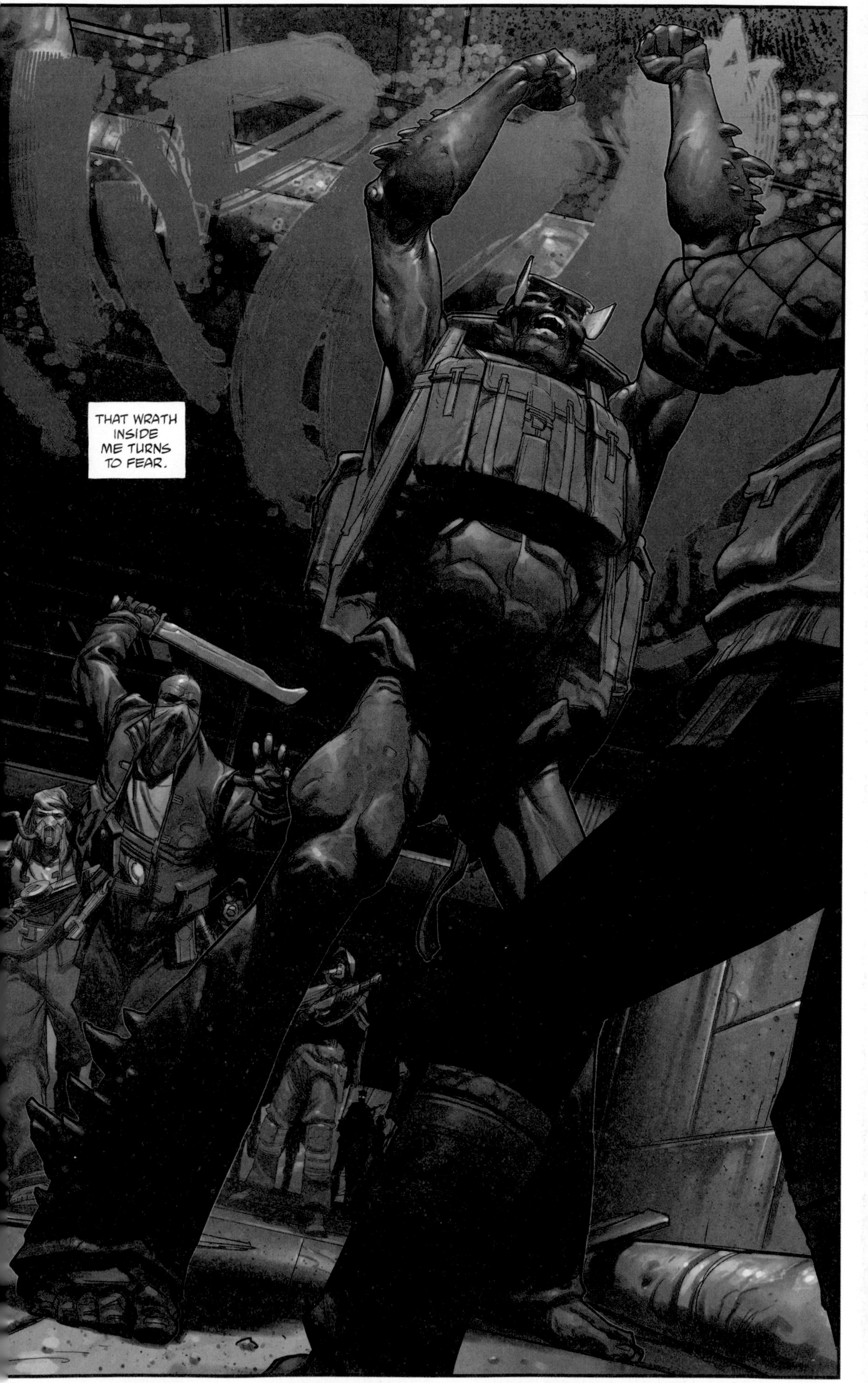
THAT WRATH INSIDE ME TURNS TO FEAR.

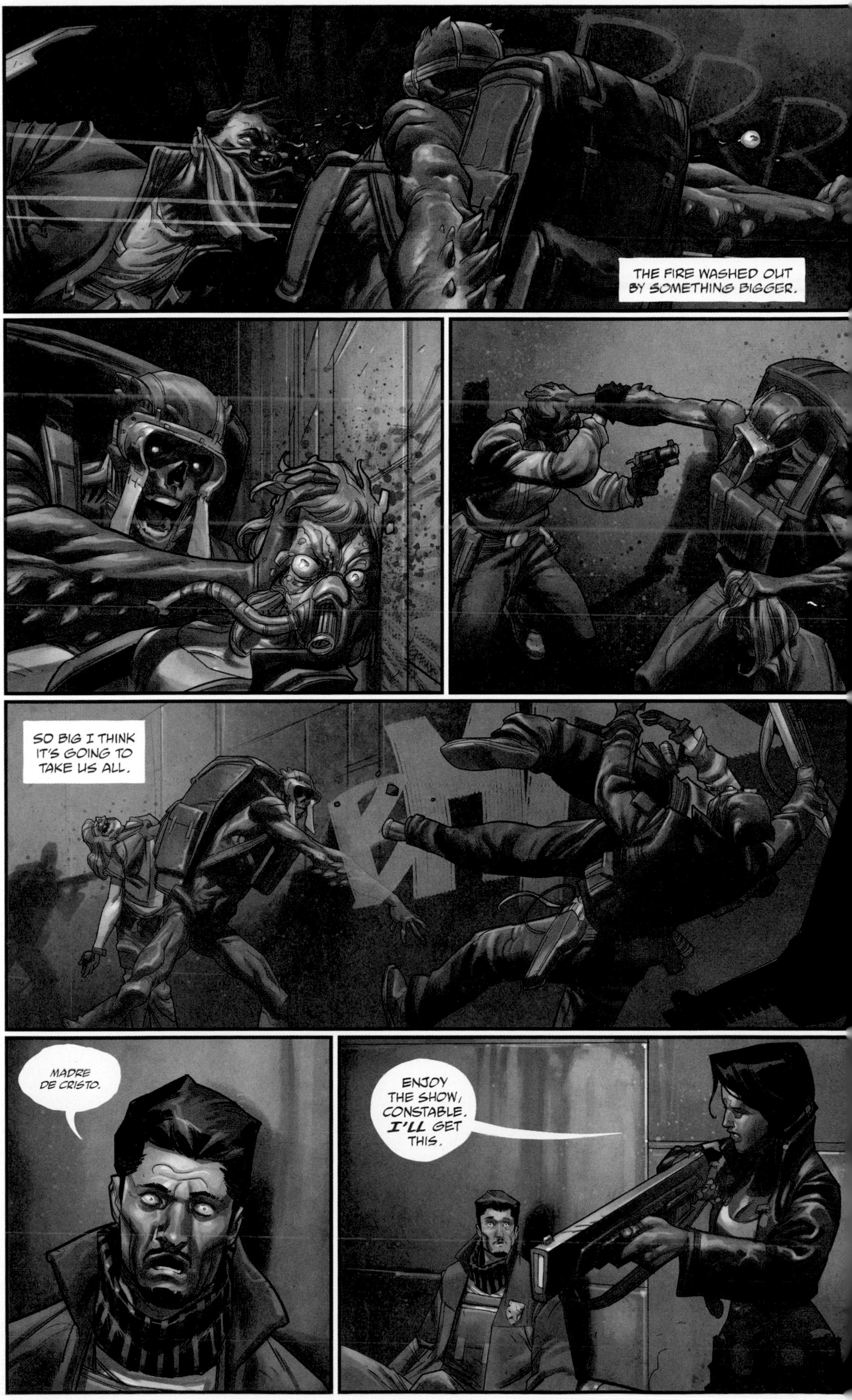
THE FIRE WASHED OUT BY SOMETHING BIGGER.
SO BIG I THINK IT'S GOING TO TAKE US ALL.
MADRE DE CRISTO.
ENJOY THE SHOW, CONSTABLE. I'LL GET THIS.

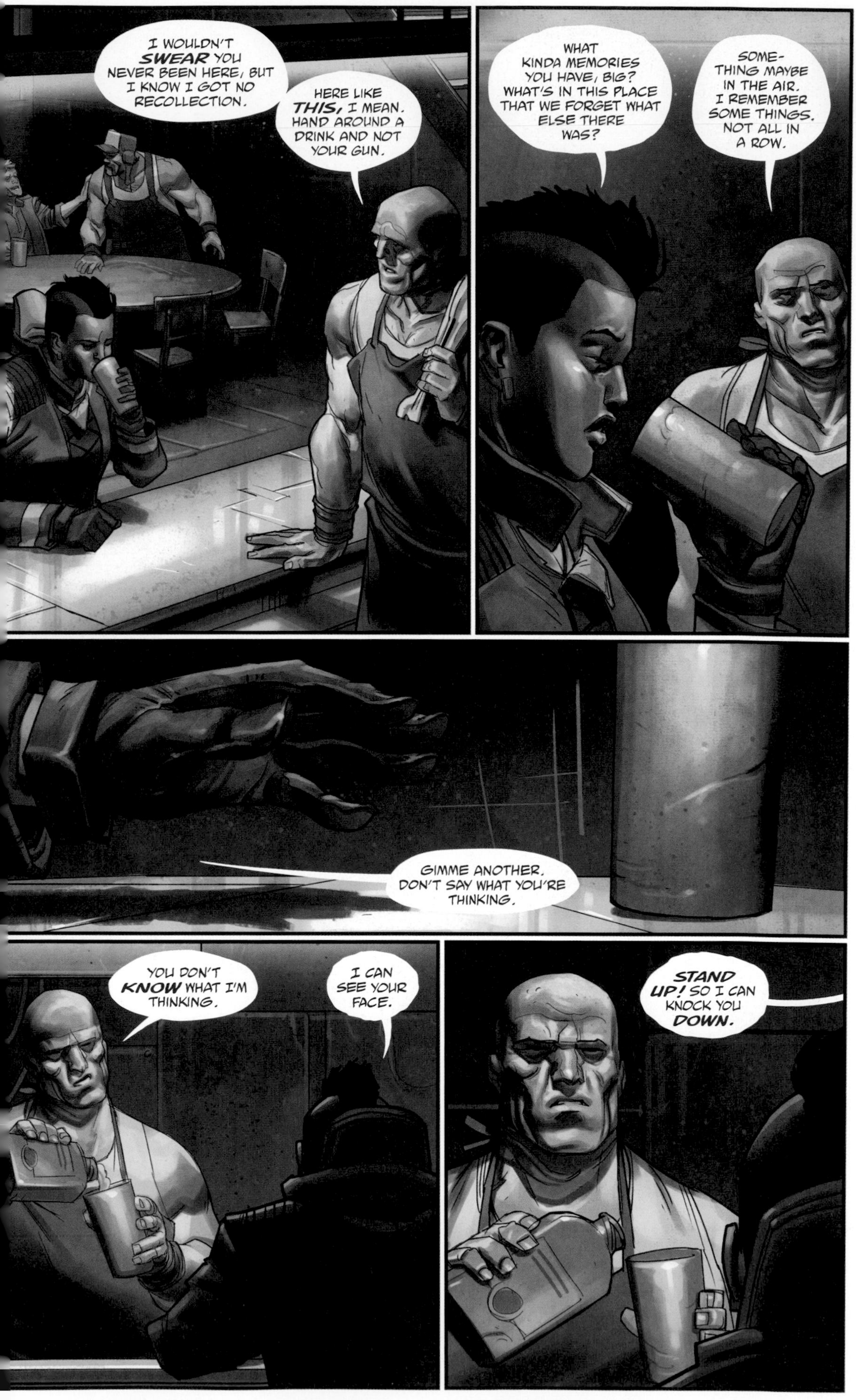
I WOULDN'T SWEAR YOU NEVER BEEN HERE, BUT I KNOW I GOT NO RECOLLECTION.
HERE LIKE THIS, I MEAN. HAND AROUND A DRINK AND NOT YOUR GUN.
WHAT KINDA MEMORIES YOU HAVE, BIG? WHAT'S IN THIS PLACE THAT WE FORGET WHAT ELSE THERE WAS?
SOME-THING MAYBE IN THE AIR. I REMEMBER SOME THINGS. NOT ALL IN A ROW.
GIMME ANOTHER. DON'T SAY WHAT YOU'RE THINKING.
YOU DON'T KNOW WHAT I'M THINKING.
I CAN SEE YOUR FACE.
STAND UP! SO I CAN KNOCK YOU DOWN.

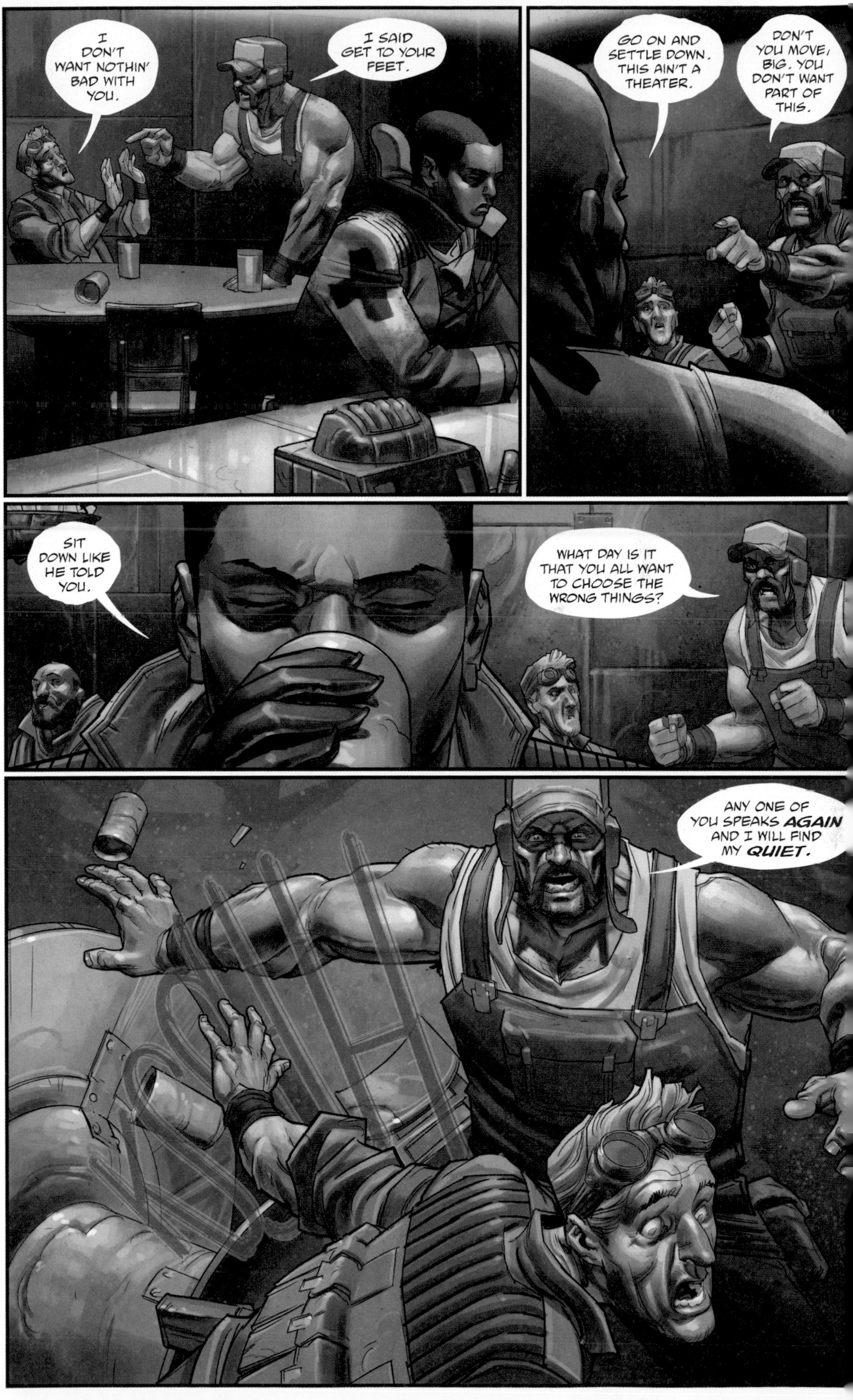
I DON'T WANT NOTHIN' BAD WITH YOU.
I SAID GET TO YOUR FEET.
GO ON AND SETTLE DOWN. THIS AIN'T A THEATER.
DON'T YOU MOVE, BIG. YOU DON'T WANT PART OF THIS.
SIT DOWN LIKE HE TOLD YOU.
WHAT DAY IS IT THAT YOU ALL WANT TO CHOOSE THE WRONG THINGS?
ANY ONE OF YOU SPEAKS AGAIN AND I WILL FIND MY QUIET.

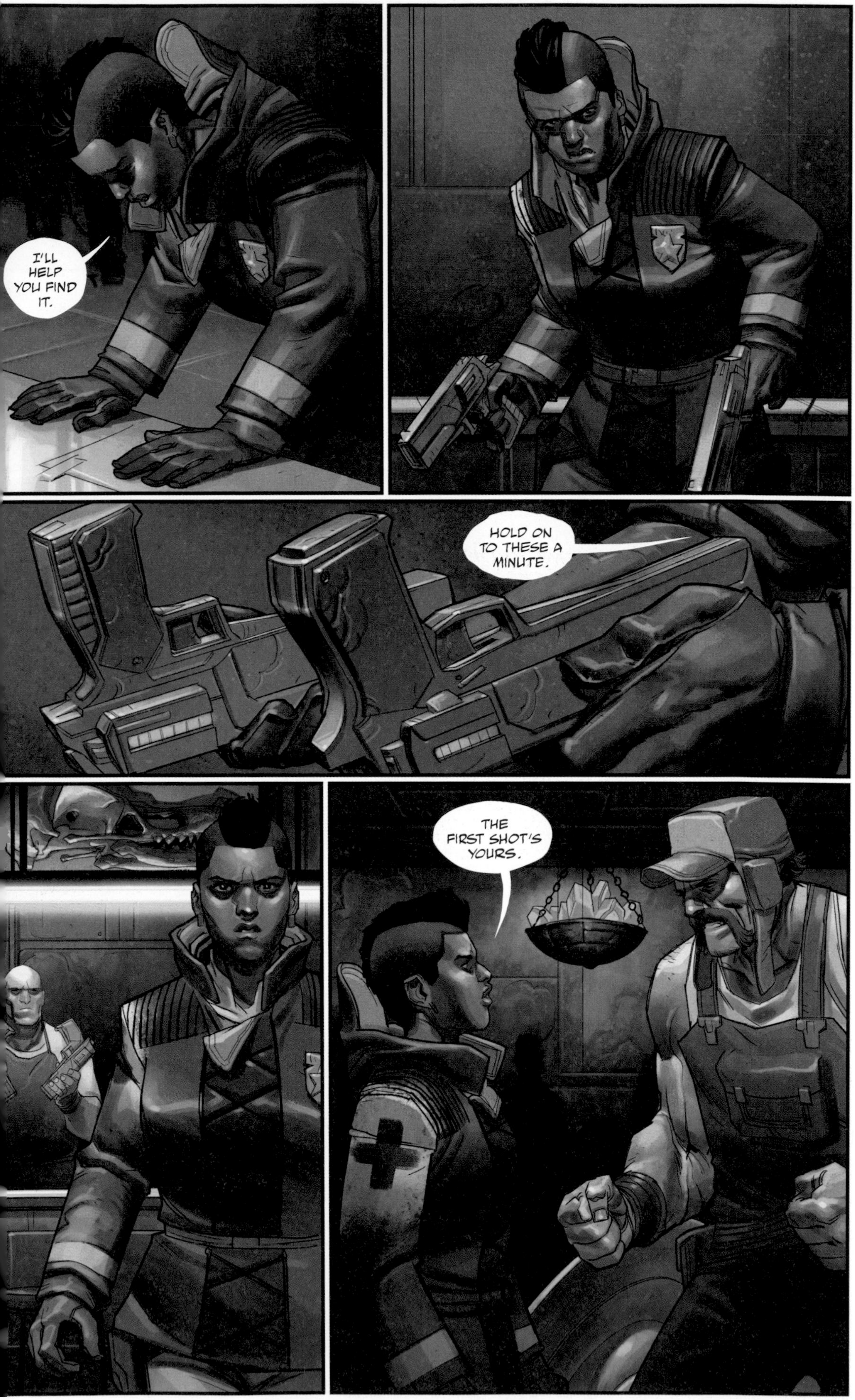
I'LL HELP YOU FIND IT.
HOLD ON TO THESE A MINUTE.
THE FIRST SHOT'S YOURS.

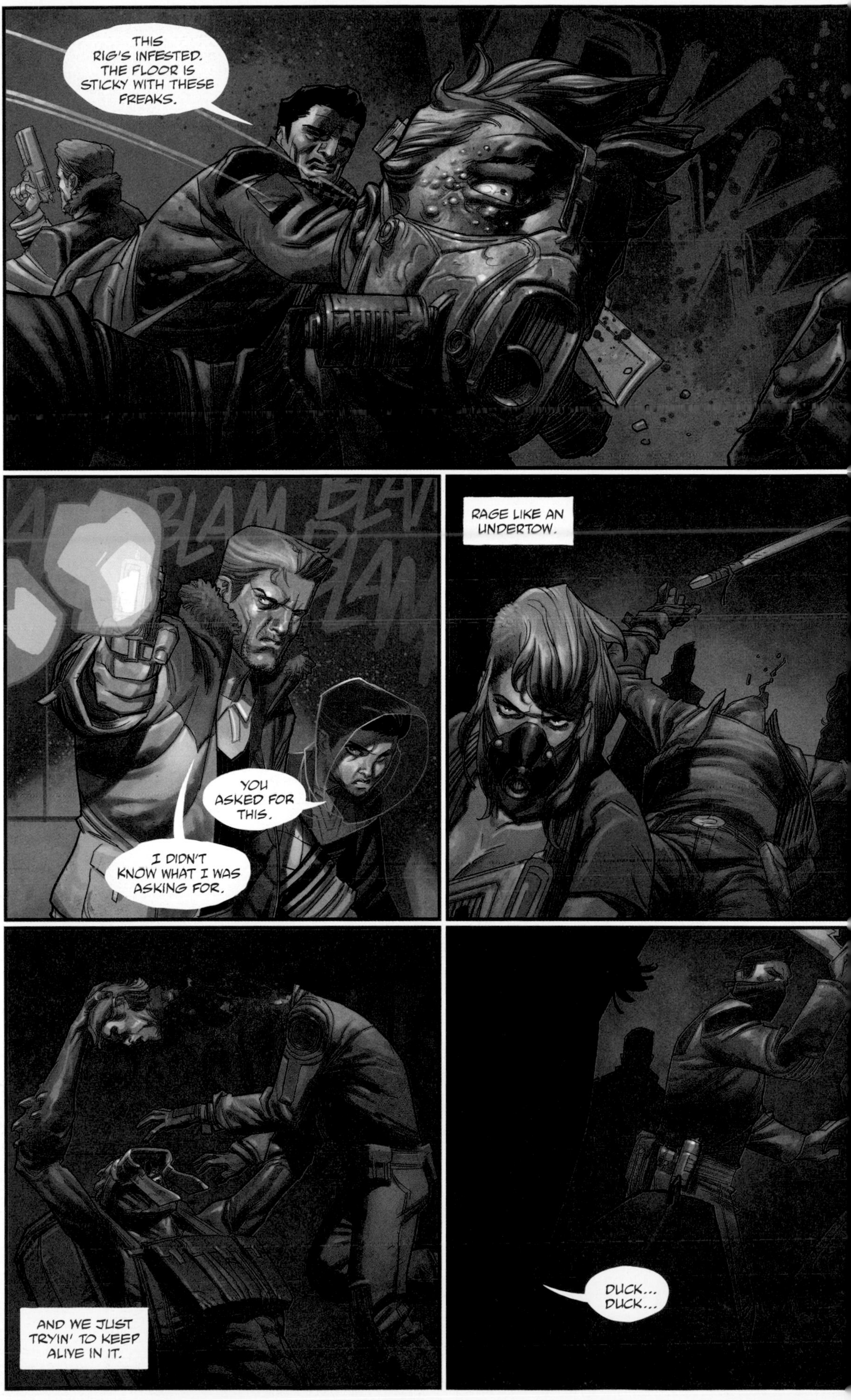
THIS RIG'S INFESTED. THE FLOOR IS STICKY WITH THESE FREAKS.
RAGE LIKE AN UNDERTOW.
YOU ASKED FOR THIS.
I DIDN'T KNOW WHAT I WAS ASKING FOR.
AND WE JUST TRYIN' TO KEEP ALIVE IN IT.
DUCK... DUCK...

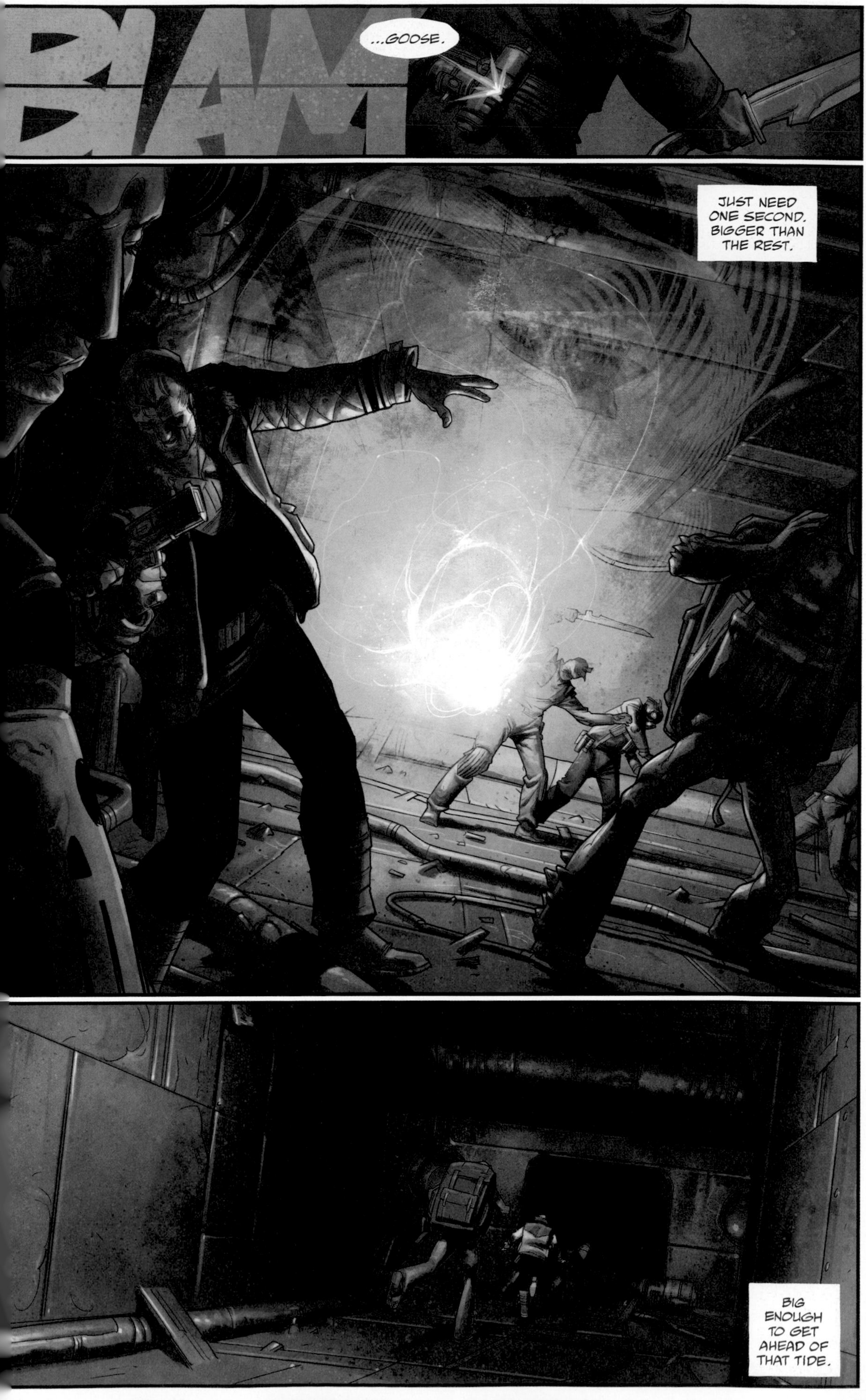
...GOOSE.
JUST NEED ONE SECOND. BIGGER THAN THE REST.
BIG ENOUGH TO GET AHEAD OF THAT TIDE.

WHERE WE CAN RUN.

I KNOW A WAY TO GET US LOOSE.

THAT LIGHT BEHIND US.

BRIGHT ENOUGH TO BURN.

REST.

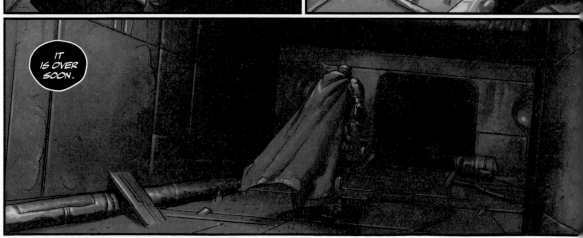

IT IS OVER SOON.

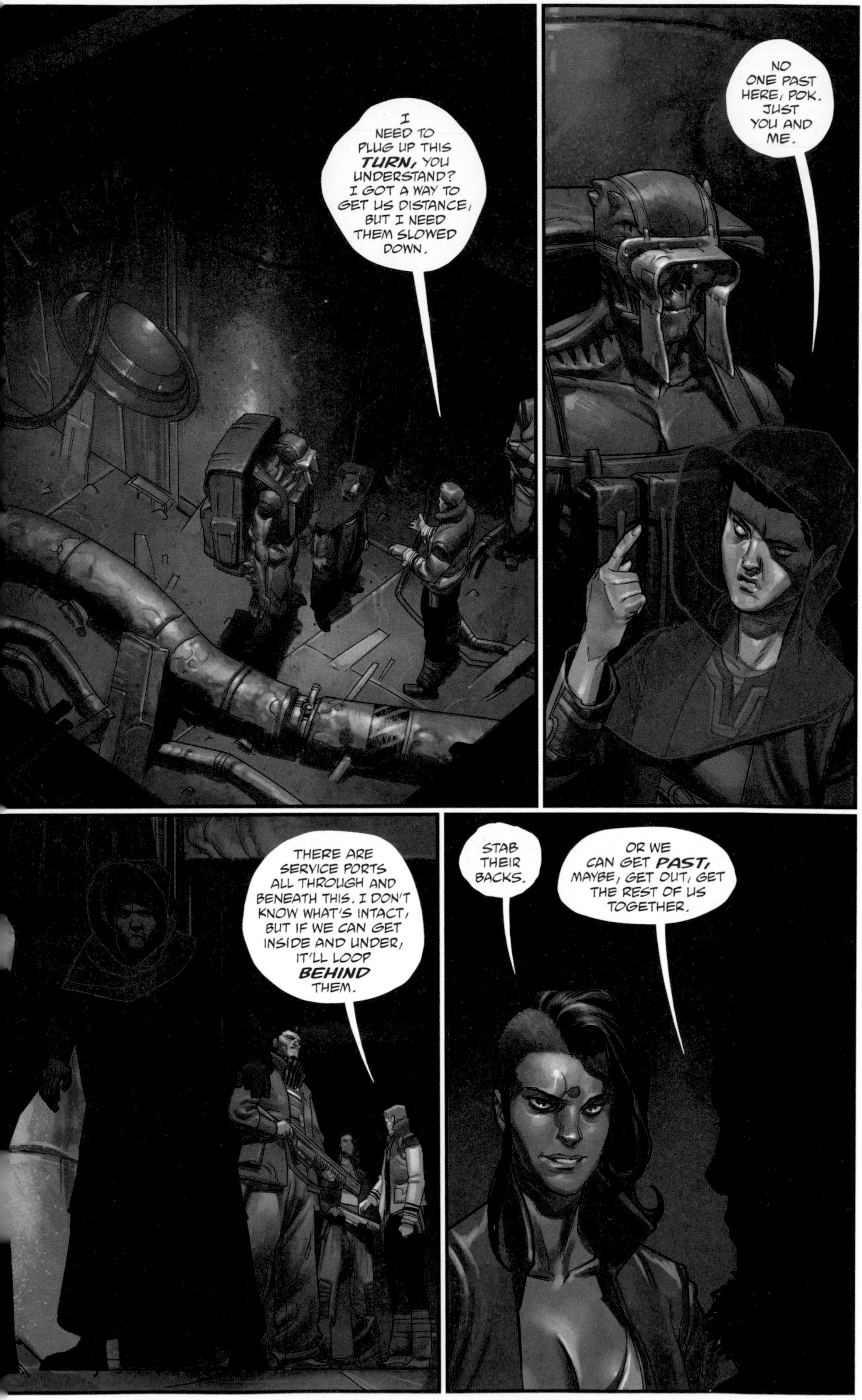
I NEED TO PLUG UP THIS TURN, YOU UNDERSTAND? I GOT A WAY TO GET US DISTANCE, BUT I NEED THEM SLOWED DOWN.
NO ONE PAST HERE, POK. JUST YOU AND ME.
THERE ARE SERVICE PORTS ALL THROUGH AND BENEATH THIS. I DON'T KNOW WHAT'S INTACT, BUT IF WE CAN GET INSIDE AND UNDER, IT'LL LOOP BEHIND THEM.
STAB THEIR BACKS.
OR WE CAN GET PAST, MAYBE, GET OUT, GET THE REST OF US TOGETHER.

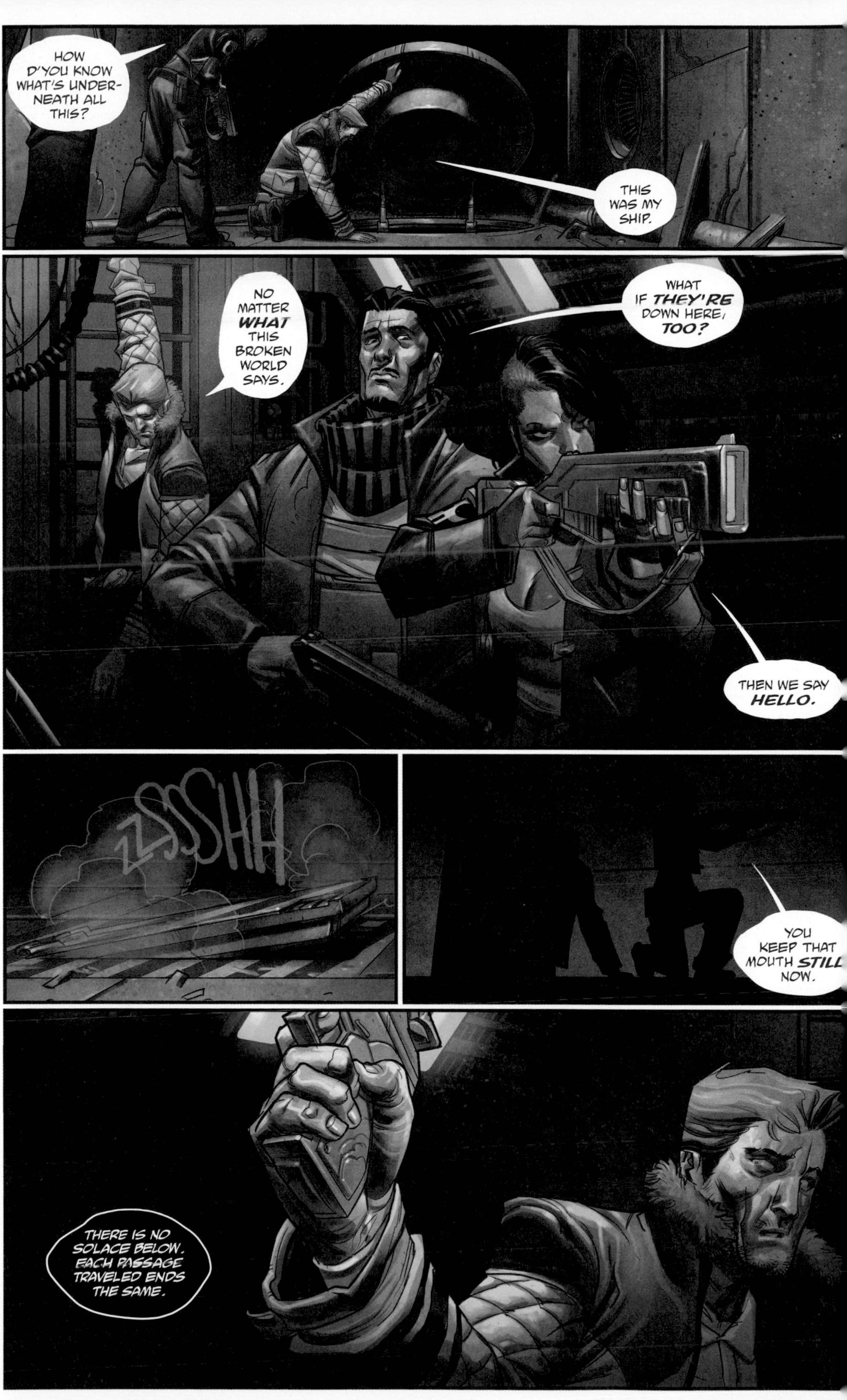
HOW D'YOU KNOW WHAT'S UNDER-NEATH ALL THIS?
THIS WAS MY SHIP.
NO MATTER WHAT THIS BROKEN WORLD SAYS.
WHAT IF THEY'RE DOWN HERE, TOO?
THEN WE SAY HELLO.
ZSSSHH
YOU KEEP THAT MOUTH STILL NOW.
THERE IS NO SOLACE BELOW. EACH PASSAGE TRAVELED ENDS THE SAME.

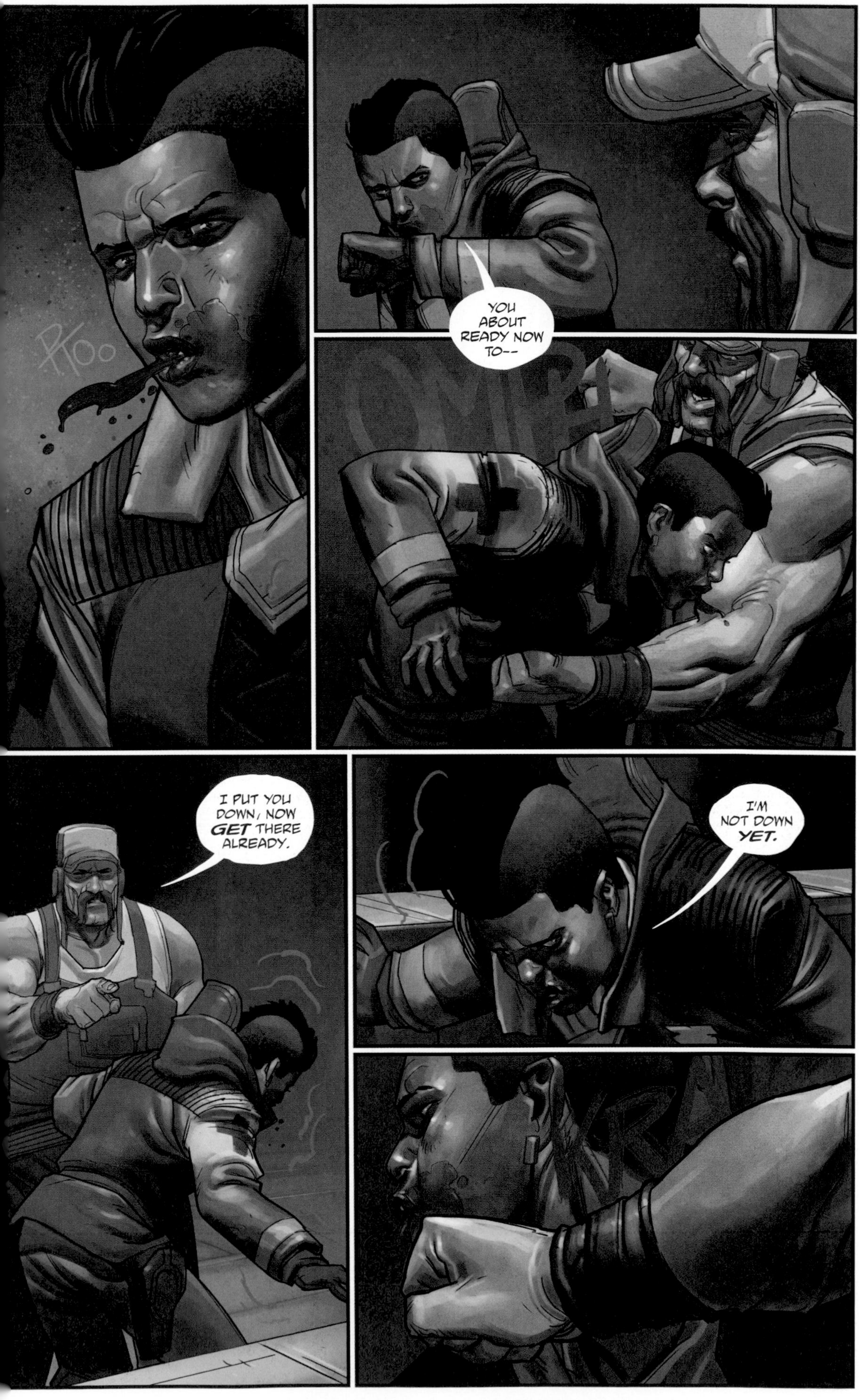
PTOO
YOU ABOUT READY NOW TO--
I PUT YOU DOWN, NOW GET THERE ALREADY.
I'M NOT DOWN YET.

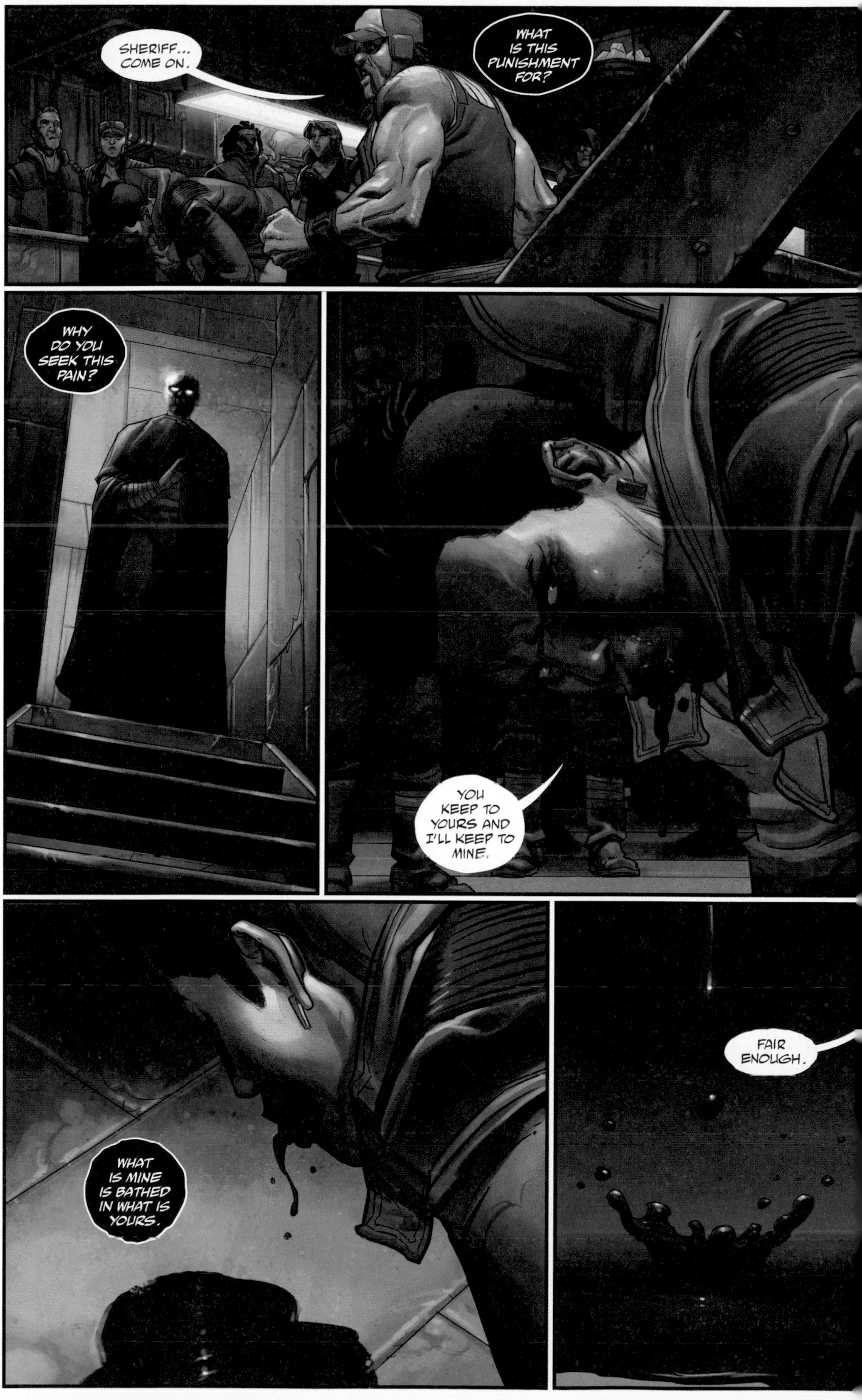
SHERIFF... COME ON.
WHAT IS THIS PUNISHMENT FOR?
WHY DO YOU SEEK THIS PAIN?
YOU KEEP TO YOURS AND I'LL KEEP TO MINE.
WHAT IS MINE IS BATHED IN WHAT IS YOURS.
FAIR ENOUGH.

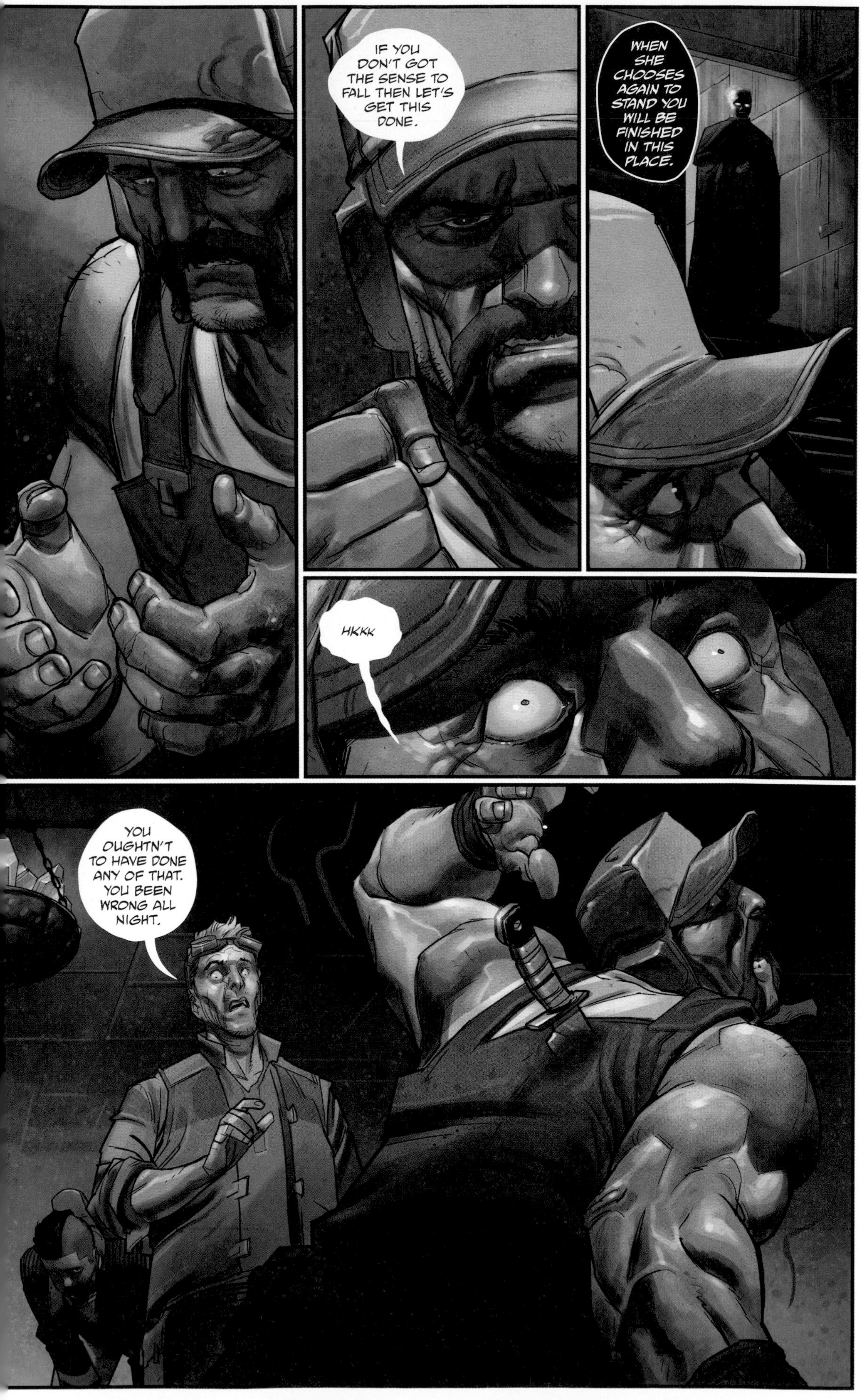
IF YOU DON'T GOT THE SENSE TO FALL THEN LET'S GET THIS DONE.
WHEN SHE CHOOSES AGAIN TO STAND YOU WILL BE FINISHED IN THIS PLACE.
HKKK
YOU OUGHTN'T TO HAVE DONE ANY OF THAT. YOU BEEN WRONG ALL NIGHT.

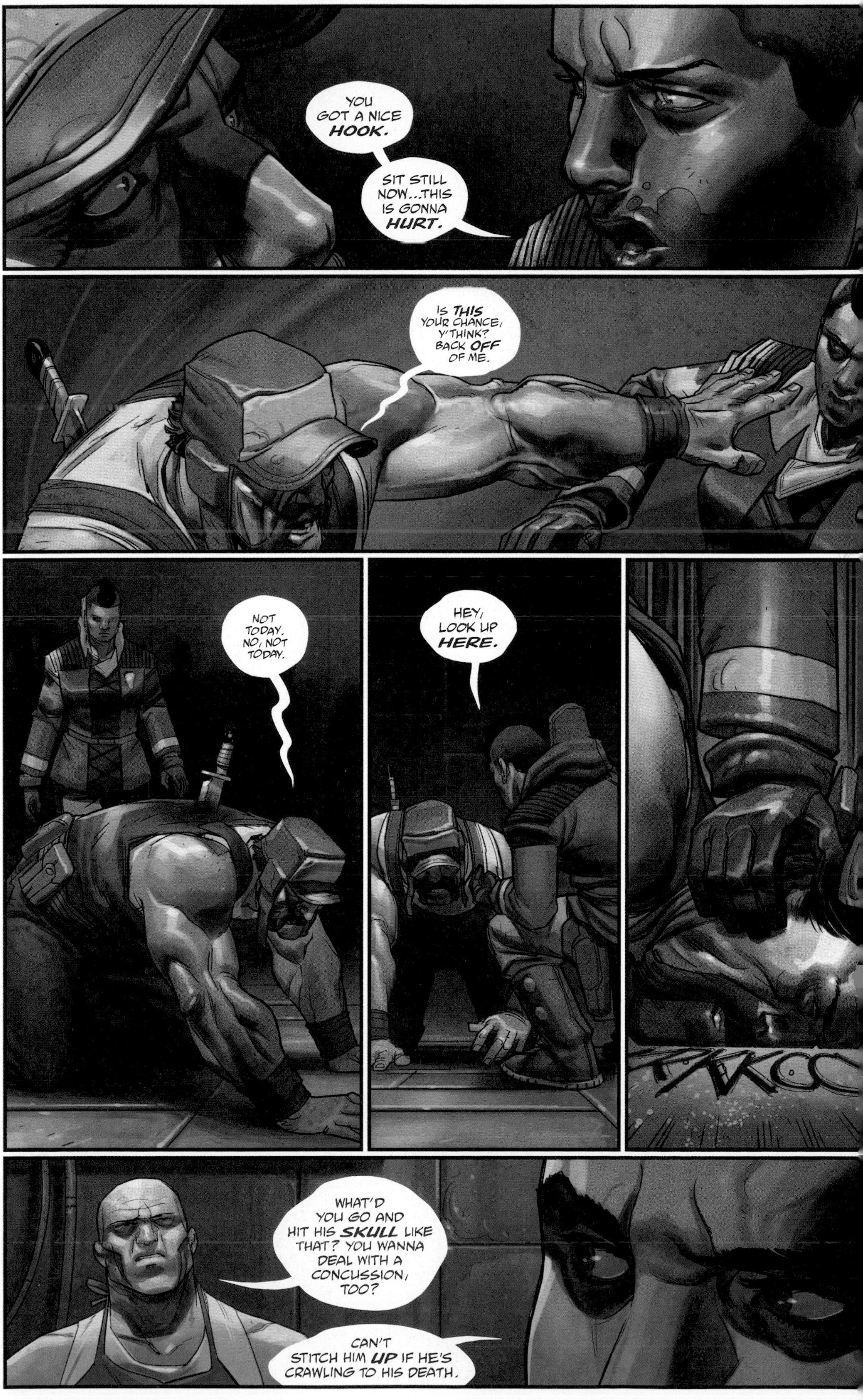

YOU GOT A NICE HOOK.
SIT STILL NOW...THIS IS GONNA HURT.
IS THIS YOUR CHANCE, Y'THINK? BACK OFF OF ME.
NOT TODAY. NO, NOT TODAY.
HEY, LOOK UP HERE.
WHAT'D YOU GO AND HIT HIS SKULL LIKE THAT? YOU WANNA DEAL WITH A CONCUSSION, TOO?
CAN'T STITCH HIM UP IF HE'S CRAWLING TO HIS DEATH.

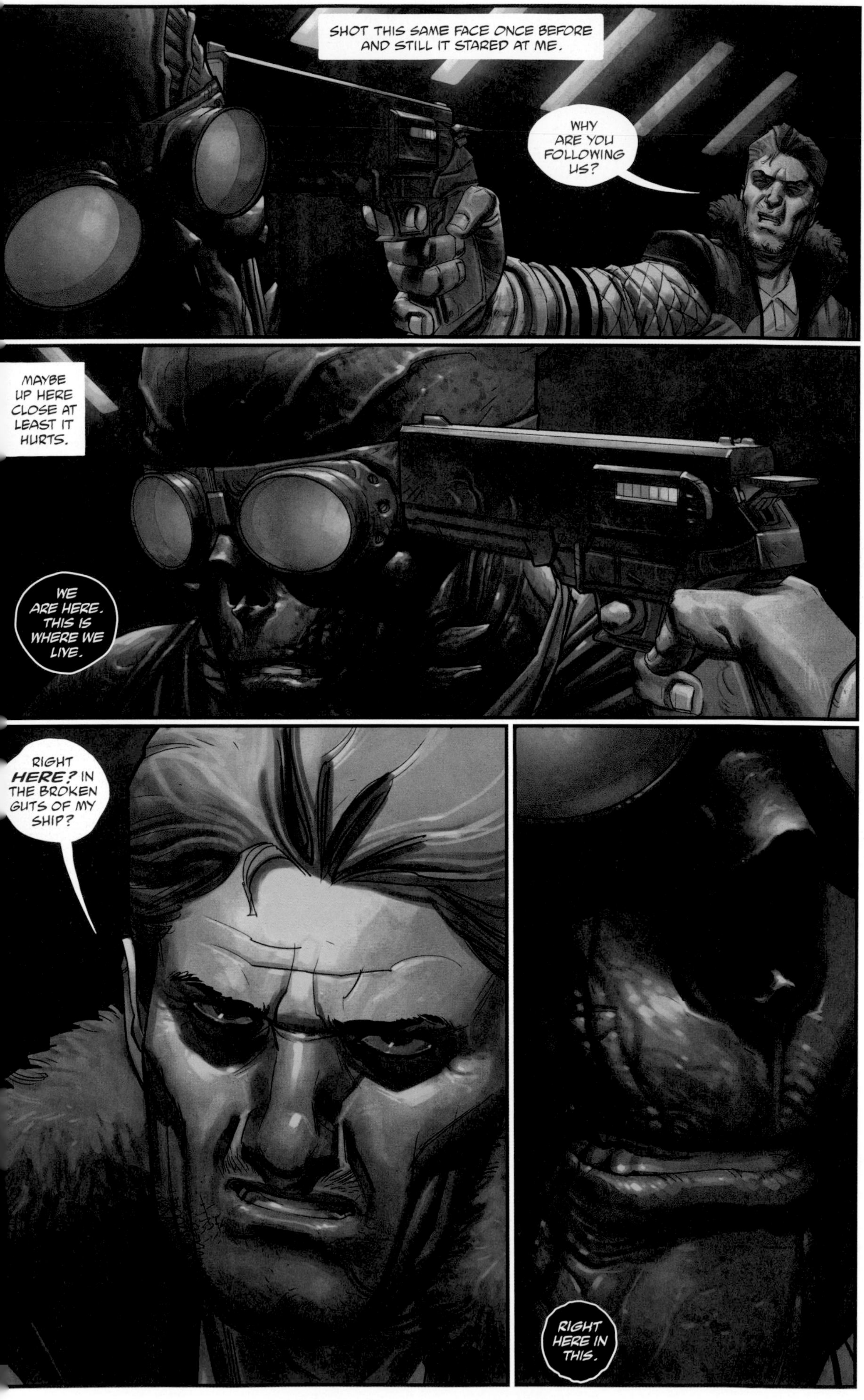
SHOT THIS SAME FACE ONCE BEFORE AND STILL IT STARED AT ME.
WHY ARE YOU FOLLOWING US?
MAYBE UP HERE CLOSE AT LEAST IT HURTS.
WE ARE HERE. THIS IS WHERE WE LIVE.
RIGHT HERE? IN THE BROKEN GUTS OF MY SHIP?
RIGHT HERE IN THIS.

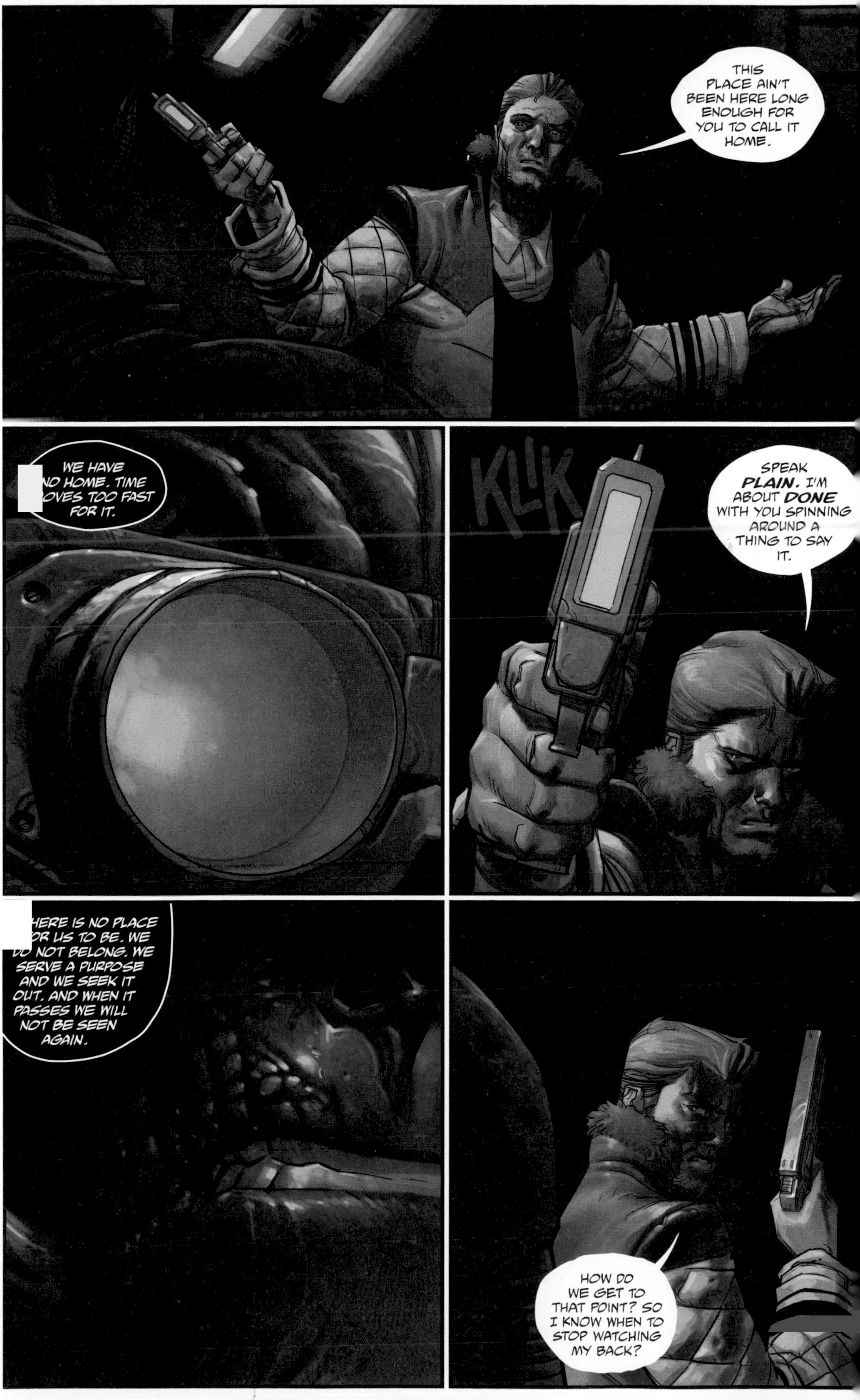
THIS PLACE AIN'T BEEN HERE LONG ENOUGH FOR YOU TO CALL IT HOME.
WE HAVE NO HOME. TIME OVES TOO FAST FOR IT.
KLIK
SPEAK **PLAIN.** I'M ABOUT **DONE** WITH YOU SPINNING AROUND A THING TO SAY IT.
HERE IS NO PLACE OR US TO BE. WE DO NOT BELONG. WE SERVE A PURPOSE AND WE SEEK IT OUT. AND WHEN IT PASSES WE WILL NOT BE SEEN AGAIN.
HOW DO WE GET TO THAT POINT? SO I KNOW WHEN TO STOP WATCHING MY BACK?

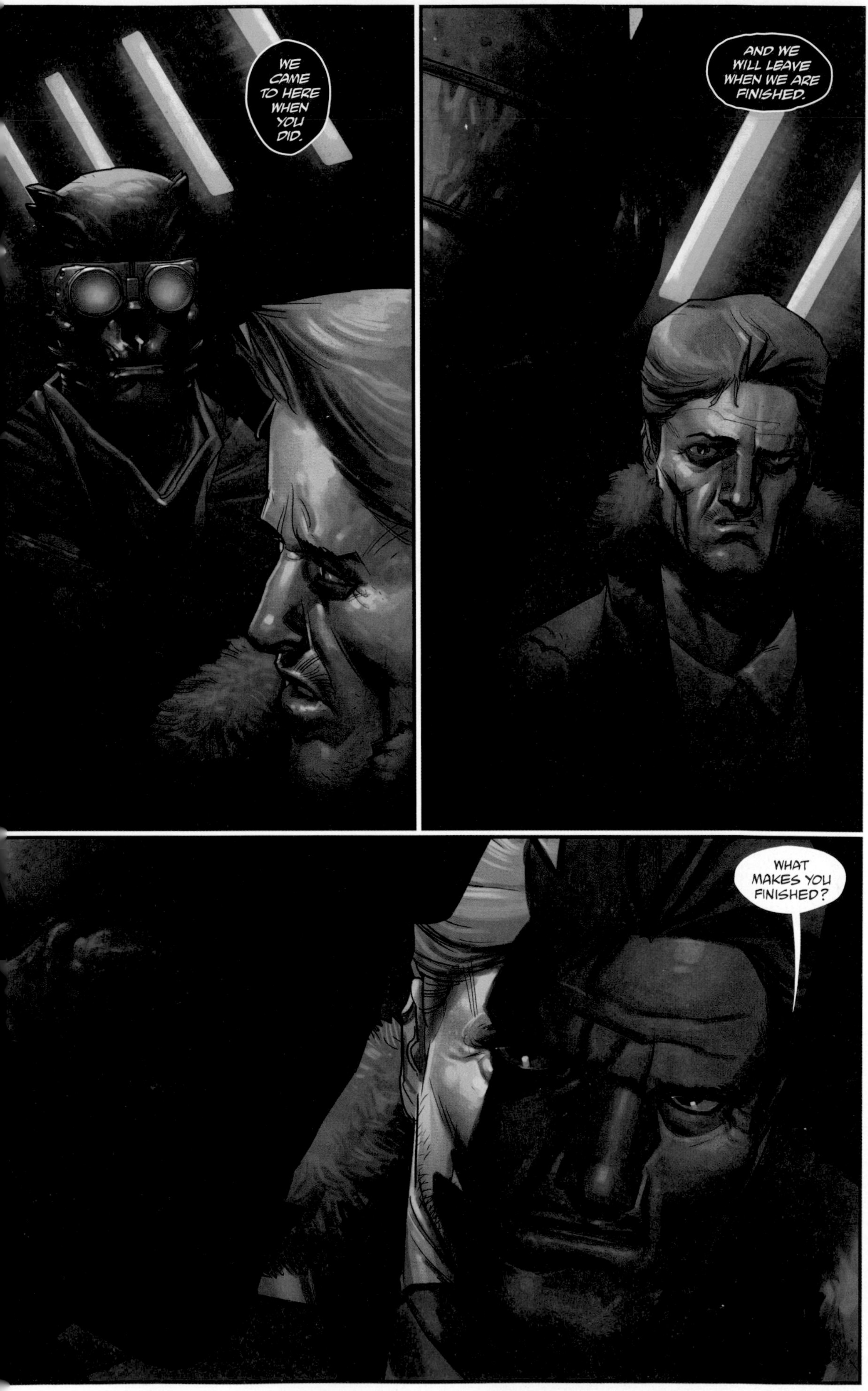
WE CAME TO HERE WHEN YOU DID.
AND WE WILL LEAVE WHEN WE ARE FINISHED.
WHAT MAKES YOU FINISHED?

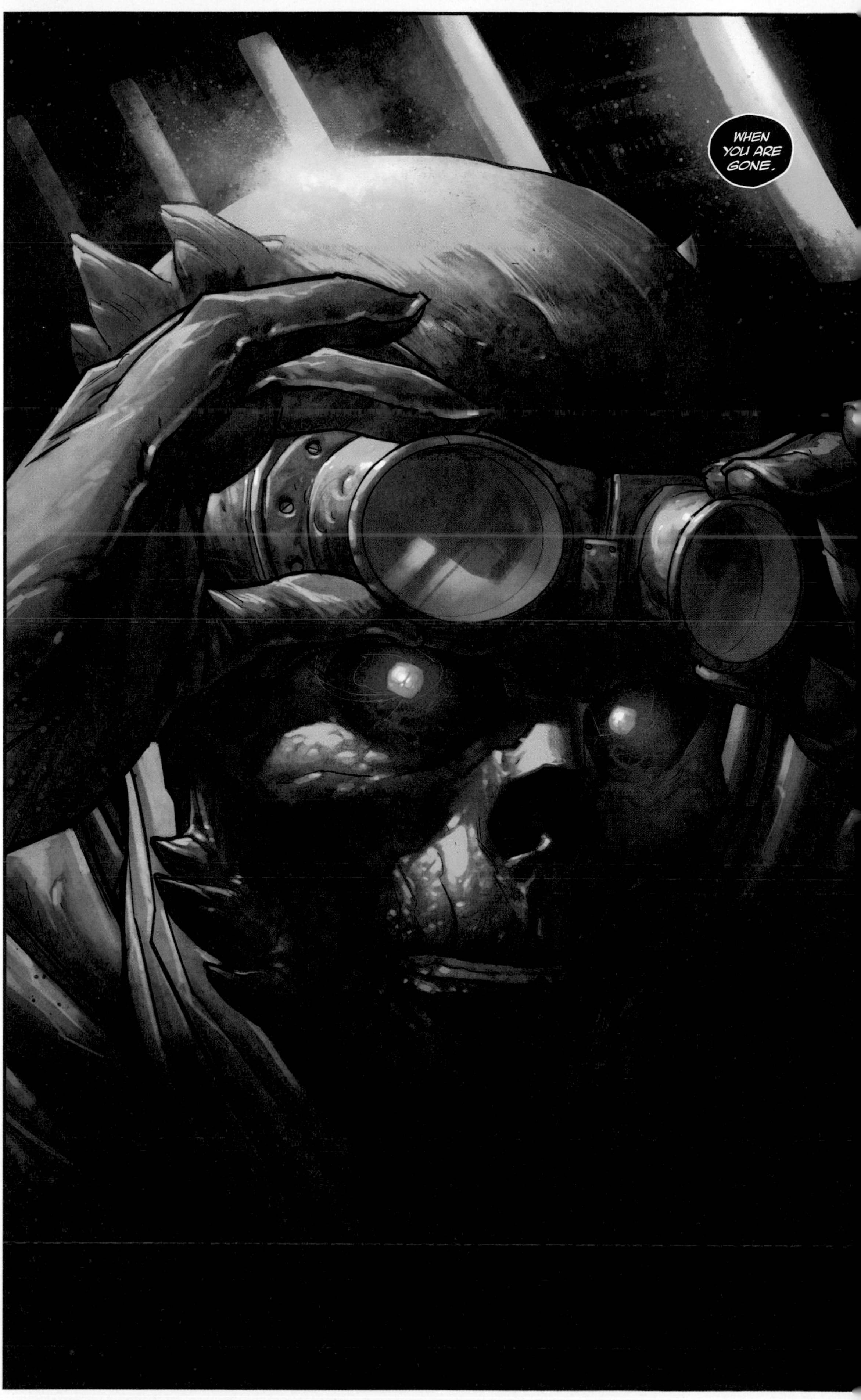
WHEN YOU ARE GONE.

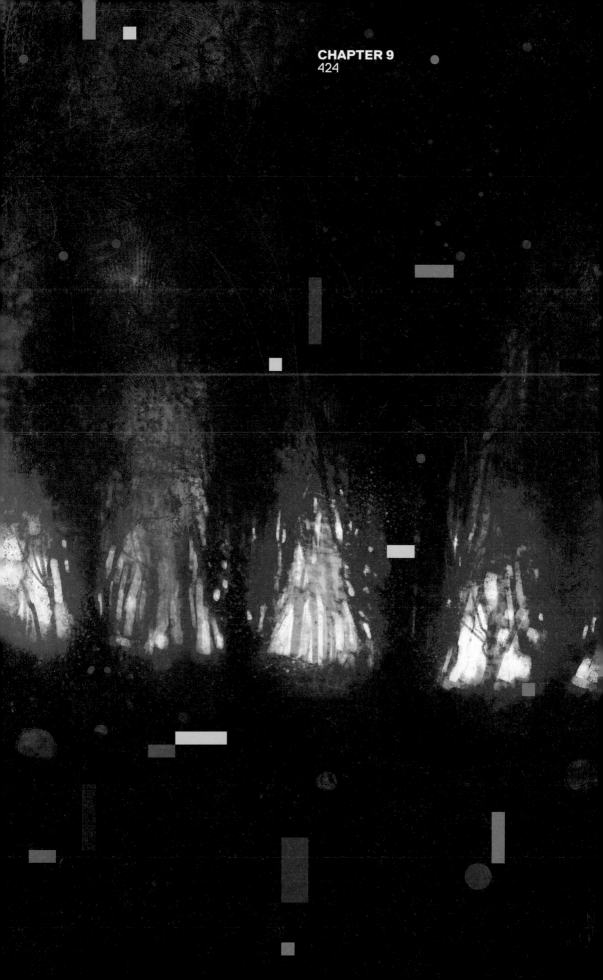

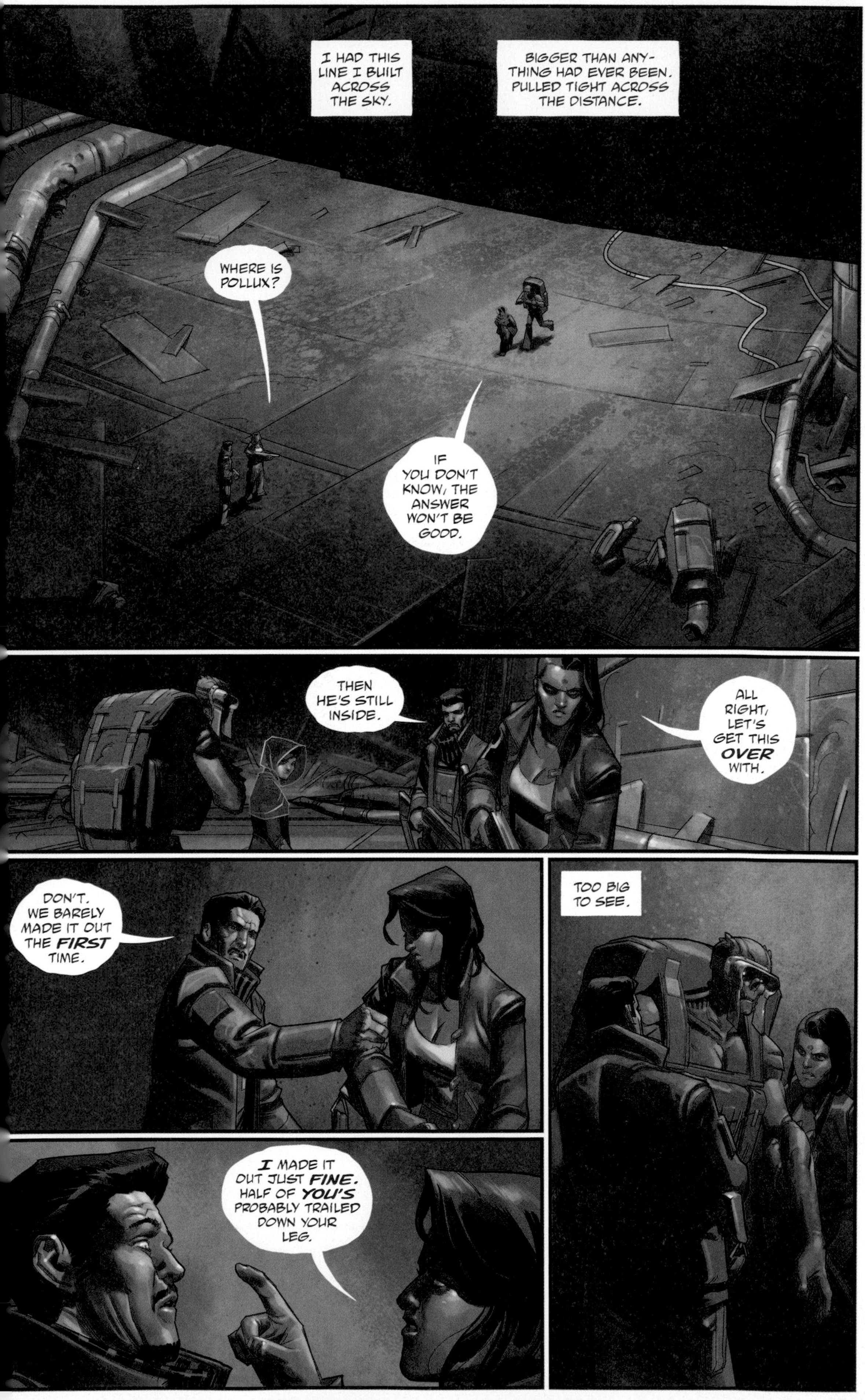
I HAD THIS LINE I BUILT ACROSS THE SKY.
BIGGER THAN ANYTHING HAD EVER BEEN. PULLED TIGHT ACROSS THE DISTANCE.
WHERE IS POLLUX?
IF YOU DON'T KNOW, THE ANSWER WON'T BE GOOD.
THEN HE'S STILL INSIDE.
ALL RIGHT, LET'S GET THIS OVER WITH.
DON'T. WE BARELY MADE IT OUT THE FIRST TIME.
I MADE IT OUT JUST FINE. HALF OF YOU'S PROBABLY TRAILED DOWN YOUR LEG.
TOO BIG TO SEE.

FELL AT EVERY STEP BUT STILL I TRIED TO WALK.

WE HAVE TO **THINK** NOW. **NOT** SPEAK. IF WE ARE WRONG, WE LOSE IT ALL.

EACH TIME THAT LINE IT PULLED AT ME.

WHOLE **TRUCK** FULL OF FRIENDLIES DOWN THE WAY. BRING THEM BACK HERE AND YOU CAN STORM THE GATES **TOGETHER**.

LIKE YOU WERE PULLING ME TO STAND AGAIN.

WE HAVE ZERO TIME FOR THIS.

WE'LL BE SUPERFAST.

PULLING ME A LITTLE CLOSER.

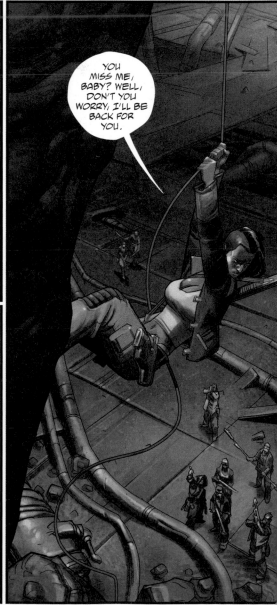

YOU MISS ME, BABY? WELL, DON'T YOU WORRY, I'LL BE BACK FOR YOU.

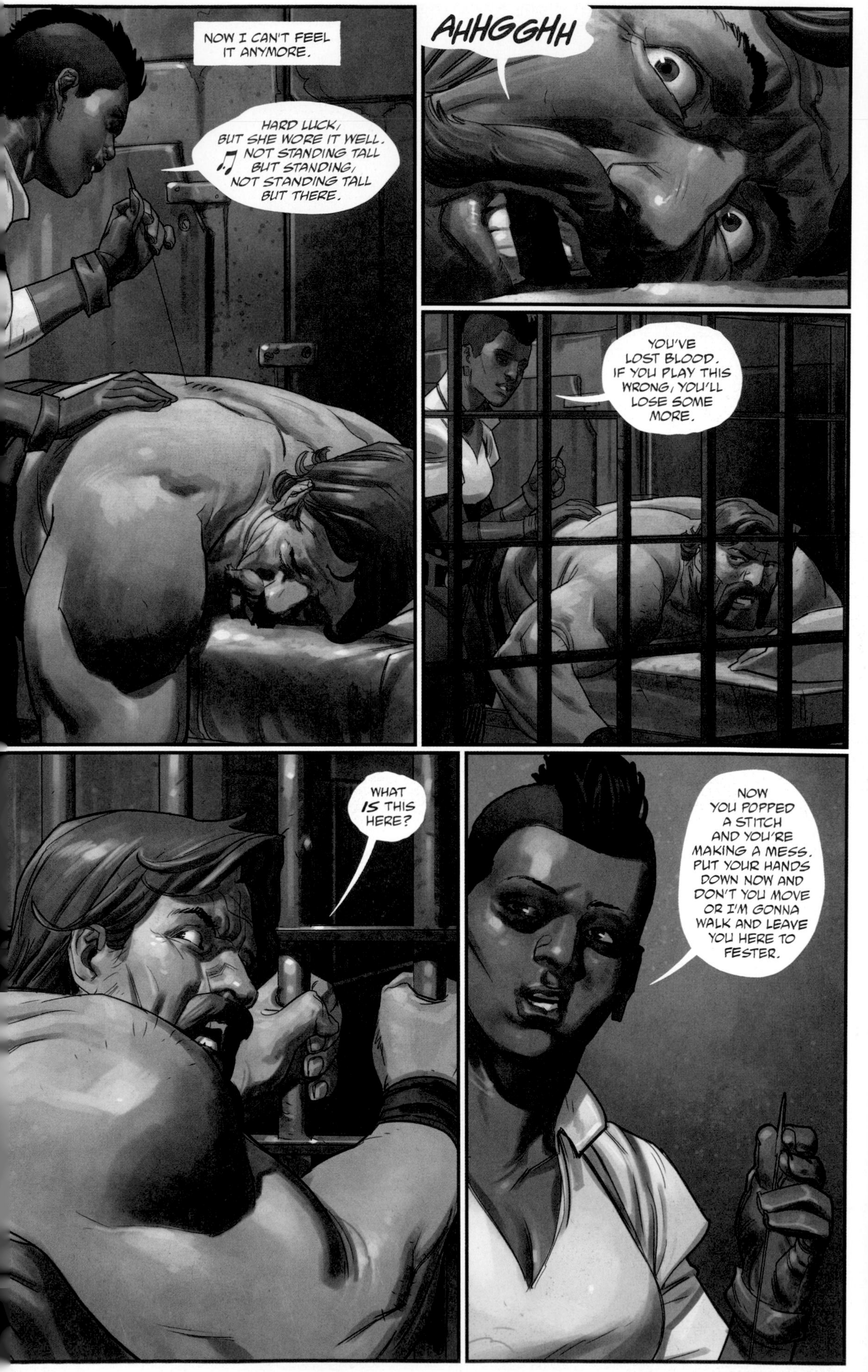
NOW I CAN'T FEEL IT ANYMORE.
HARD LUCK, BUT SHE WORE IT WELL. ♫ NOT STANDING TALL BUT STANDING, NOT STANDING TALL BUT THERE.
AHHGGHH
YOU'VE LOST BLOOD. IF YOU PLAY THIS WRONG, YOU'LL LOSE SOME MORE.
WHAT *IS* THIS HERE?
NOW YOU POPPED A STITCH AND YOU'RE MAKING A MESS. PUT YOUR HANDS DOWN NOW AND DON'T YOU MOVE OR I'M GONNA WALK AND LEAVE YOU HERE TO FESTER.

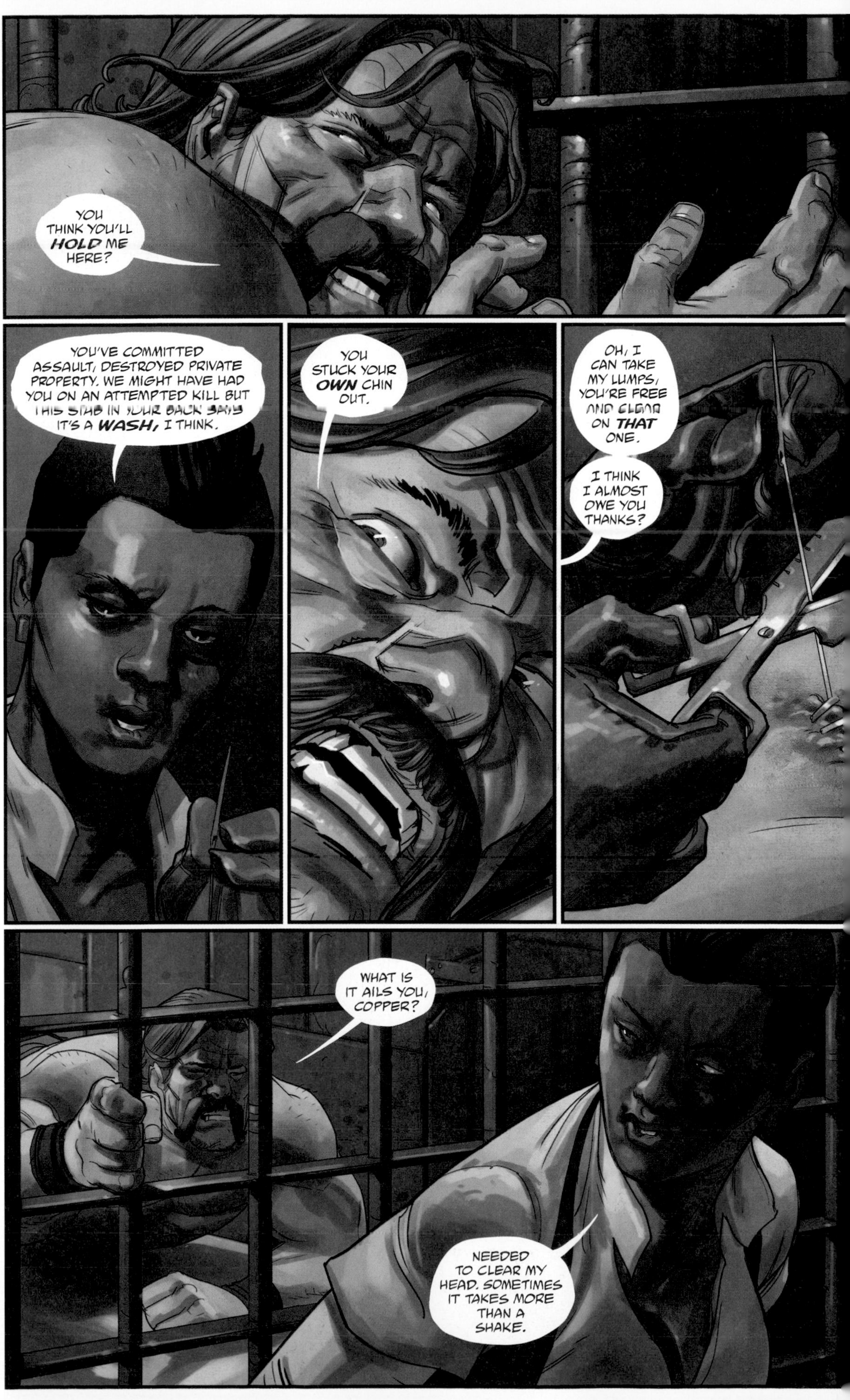
YOU THINK YOU'LL **HOLD** ME HERE?
YOU'VE COMMITTED ASSAULT, DESTROYED PRIVATE PROPERTY. WE MIGHT HAVE HAD YOU ON AN ATTEMPTED KILL BUT THIS STAB IN YOUR BACK SAYS IT'S A **WASH,** I THINK.
YOU STUCK YOUR **OWN** CHIN OUT.
OH, I CAN TAKE MY LUMPS, YOU'RE FREE AND CLEAR ON **THAT** ONE.
I THINK I ALMOST OWE YOU THANKS?
WHAT IS IT AILS YOU, COPPER?
NEEDED TO CLEAR MY HEAD. SOMETIMES IT TAKES MORE THAN A SHAKE.

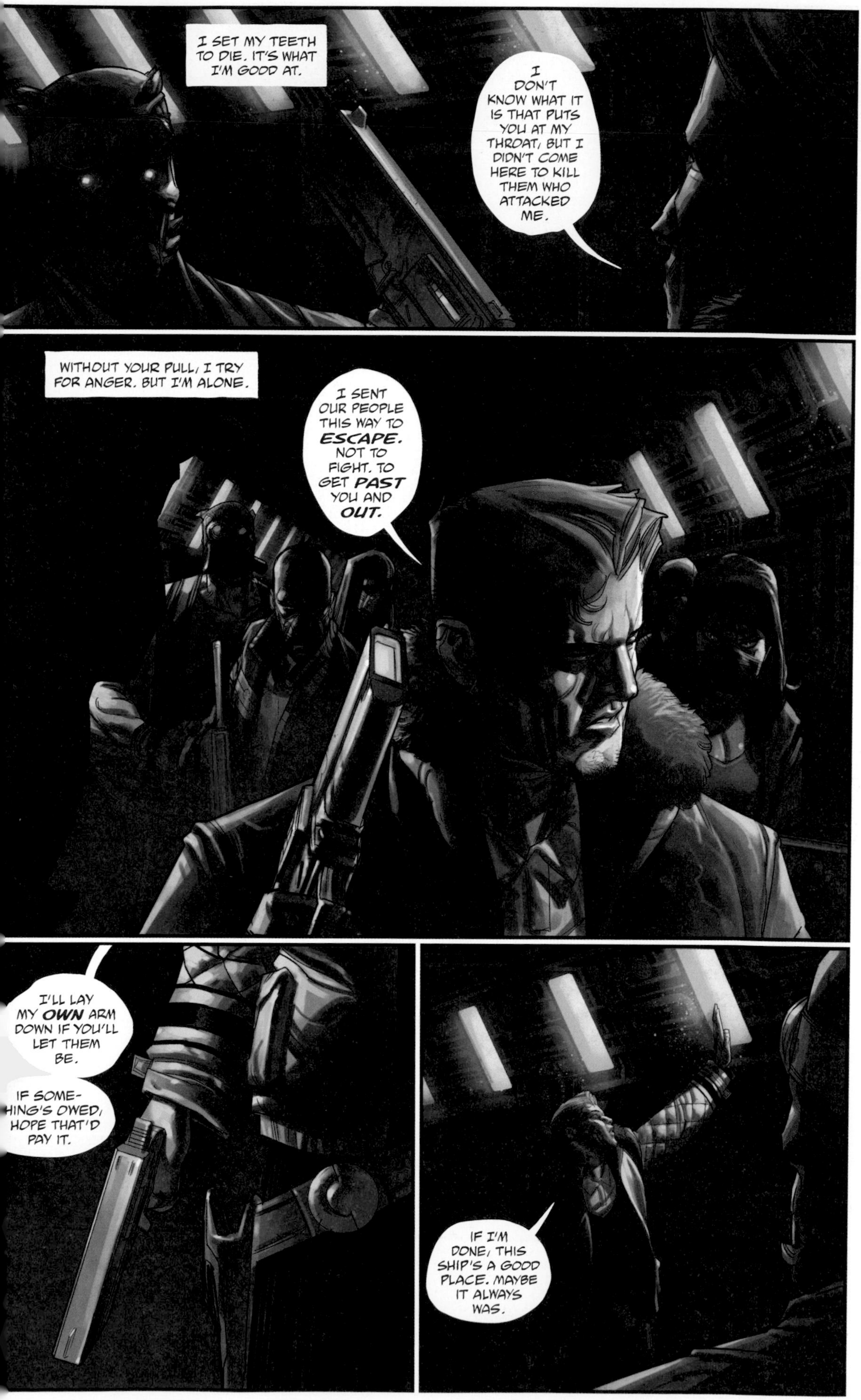

I SET MY TEETH TO DIE. IT'S WHAT I'M GOOD AT.
I DON'T KNOW WHAT IT IS THAT PUTS YOU AT MY THROAT, BUT I DIDN'T COME HERE TO KILL THEM WHO ATTACKED ME.
WITHOUT YOUR PULL, I TRY FOR ANGER. BUT I'M ALONE.
I SENT OUR PEOPLE THIS WAY TO ESCAPE. NOT TO FIGHT. TO GET PAST YOU AND OUT.
I'LL LAY MY OWN ARM DOWN IF YOU'LL LET THEM BE.
IF SOME-HING'S OWED, HOPE THAT'D PAY IT.
IF I'M DONE, THIS SHIP'S A GOOD PLACE. MAYBE IT ALWAYS WAS.

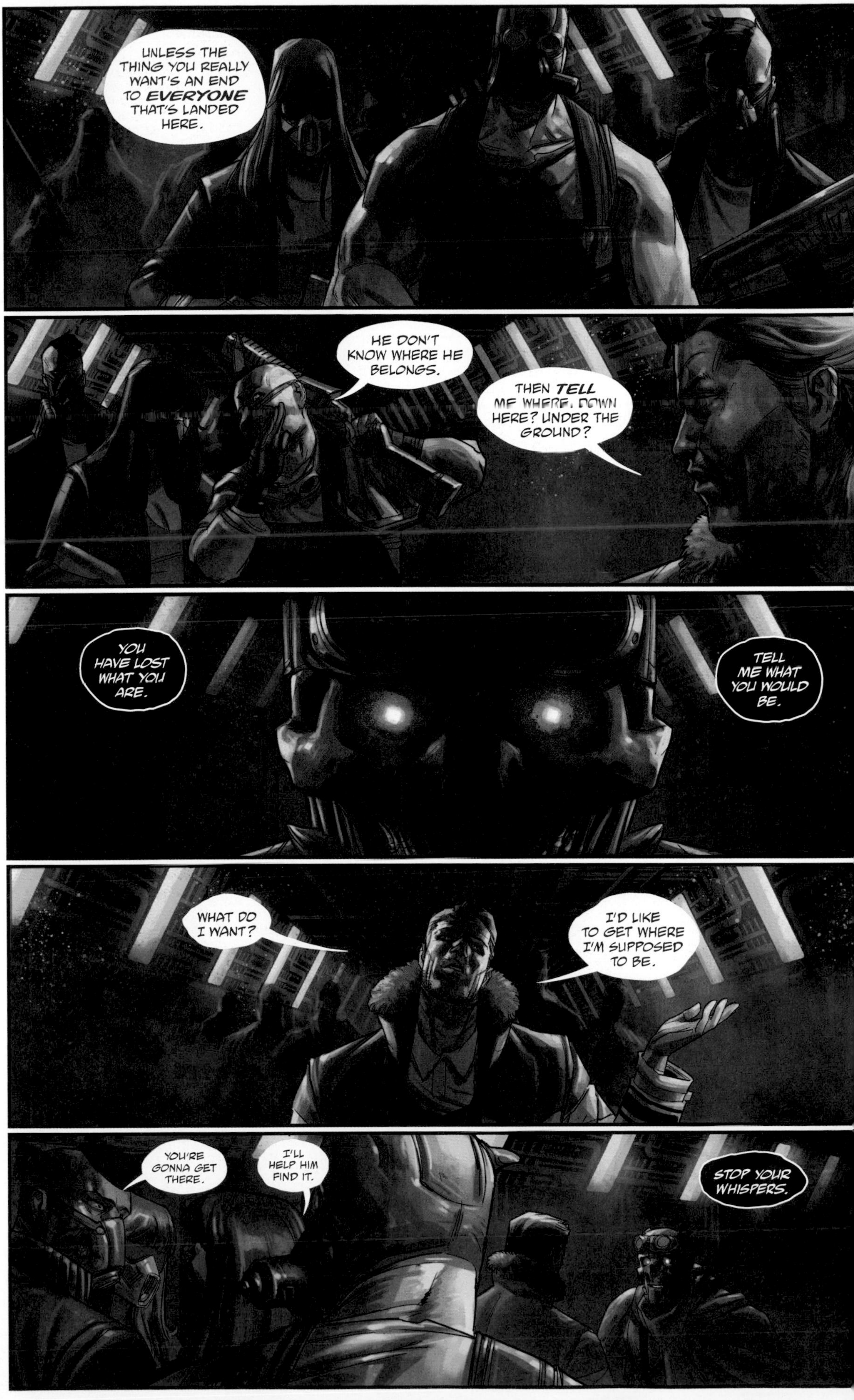
UNLESS THE THING YOU REALLY WANT'S AN END TO EVERYONE THAT'S LANDED HERE.
HE DON'T KNOW WHERE HE BELONGS.
THEN TELL ME WHERE. DOWN HERE? UNDER THE GROUND?
YOU HAVE LOST WHAT YOU ARE.
TELL ME WHAT YOU WOULD BE.
WHAT DO I WANT?
I'D LIKE TO GET WHERE I'M SUPPOSED TO BE.
YOU'RE GONNA GET THERE.
I'LL HELP HIM FIND IT.
STOP YOUR WHISPERS.

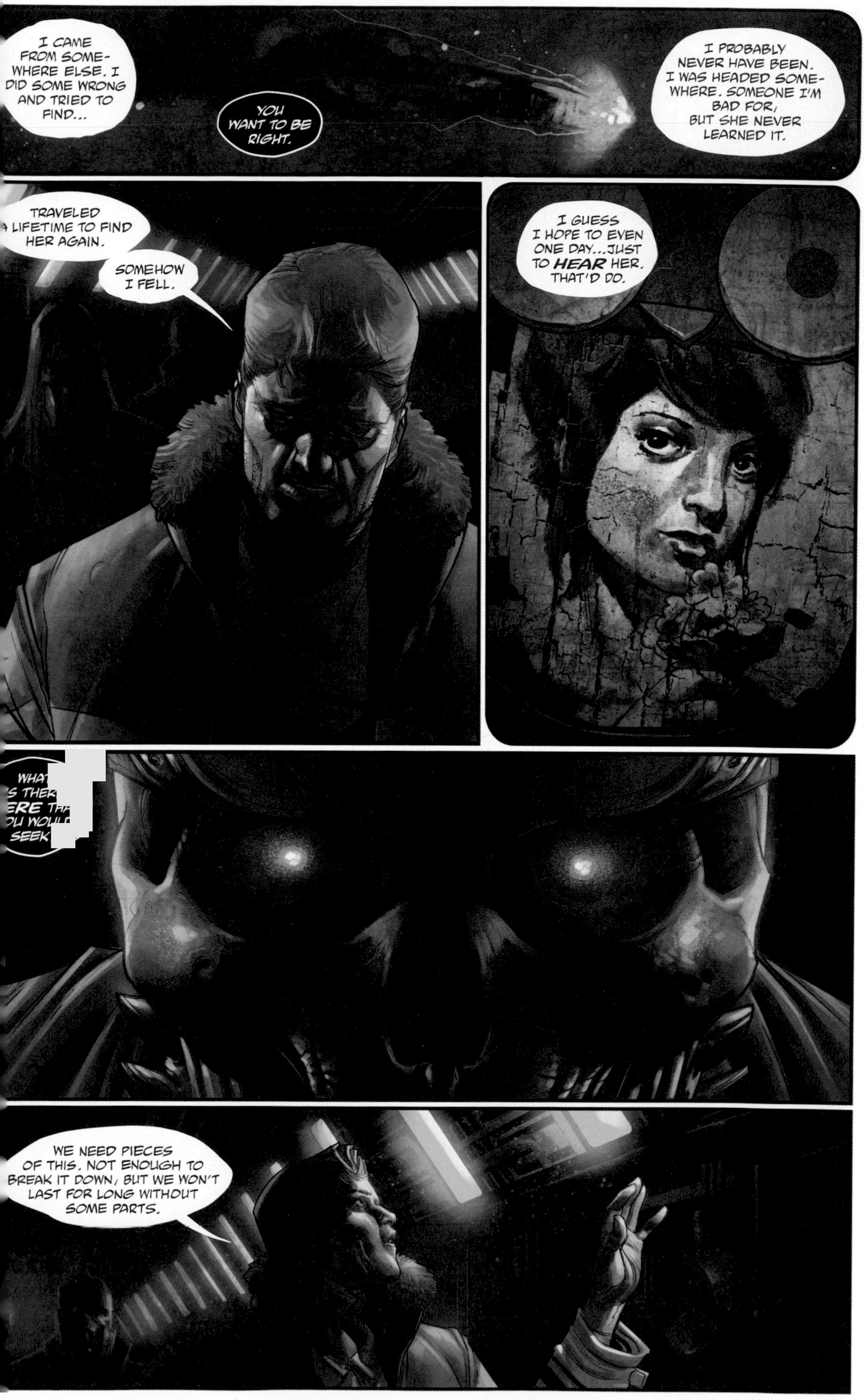
I CAME FROM SOMEWHERE ELSE. I DID SOME WRONG AND TRIED TO FIND...
YOU WANT TO BE RIGHT.
I PROBABLY NEVER HAVE BEEN. I WAS HEADED SOMEWHERE. SOMEONE I'M BAD FOR, BUT SHE NEVER LEARNED IT.
TRAVELED A LIFETIME TO FIND HER AGAIN.
SOMEHOW I FELL.
I GUESS I HOPE TO EVEN ONE DAY...JUST TO HEAR HER. THAT'D DO.
WE NEED PIECES OF THIS. NOT ENOUGH TO BREAK IT DOWN, BUT WE WON'T LAST FOR LONG WITHOUT SOME PARTS.

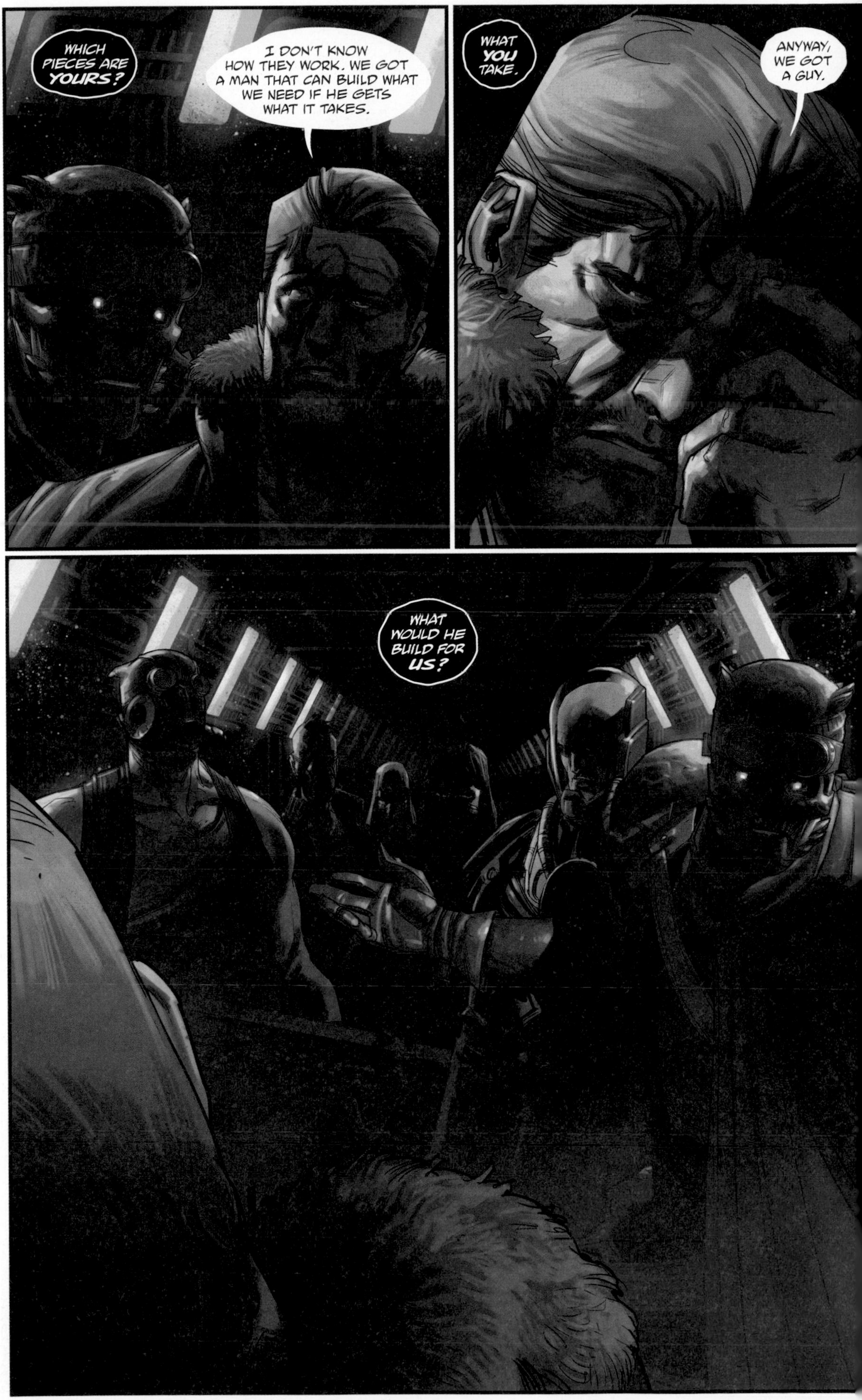
WHICH PIECES ARE YOURS?
I DON'T KNOW HOW THEY WORK. WE GOT A MAN THAT CAN BUILD WHAT WE NEED IF HE GETS WHAT IT TAKES.
WHAT YOU TAKE.
ANYWAY, WE GOT A GUY.
WHAT WOULD HE BUILD FOR US?

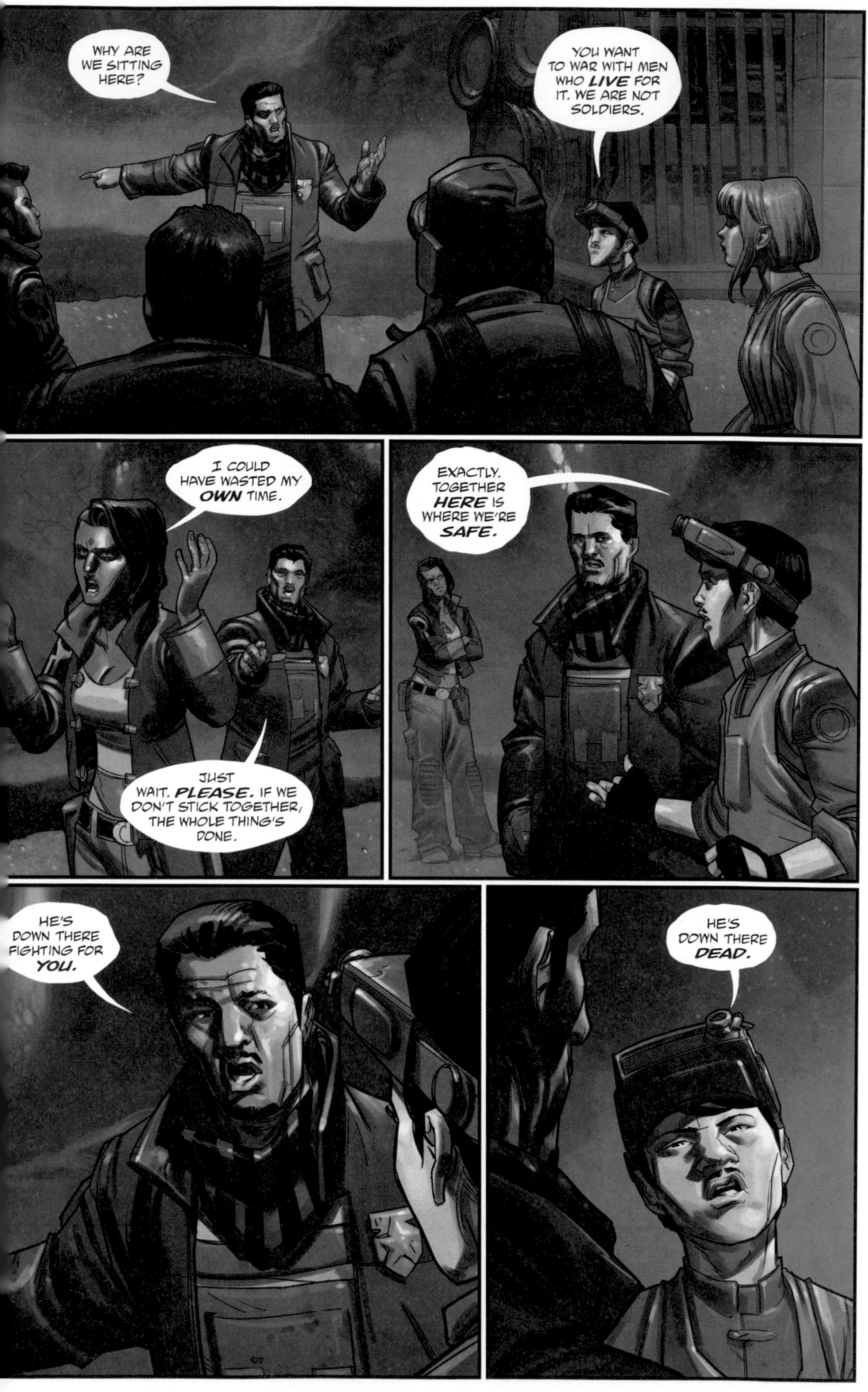
WHY ARE WE SITTING HERE?
YOU WANT TO WAR WITH MEN WHO LIVE FOR IT. WE ARE NOT SOLDIERS.
I COULD HAVE WASTED MY OWN TIME.
JUST WAIT. PLEASE. IF WE DON'T STICK TOGETHER, THE WHOLE THING'S DONE.
EXACTLY. TOGETHER HERE IS WHERE WE'RE SAFE.
HE'S DOWN THERE FIGHTING FOR YOU.
HE'S DOWN THERE DEAD.

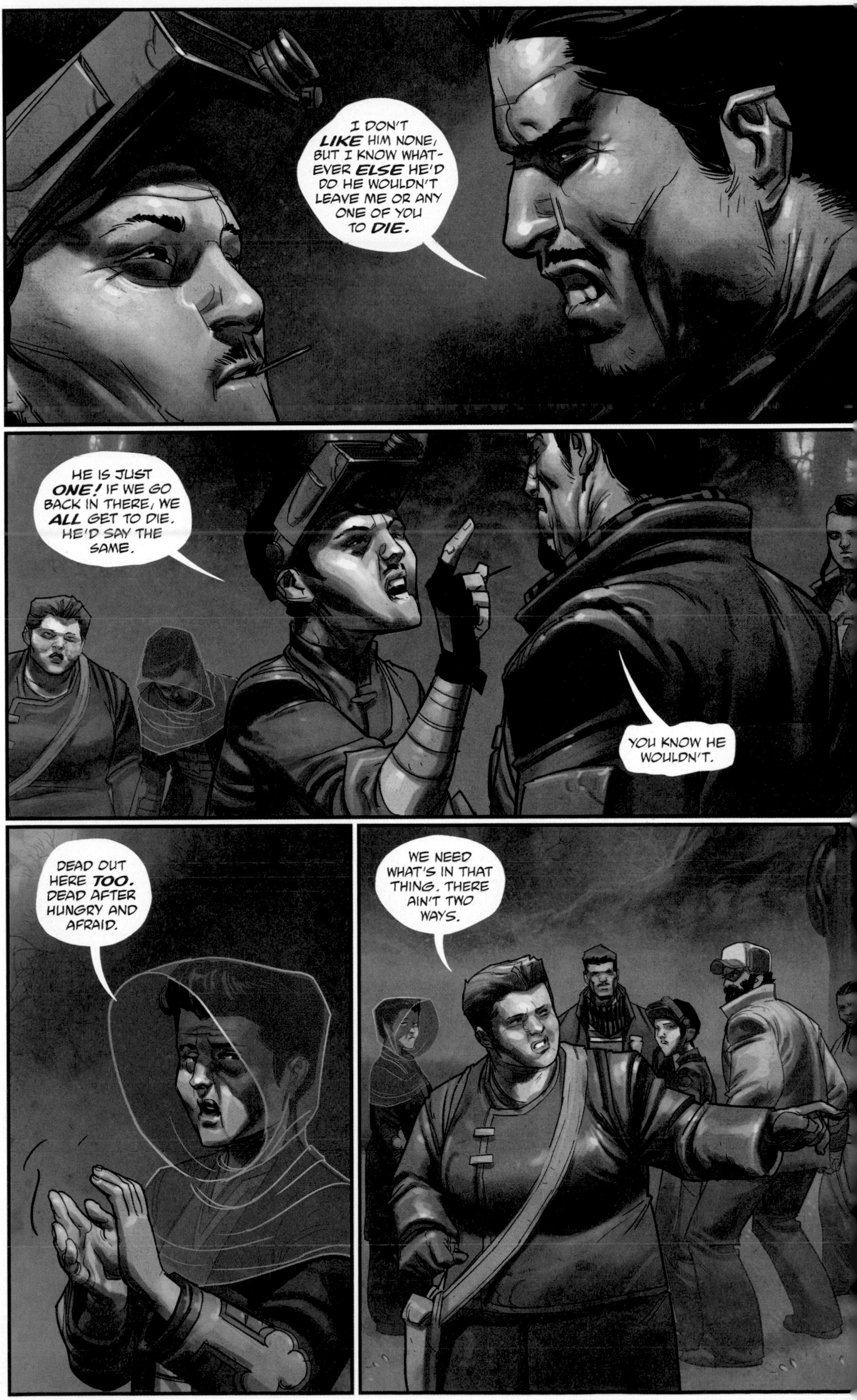
I DON'T LIKE HIM NONE, BUT I KNOW WHAT-EVER ELSE HE'D DO HE WOULDN'T LEAVE ME OR ANY ONE OF YOU TO DIE.
HE IS JUST ONE! IF WE GO BACK IN THERE, WE ALL GET TO DIE. HE'D SAY THE SAME.
YOU KNOW HE WOULDN'T.
DEAD OUT HERE TOO. DEAD AFTER HUNGRY AND AFRAID.
WE NEED WHAT'S IN THAT THING. THERE AIN'T TWO WAYS.

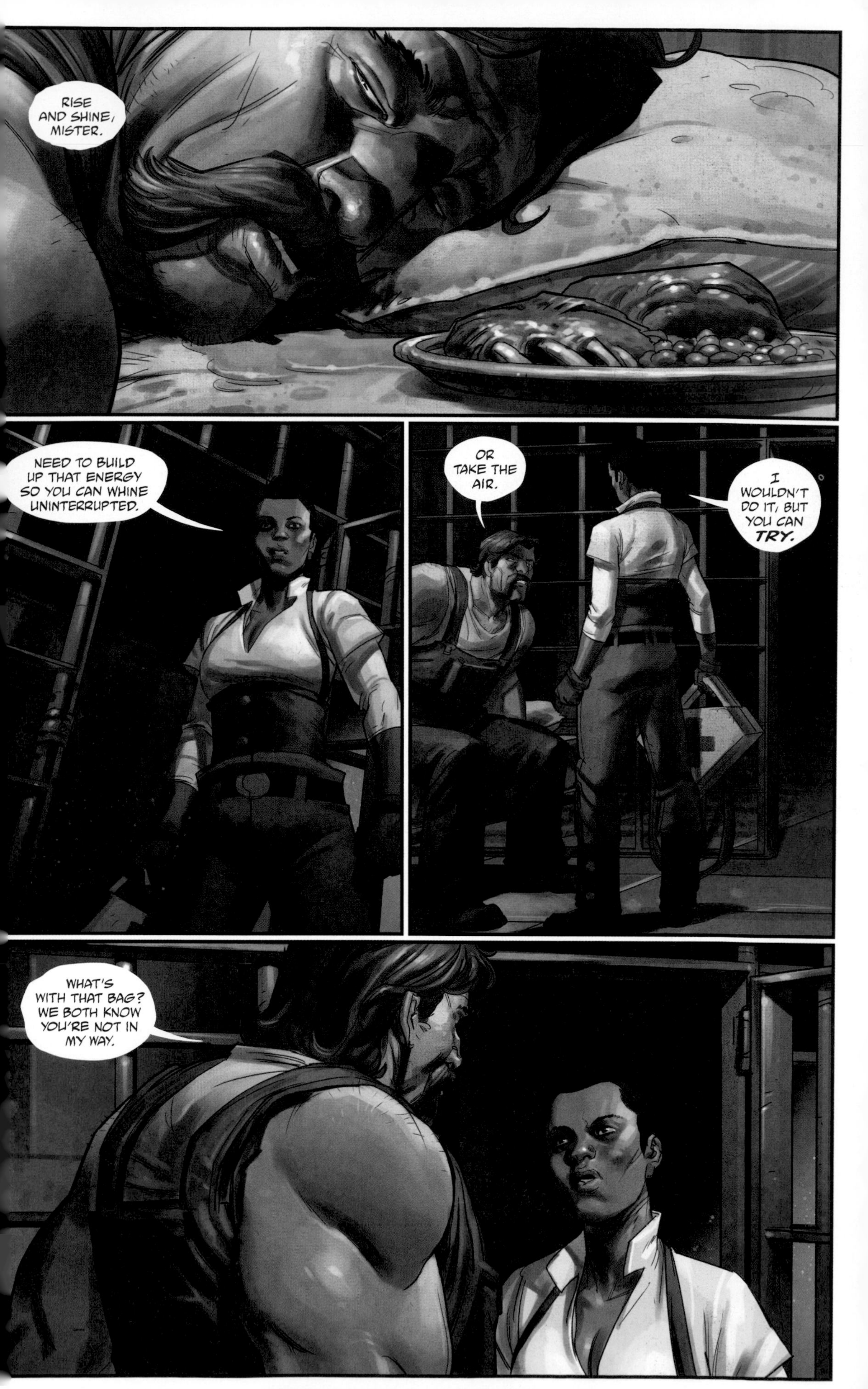
RISE AND SHINE, MISTER.
NEED TO BUILD UP THAT ENERGY SO YOU CAN WHINE UNINTERRUPTED.
OR TAKE THE AIR.
I WOULDN'T DO IT, BUT YOU CAN TRY.
WHAT'S WITH THAT BAG? WE BOTH KNOW YOU'RE NOT IN MY WAY.

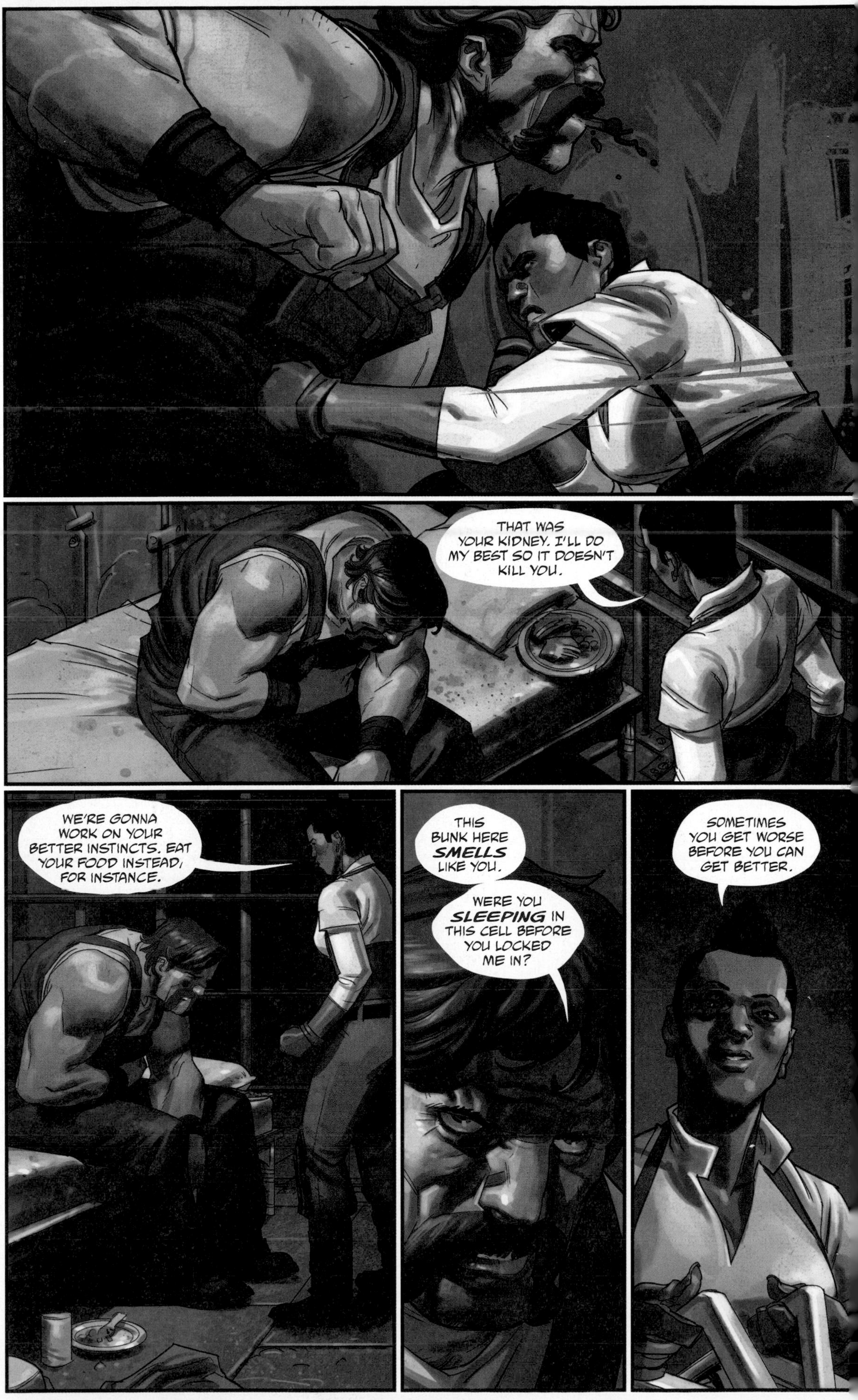
THAT WAS YOUR KIDNEY. I'LL DO MY BEST SO IT DOESN'T KILL YOU.
WE'RE GONNA WORK ON YOUR BETTER INSTINCTS. EAT YOUR FOOD INSTEAD, FOR INSTANCE.
THIS BUNK HERE SMELLS LIKE YOU.
WERE YOU SLEEPING IN THIS CELL BEFORE YOU LOCKED ME IN?
SOMETIMES YOU GET WORSE BEFORE YOU CAN GET BETTER.

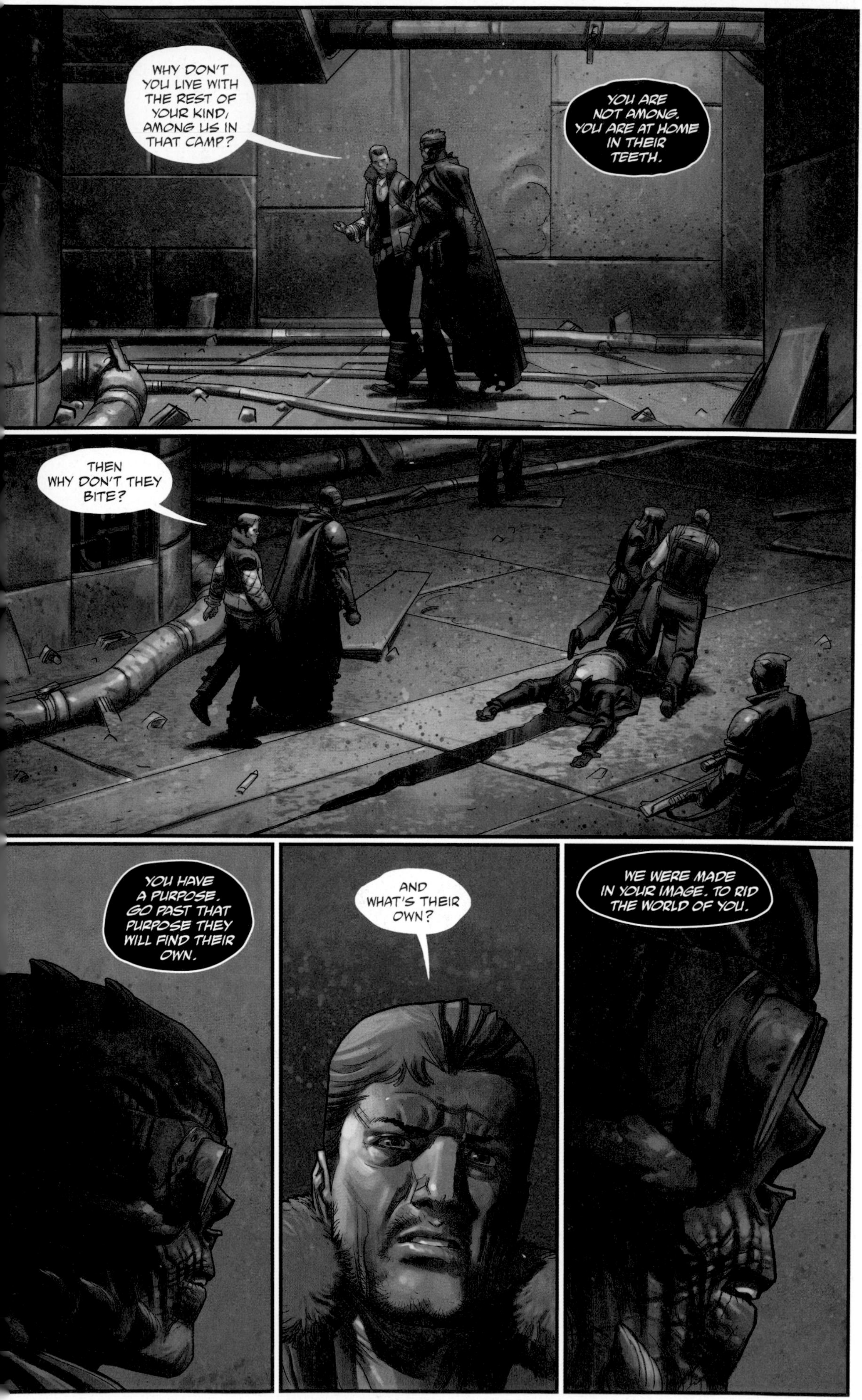
WHY DON'T YOU LIVE WITH THE REST OF YOUR KIND, AMONG US IN THAT CAMP?
YOU ARE NOT AMONG. YOU ARE AT HOME IN THEIR TEETH.
THEN WHY DON'T THEY BITE?
YOU HAVE A PURPOSE. GO PAST THAT PURPOSE THEY WILL FIND THEIR OWN.
AND WHAT'S THEIR OWN?
WE WERE MADE IN YOUR IMAGE. TO RID THE WORLD OF YOU.

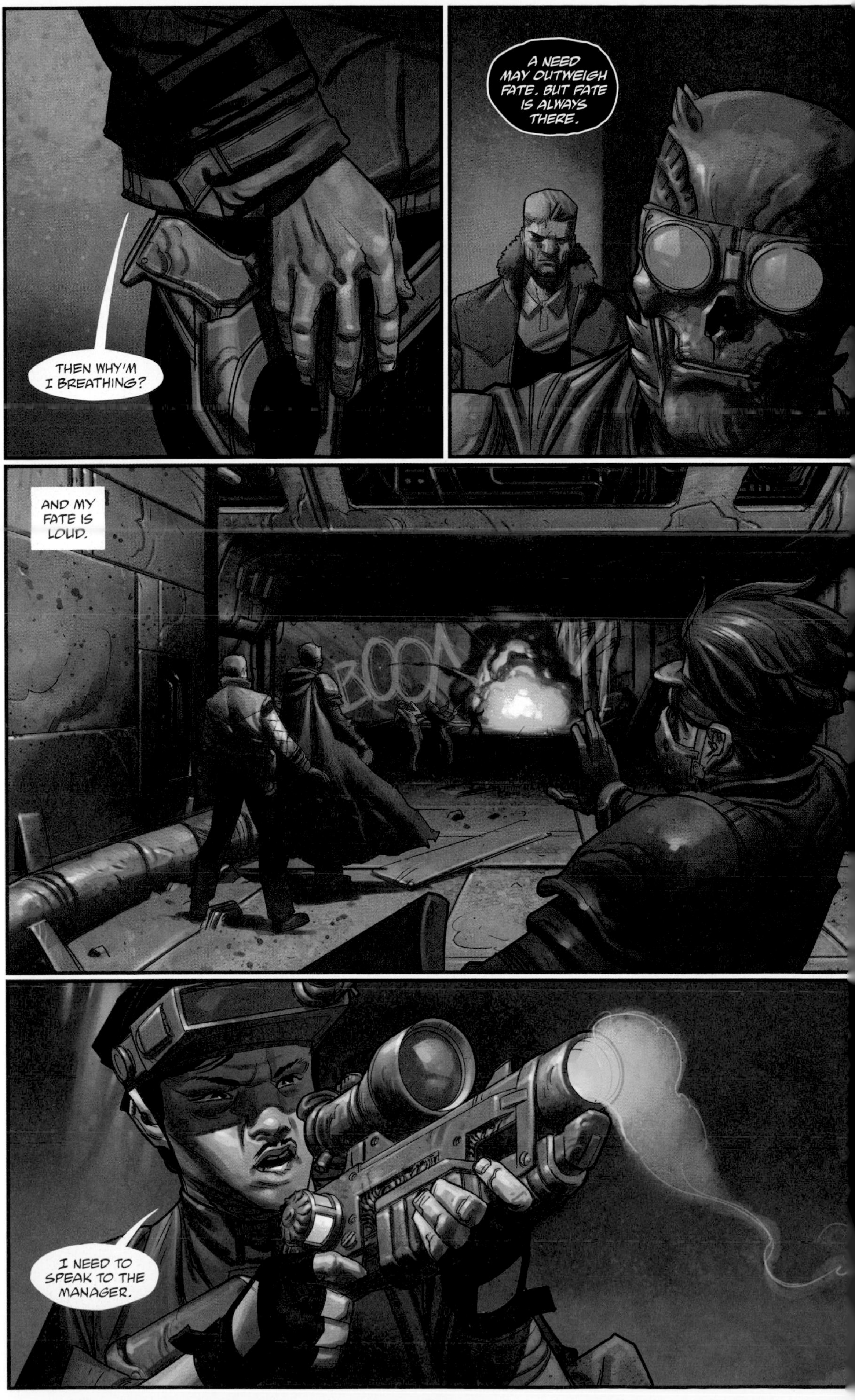
THEN WHY'M I BREATHING?
A NEED MAY OUTWEIGH FATE. BUT FATE IS ALWAYS THERE.
AND MY FATE IS LOUD.
I NEED TO SPEAK TO THE MANAGER.

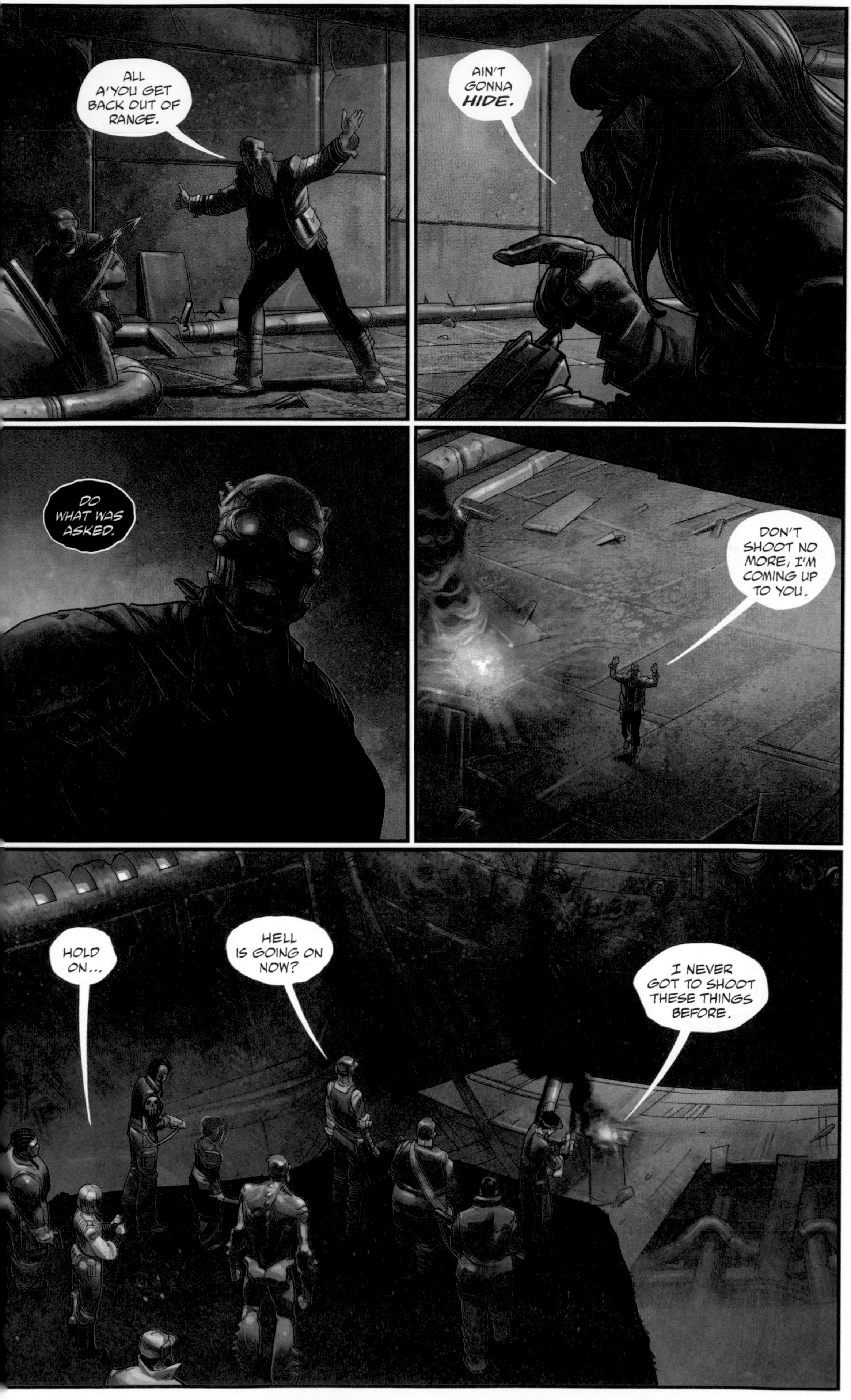
ALL A'YOU GET BACK OUT OF RANGE.
AIN'T GONNA HIDE.
DO WHAT WAS ASKED.
DON'T SHOOT NO MORE, I'M COMING UP TO YOU.
HOLD ON...
HELL IS GOING ON NOW?
I NEVER GOT TO SHOOT THESE THINGS BEFORE.

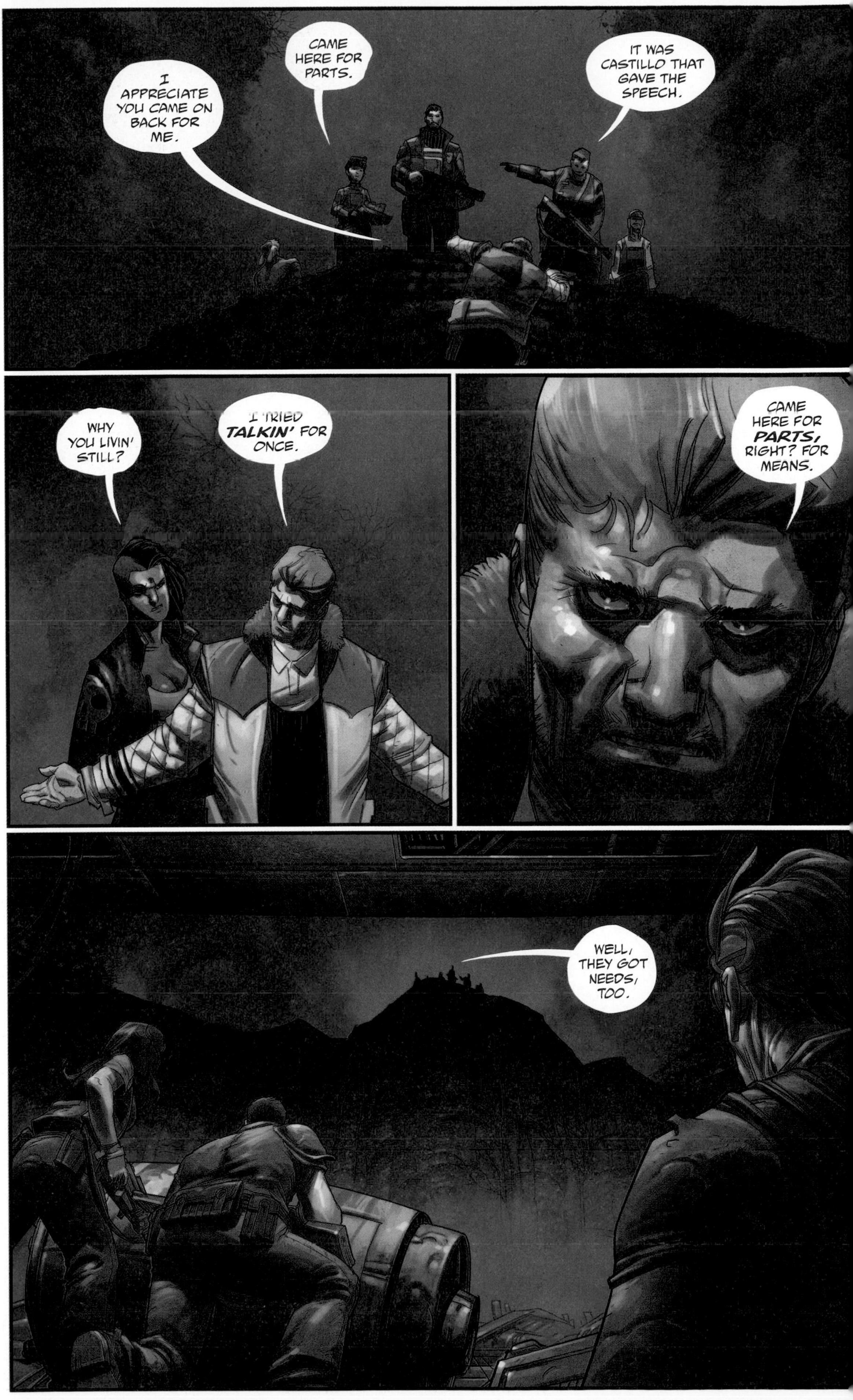
I APPRECIATE YOU CAME ON BACK FOR ME.
CAME HERE FOR PARTS.
IT WAS CASTILLO THAT GAVE THE SPEECH.
WHY YOU LIVIN' STILL?
I TRIED *TALKIN'* FOR ONCE.
CAME HERE FOR *PARTS,* RIGHT? FOR MEANS.
WELL, THEY GOT NEEDS, TOO.

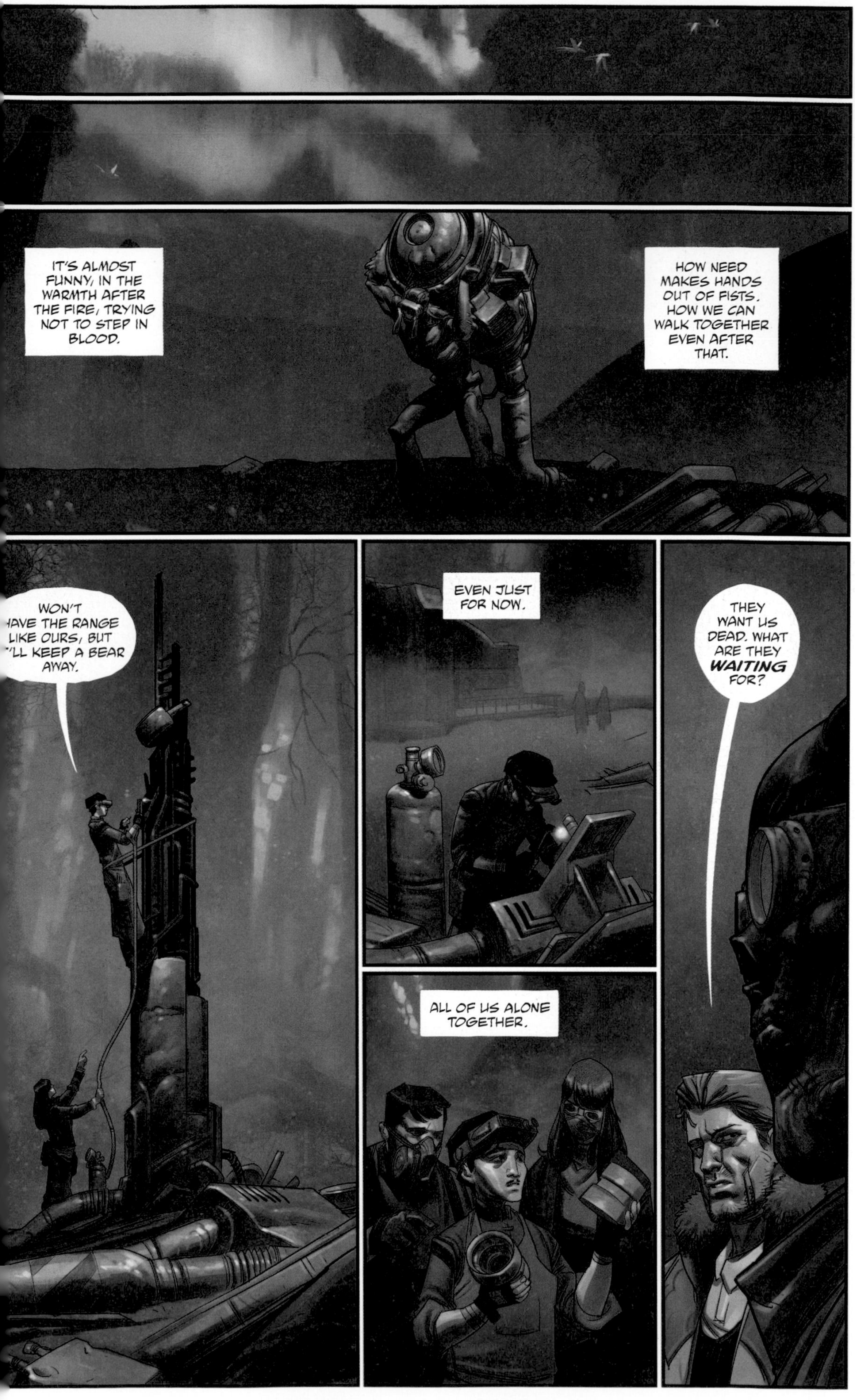
IT'S ALMOST FUNNY, IN THE WARMTH AFTER THE FIRE, TRYING NOT TO STEP IN BLOOD.
HOW NEED MAKES HANDS OUT OF FISTS. HOW WE CAN WALK TOGETHER EVEN AFTER THAT.
WON'T HAVE THE RANGE LIKE OURS, BUT 'LL KEEP A BEAR AWAY.
EVEN JUST FOR NOW.
THEY WANT US DEAD. WHAT ARE THEY WAITING FOR?
ALL OF US ALONE TOGETHER.

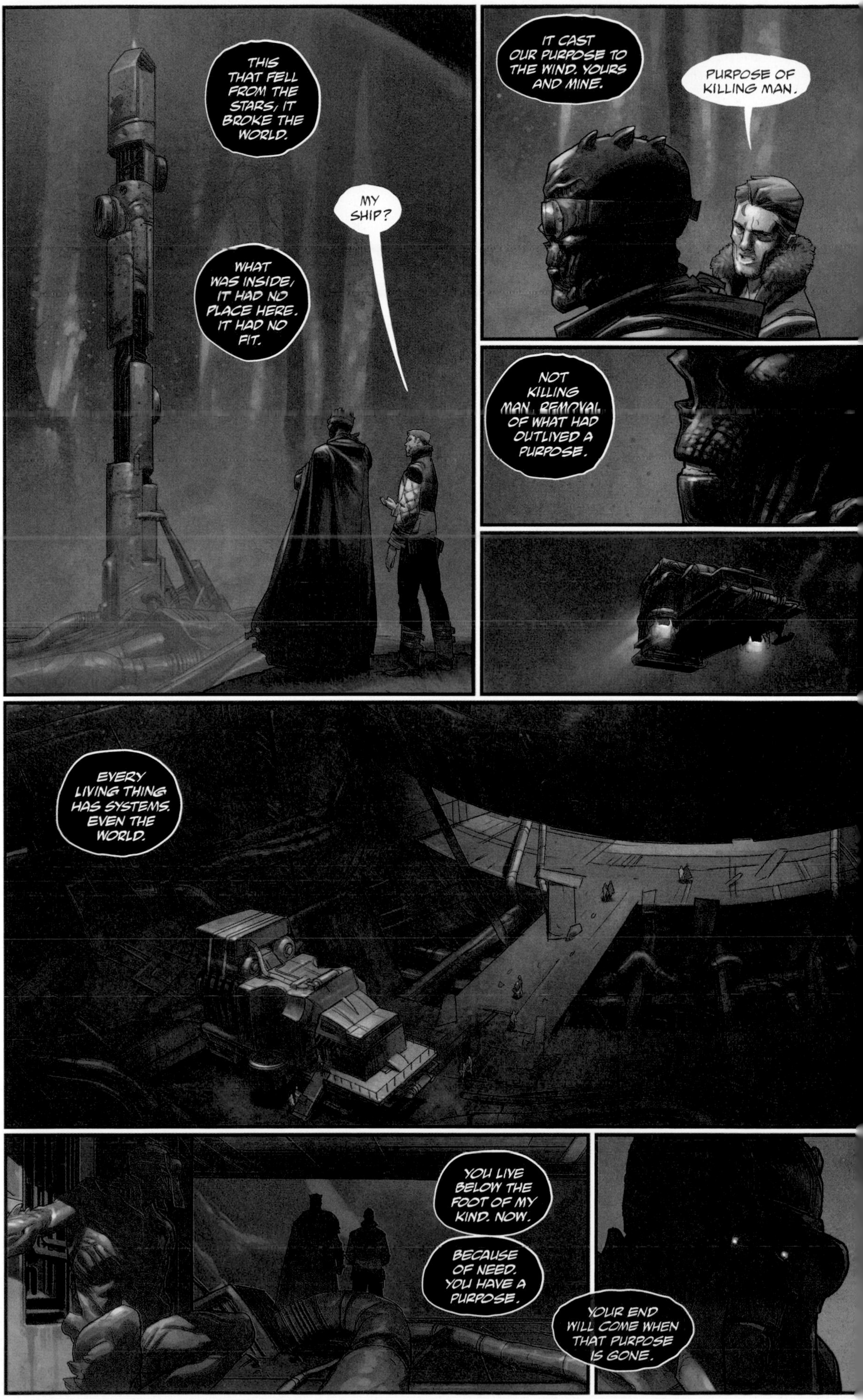
THIS THAT FELL FROM THE STARS, IT BROKE THE WORLD.
MY SHIP?
WHAT WAS INSIDE, IT HAD NO PLACE HERE. IT HAD NO FIT.
IT CAST OUR PURPOSE TO THE WIND. YOURS AND MINE.
PURPOSE OF KILLING MAN.
NOT KILLING MAN. REMOVAL OF WHAT HAD OUTLIVED A PURPOSE.
EVERY LIVING THING HAS SYSTEMS. EVEN THE WORLD.
YOU LIVE BELOW THE FOOT OF MY KIND. NOW.
BECAUSE OF NEED. YOU HAVE A PURPOSE.
YOUR END WILL COME WHEN THAT PURPOSE IS GONE.

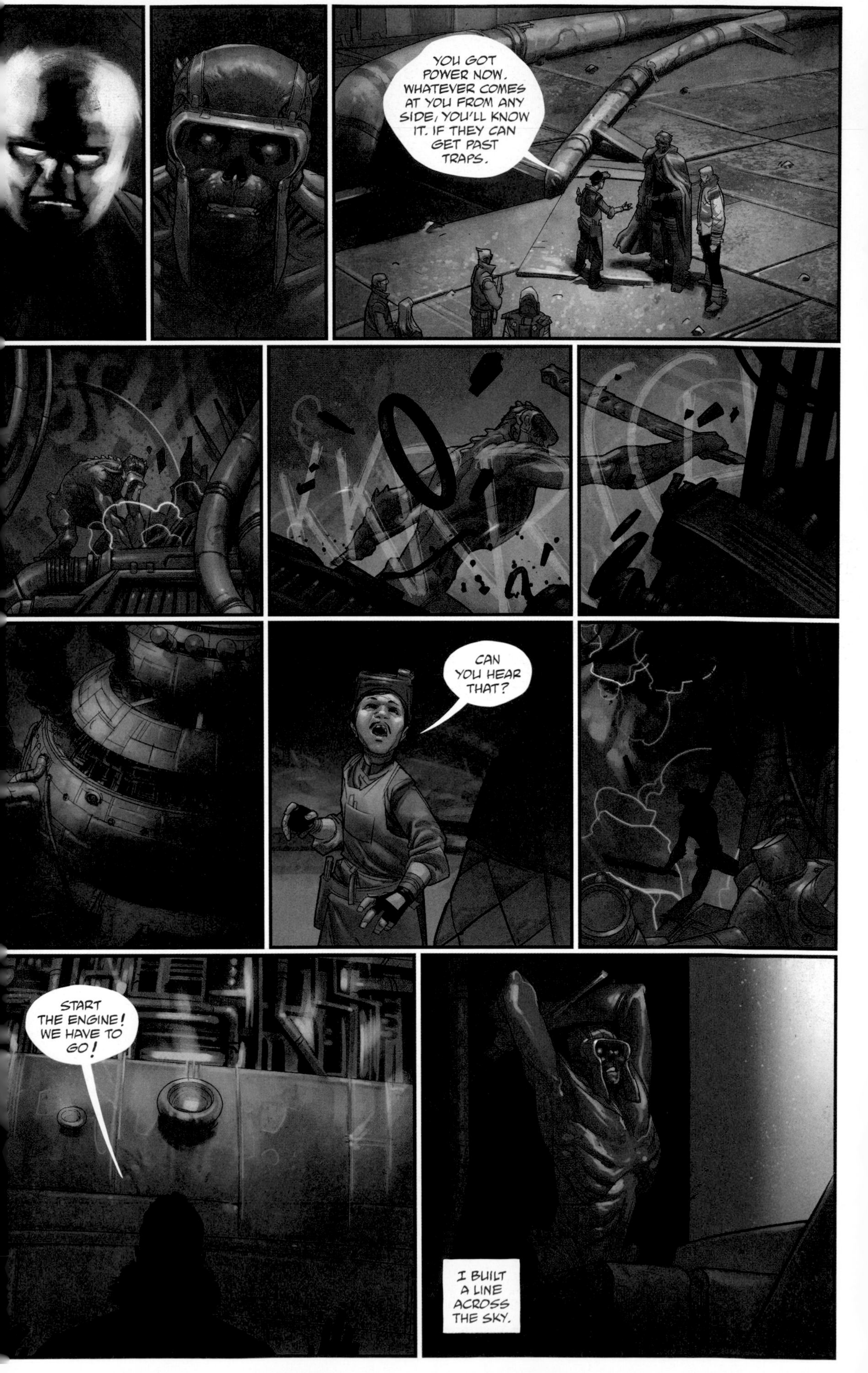
YOU GOT POWER NOW. WHATEVER COMES AT YOU FROM ANY SIDE, YOU'LL KNOW IT. IF THEY CAN GET PAST TRAPS.
CAN YOU HEAR THAT?
START THE ENGINE! WE HAVE TO GO!
I BUILT A LINE ACROSS THE SKY.

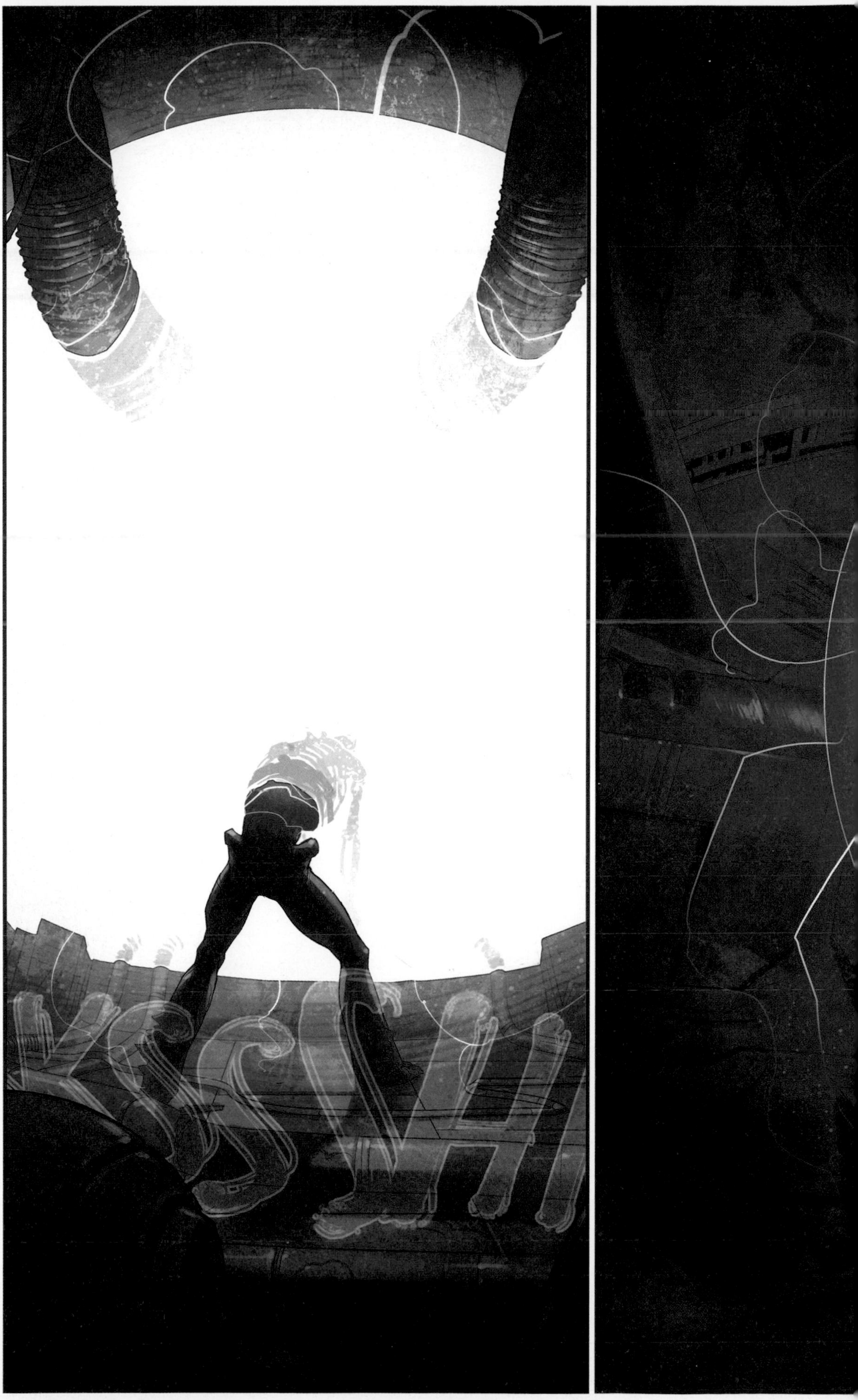
KSSH

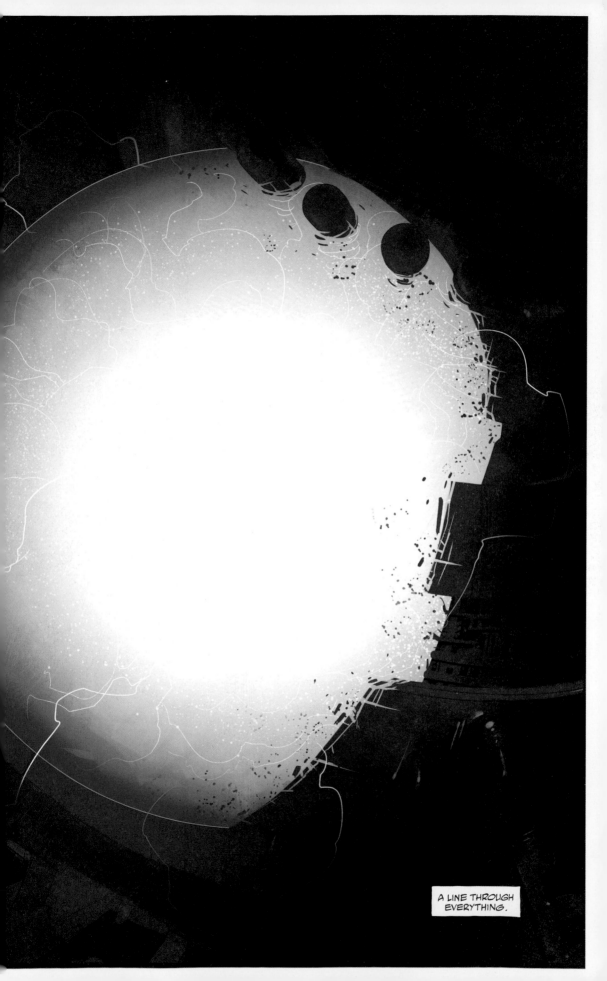

A LINE THROUGH
EVERYTHING.

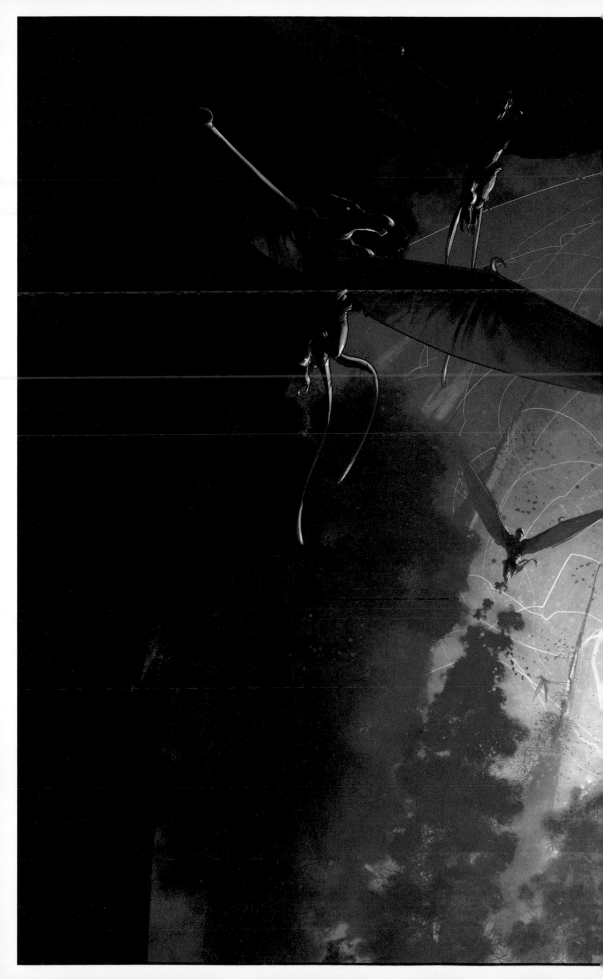

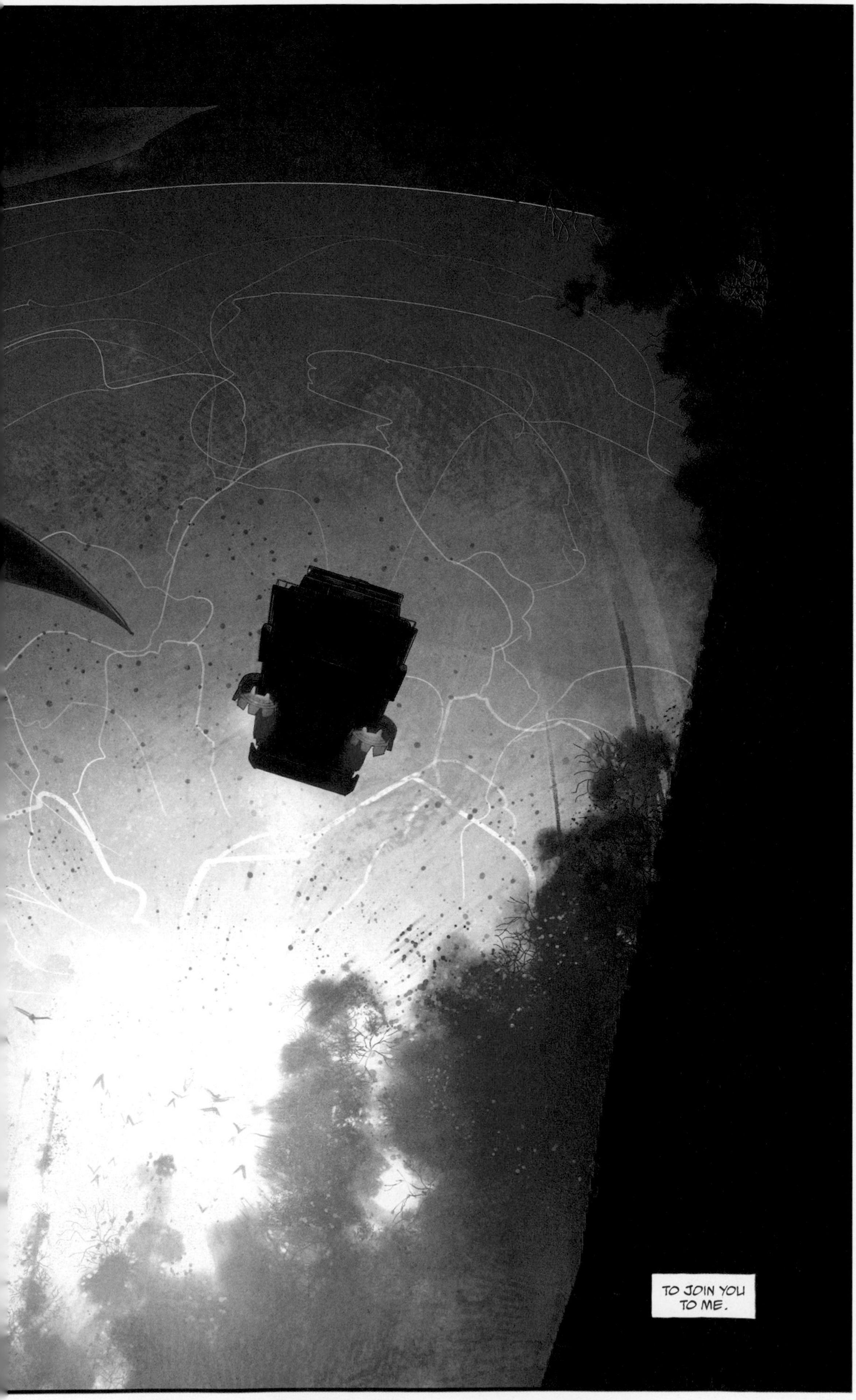
TO JOIN YOU
TO ME.

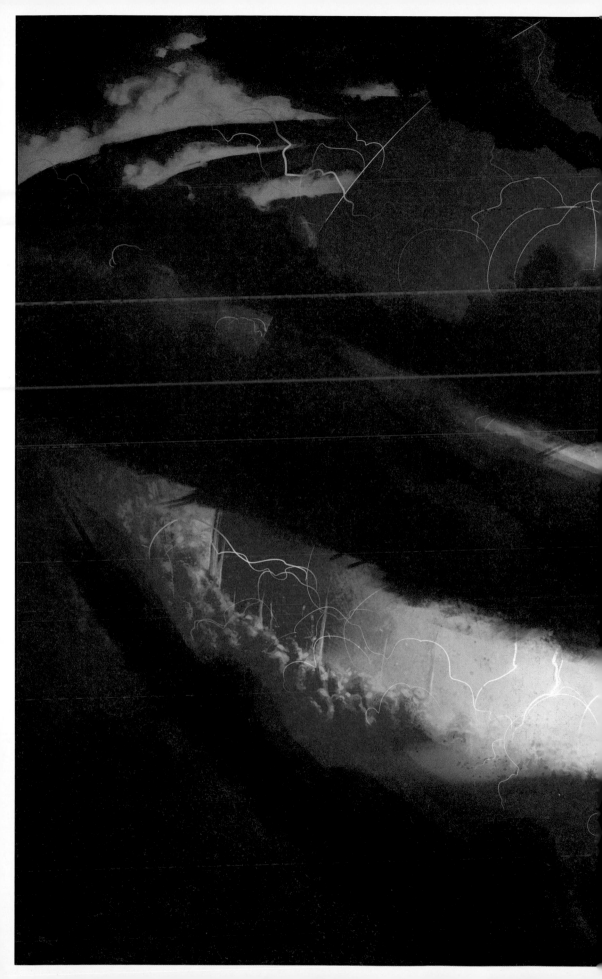

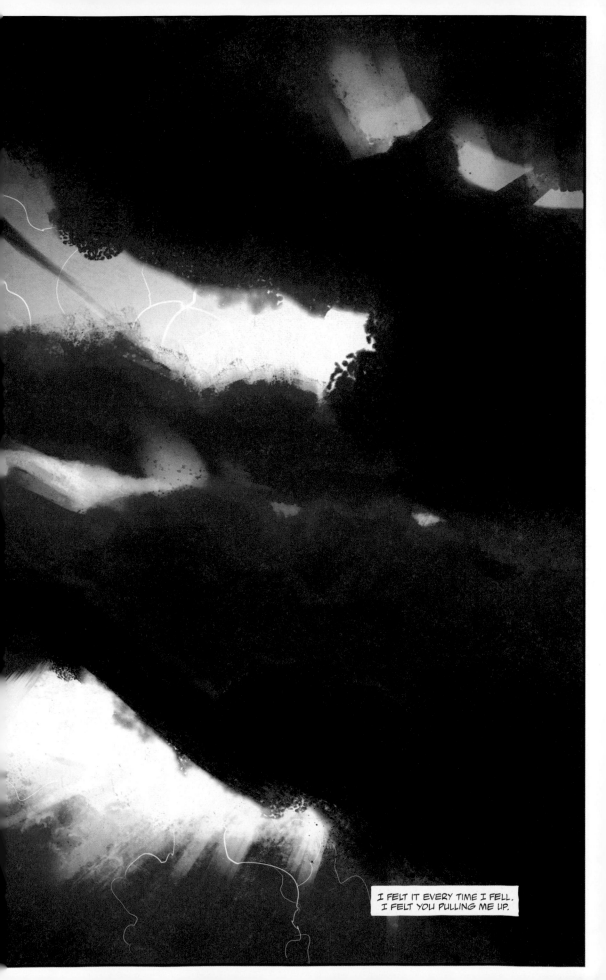

I FELT IT EVERY TIME I FELL.
I FELT YOU PULLING ME UP.

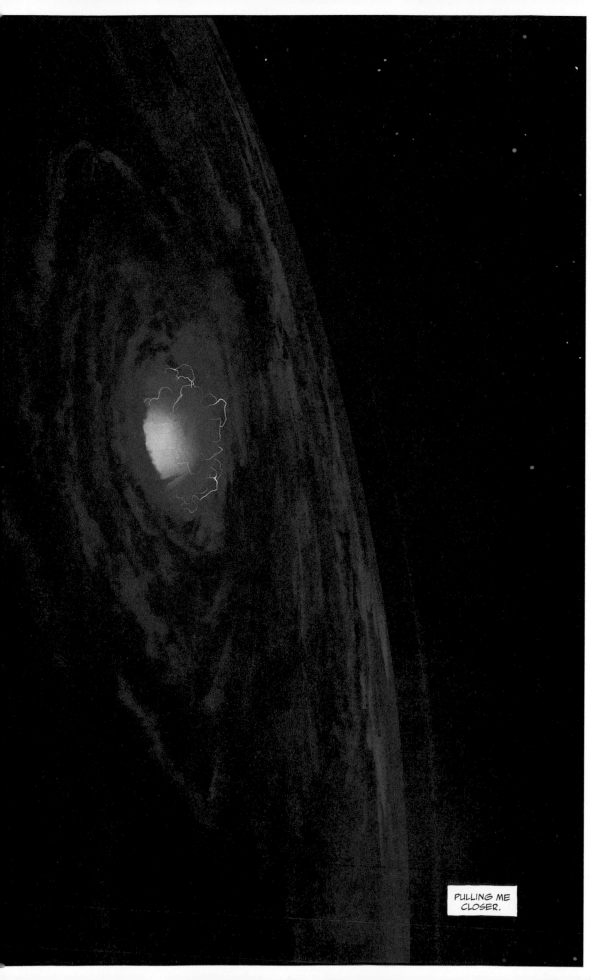

PULLING ME
CLOSER.

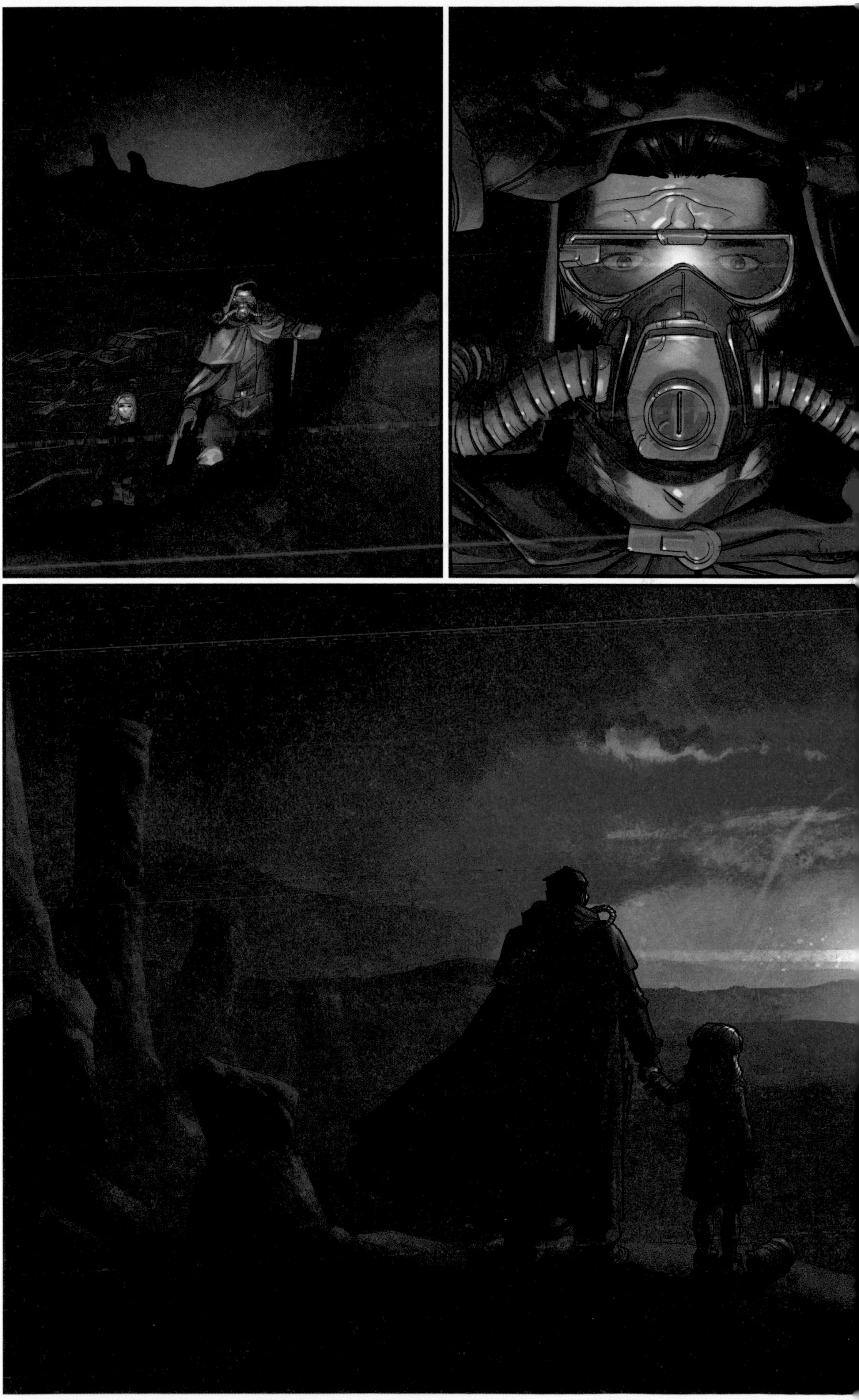

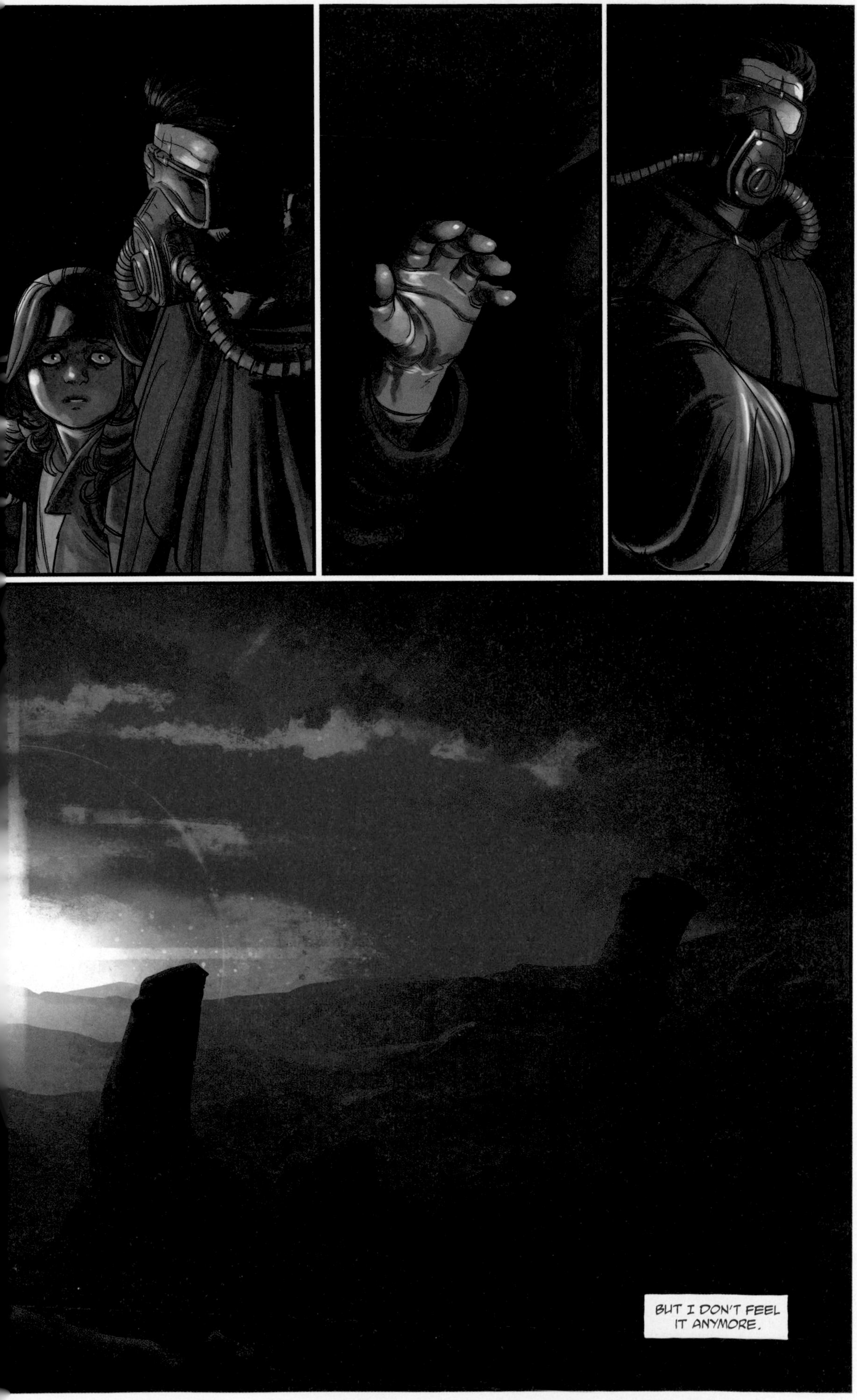
BUT I DON'T FEEL IT ANYMORE.

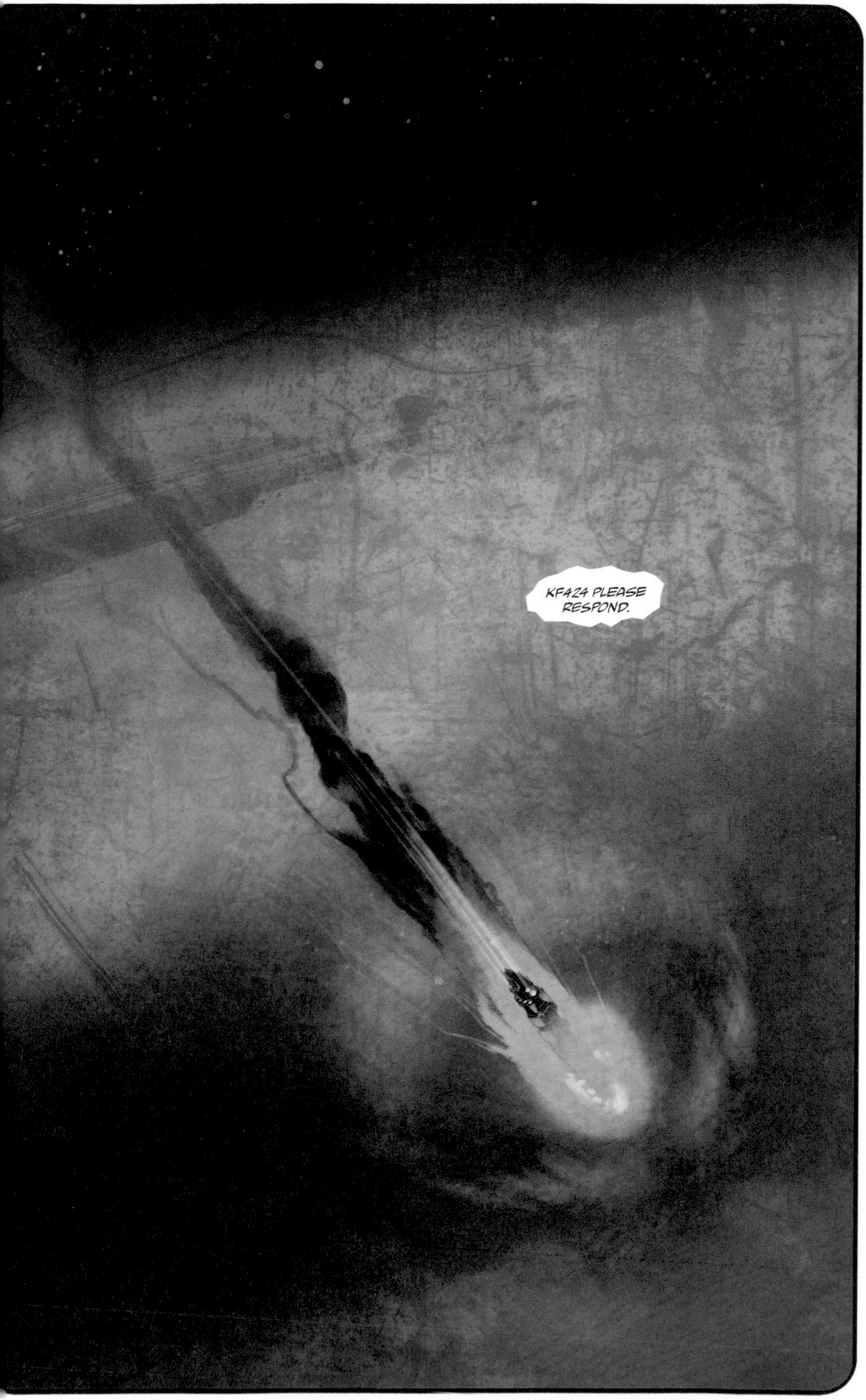
KF424 PLEASE RESPOND.

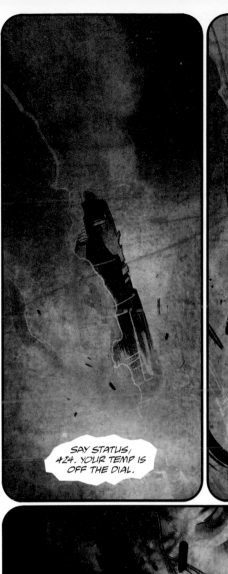

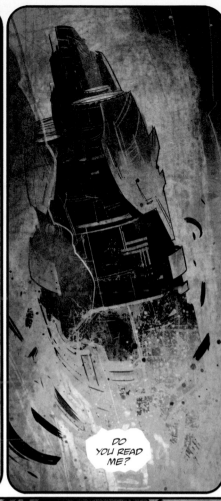

SAY STATUS, 424. YOUR TEMP IS OFF THE DIAL.

DO YOU READ ME?

CSO EMMERICH. DO YOU READ?

EMMERICH. PLEASE RESPOND.

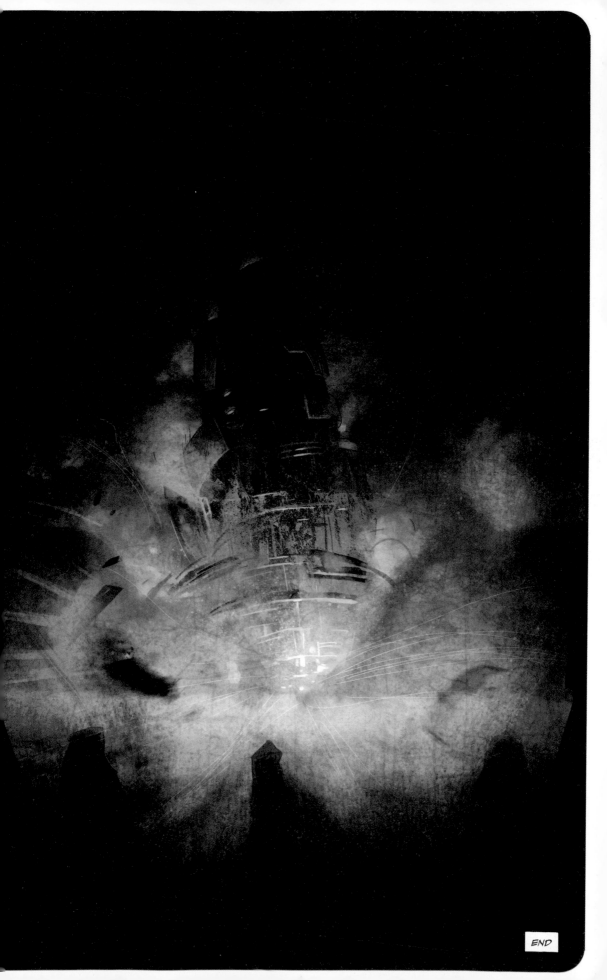

END

COVER GALLERY

Eduardo Risso, Tom Muller,
Daniel Krall, and Paul Azaceta

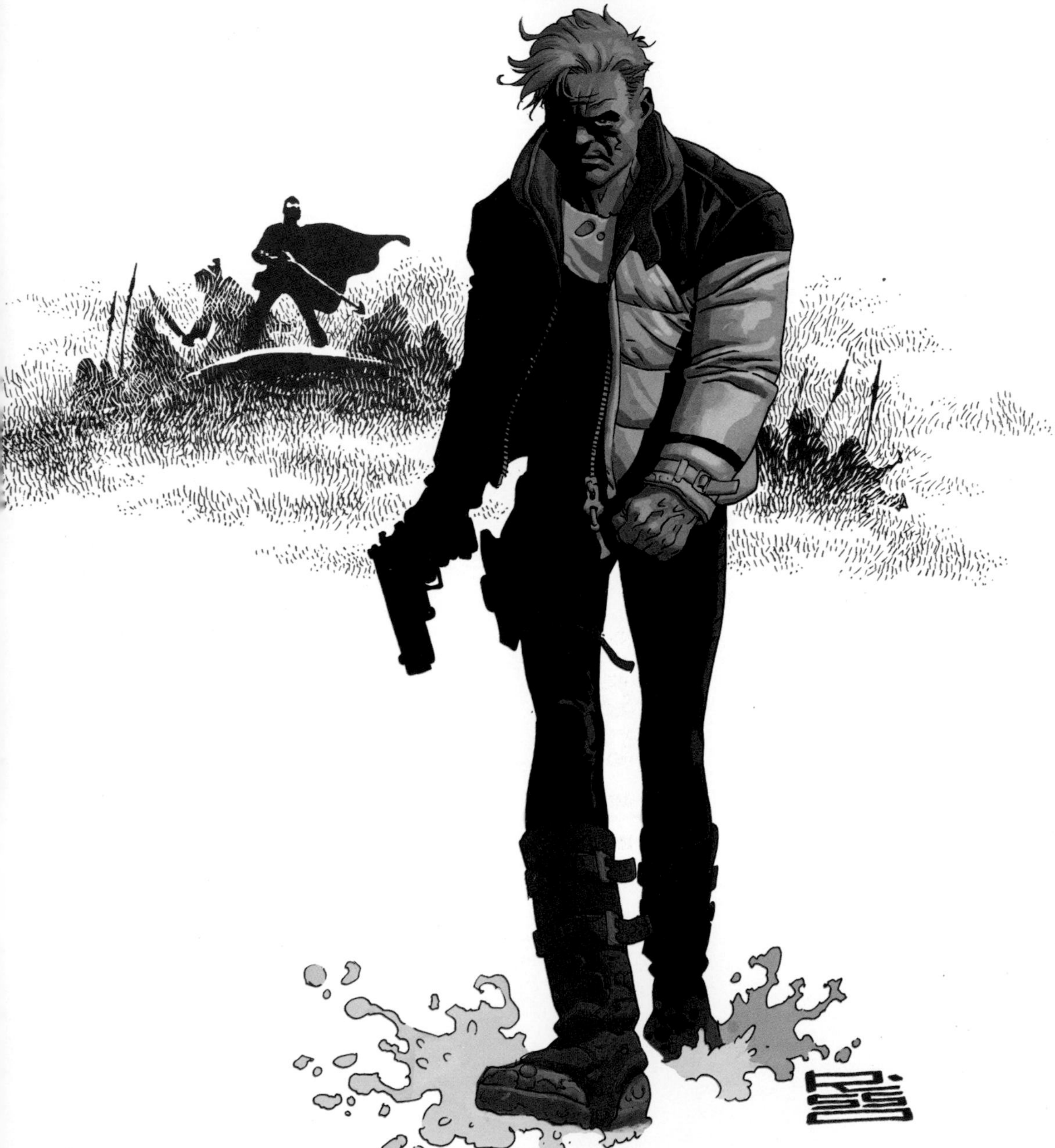

Eduardo Risso

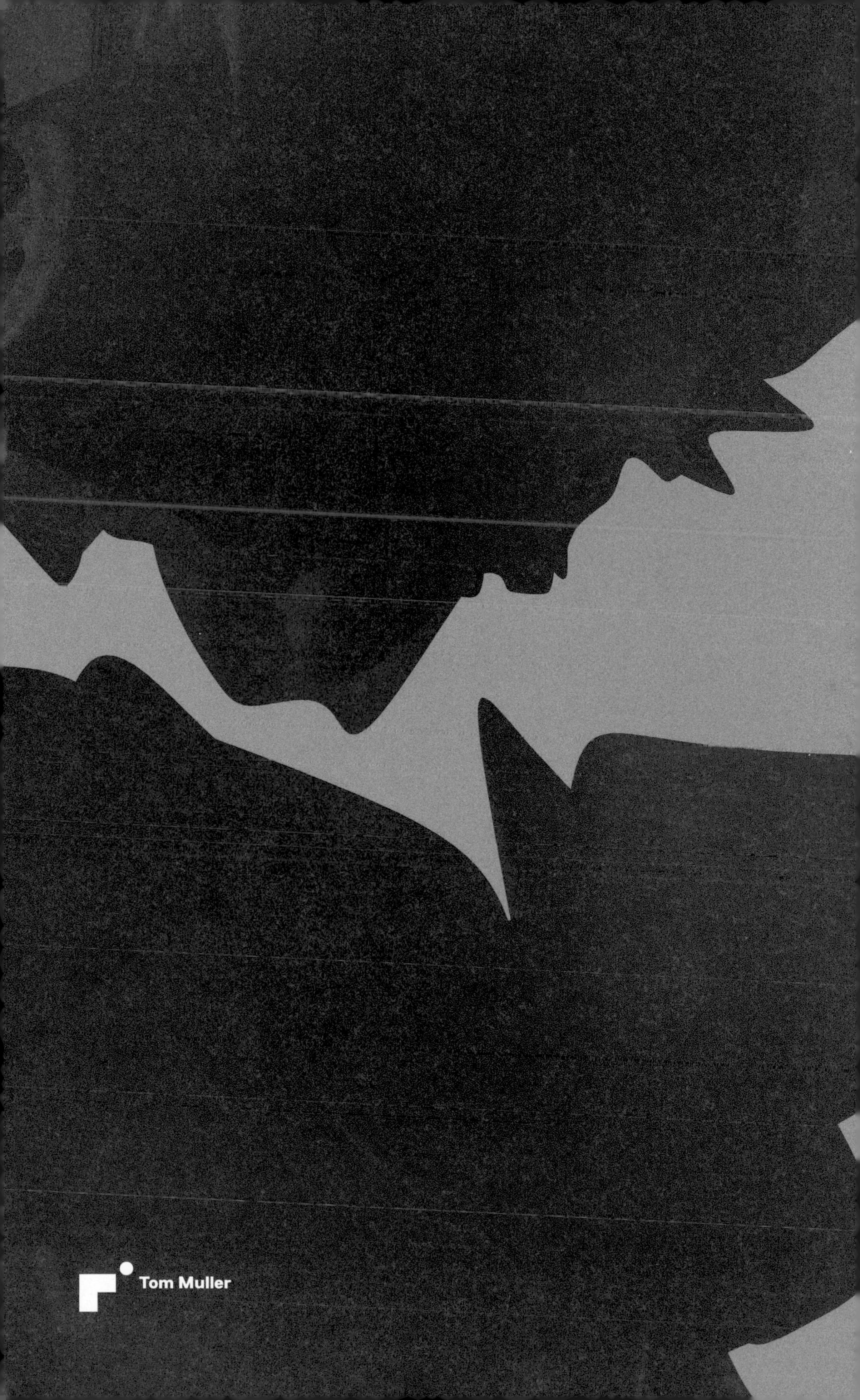
Tom Muller

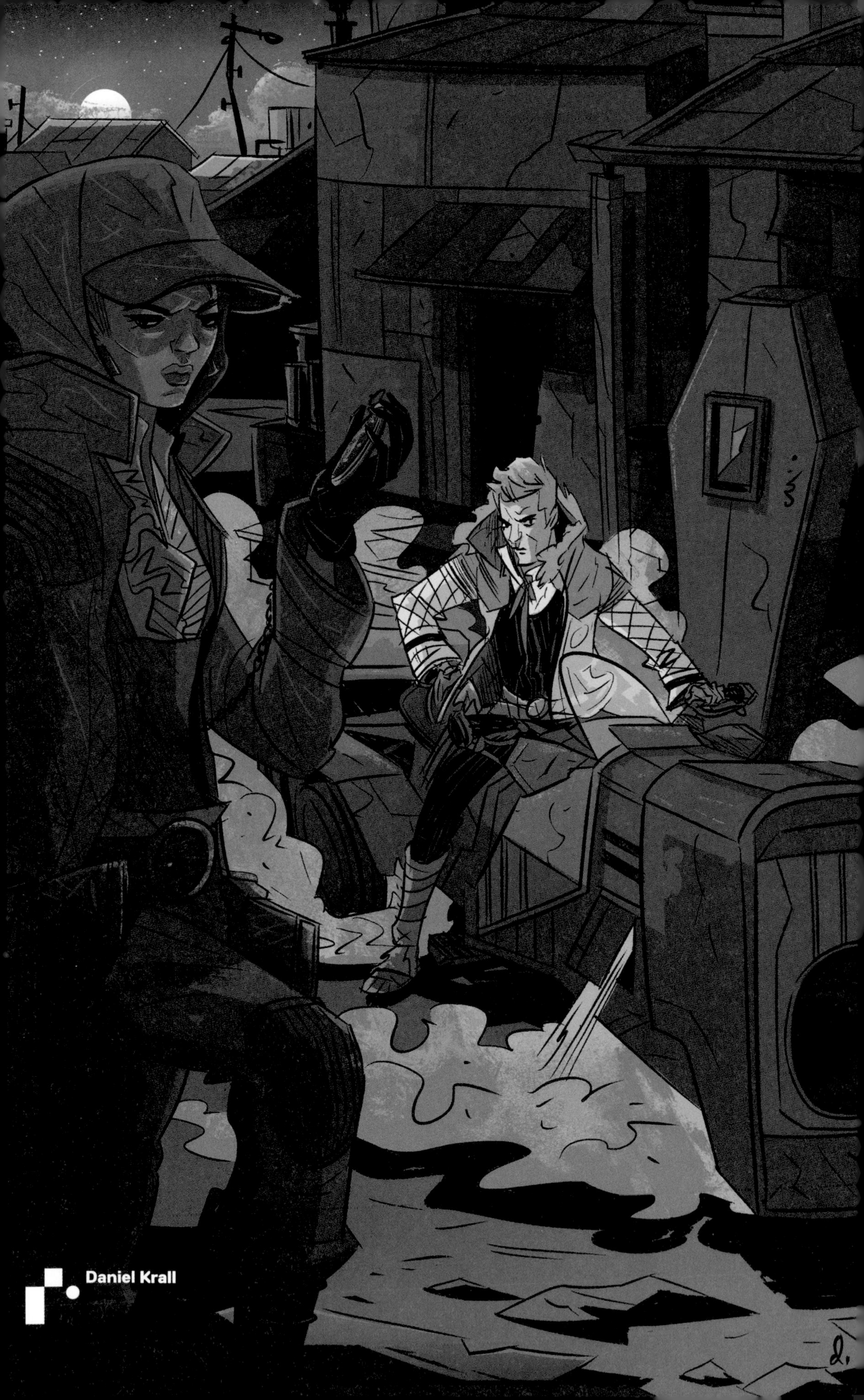
Daniel Krall

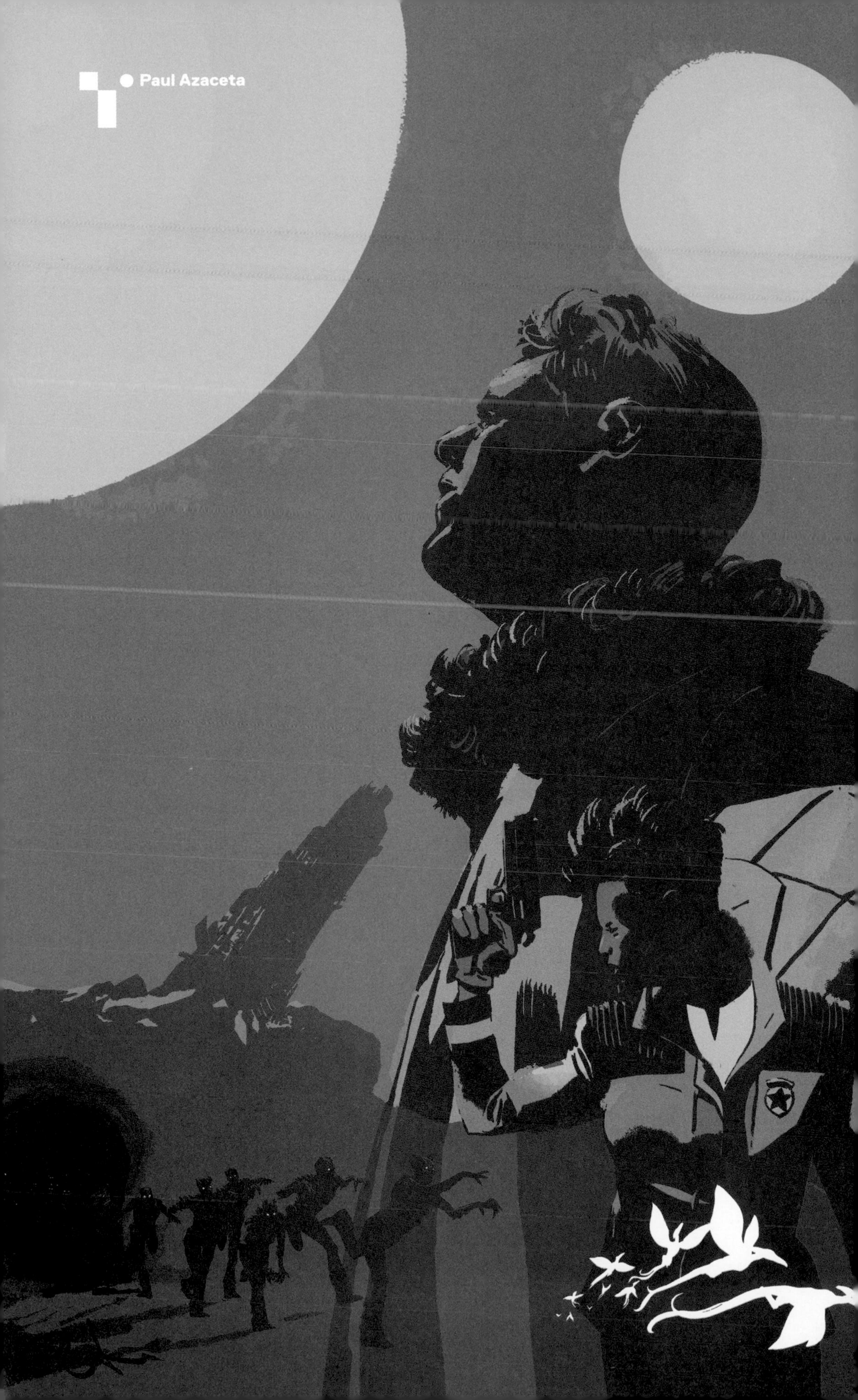
Paul Azaceta

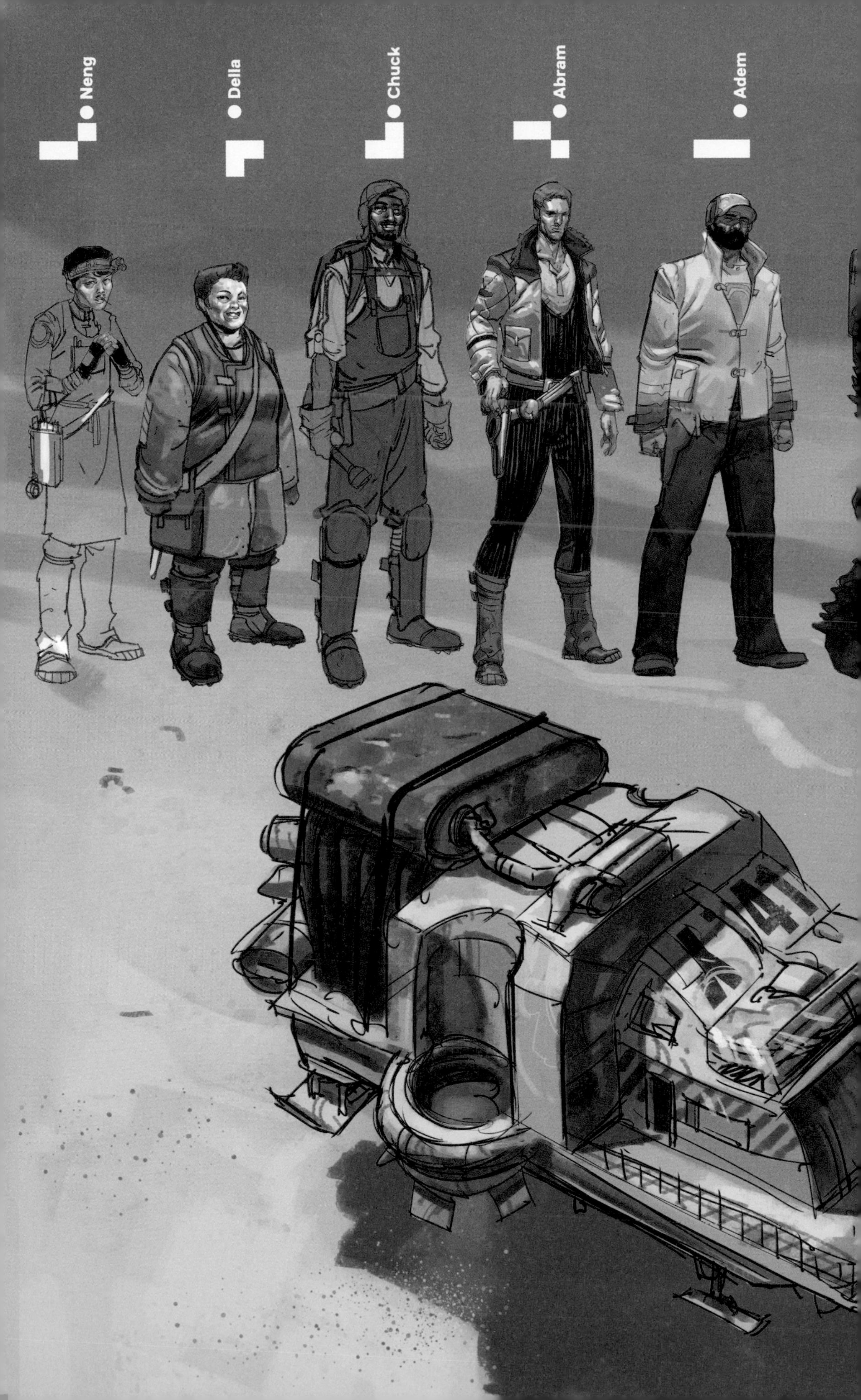
Neng
Della
Chuck
Abram
Adem

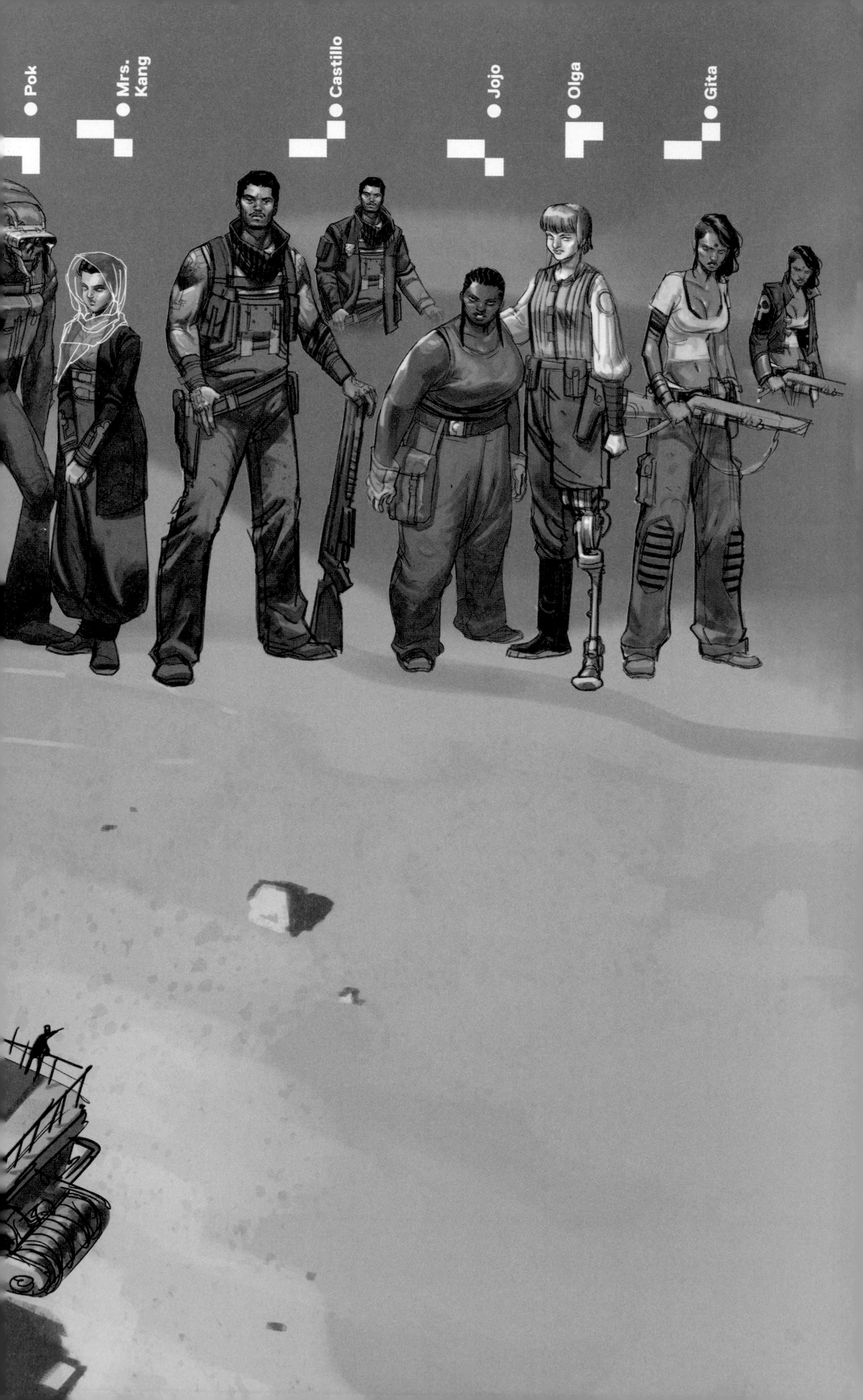
Pok
Mrs. Kang
Castillo
Jojo
Olga
Gita

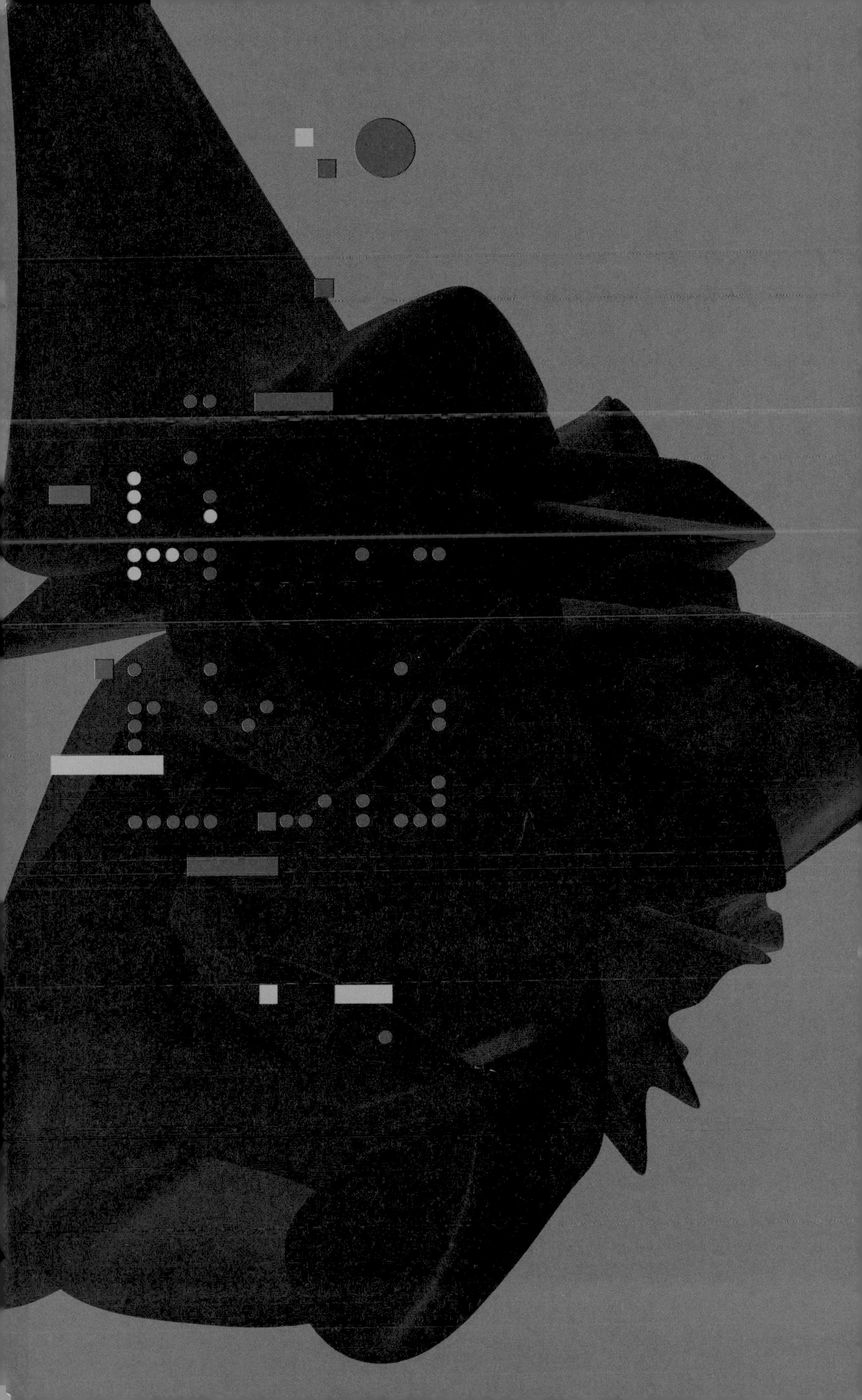

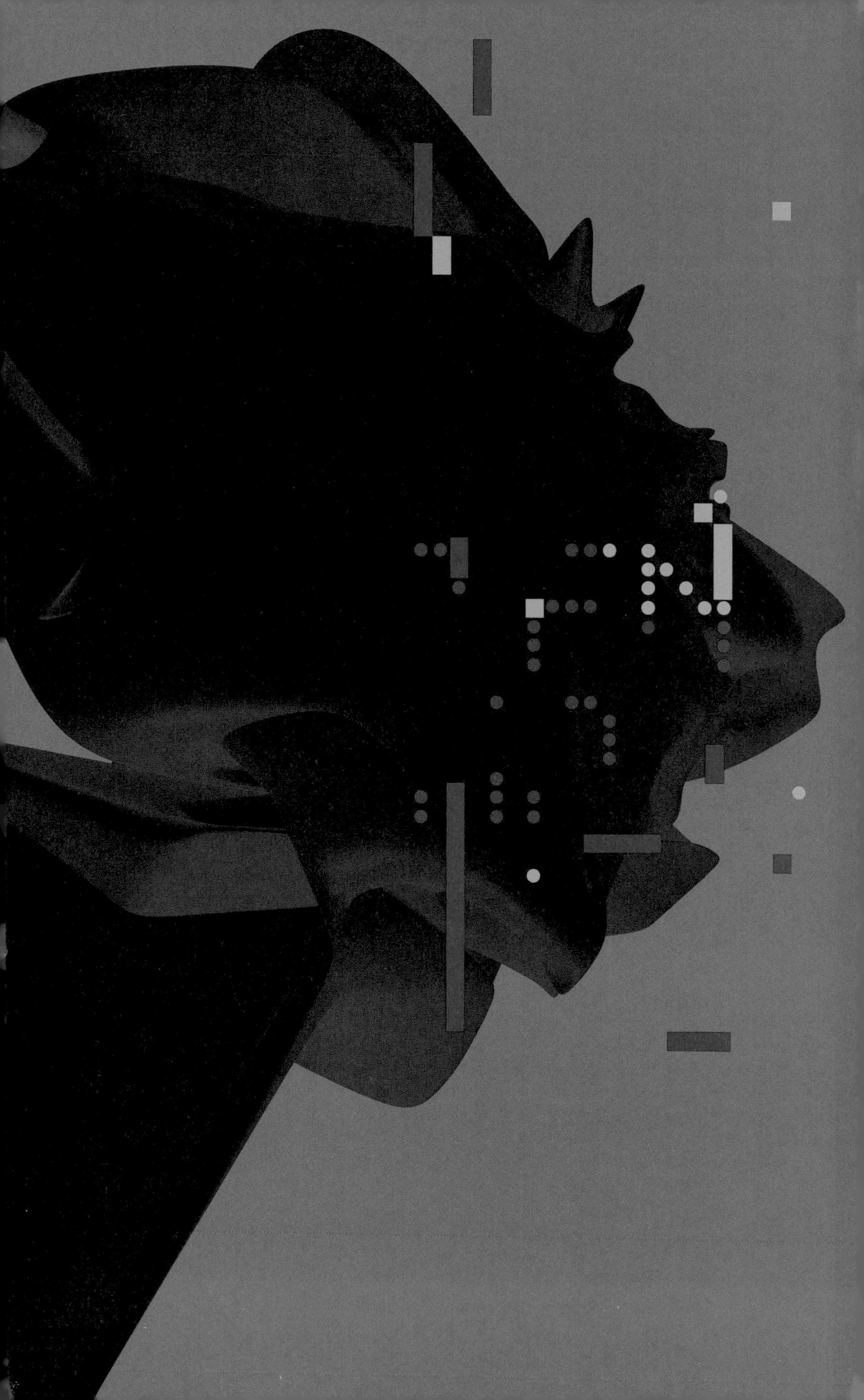

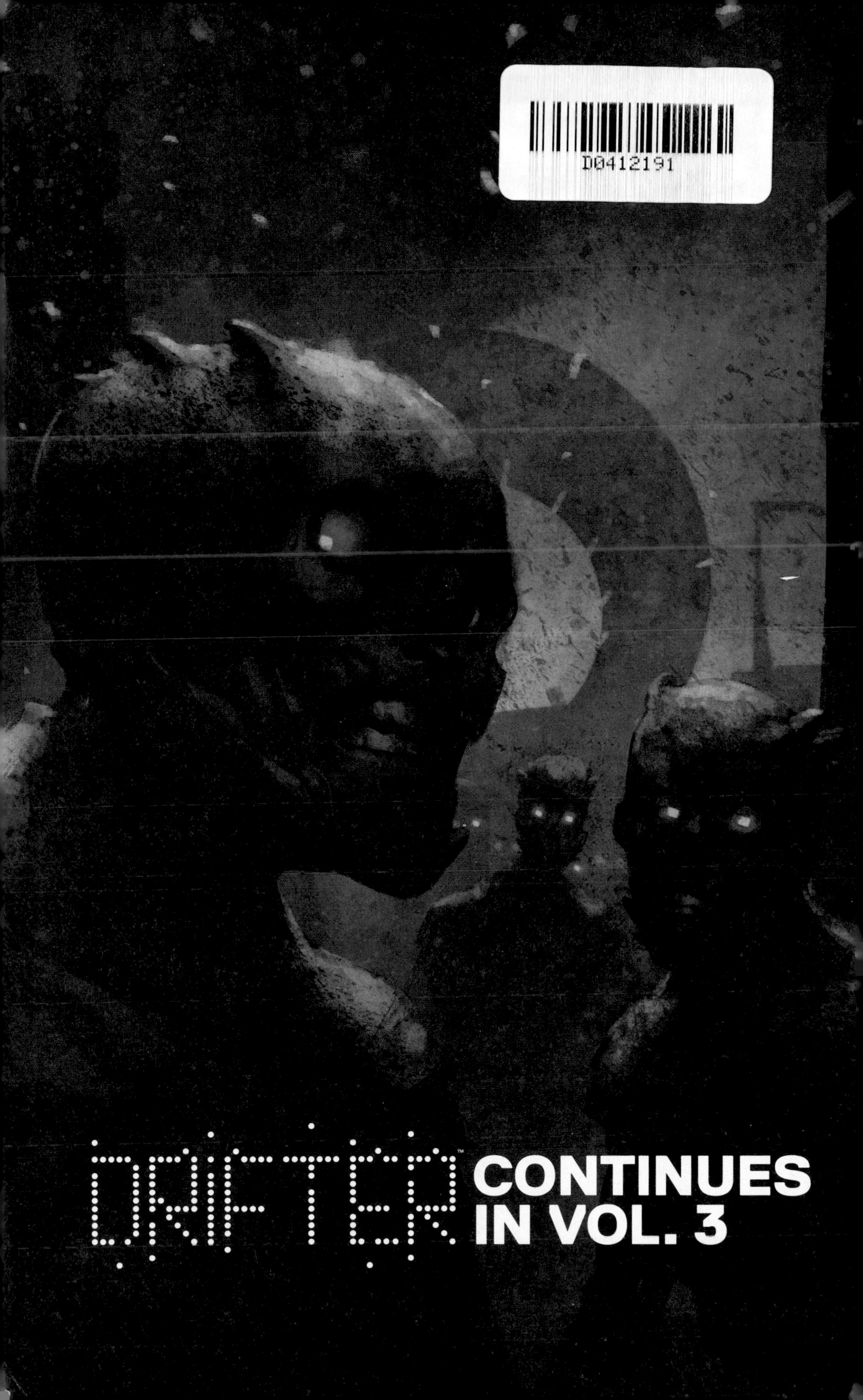
DRIFTER™
CONTINUES
IN VOL. 3